Richard Woodman

Beneath the Aurora

A *Warner* Book

First published in Great Britain
by John Murray (Publishers) Ltd in 1995
This edition published by Warner Books in 1996

A CIP catalogue record for this book is available from the British Library.

ISBN 0 7515 1142 0

Typeset by M Rules
Printed in England by Clays Ltd, St Ives plc

Warner Books
A Division of
Little, Brown and Company (UK)
Brettenham House
Lancaster Place
London WC2E 7EN

For
Rozelle and Dick Raynes and their ships
Martha McGilda and *Roskilde*

Contents

PART ONE

A Distant Treachery

'We may pick up a Marshal or two, but nothing worth
a damn.'

WELLINGTON

A Person of Some Importance
September 1813

Lieutenant Sparkman eased off the second of his mud-spattered boots with a relieved grunt, and kicked it beside its companion. Leaning back in the chair he wriggled his toes, picked up the tankard beside him and gulped the hot rum flip with greedy satisfaction. The heat of the fire drew steam from the neglected boots and a faintly distasteful aroma from his own feet. The woollen stockings were damp, damned near as damp as the Essex salt-marsh alongside which he had ridden that afternoon. Boots were no attire for a sea-officer, he reflected, though he had heard hessians were increasingly fashionable among the young blades that inhabited His Majesty's quarterdecks nowadays. But as an Inspector of Fencibles, Sparkman was no longer what might, with justice, be called a 'sea-officer'. His sore arse testified to the time he spent in the saddle and he promptly set the thought aside. He avoided disquieting recollections, having learnt the wisdom of jettisoning them before they took root and corroded a man's good temper.

True he had been disappointed in his expectations in the naval service, but he had little to complain about since swallowing the anchor. After all, the path of duty was not arduous: the Red Lion at Kirby-le-Soken was a comfortable enough house and the landlord a convivial fellow, having once been at sea himself. They would doubtless share a glass or two before the night was out. Sparkman stretched himself again and swallowed more rum; he should reach Harwich before noon next day, which was time enough; he had no intention of starting early, for the weather had turned foul and there was little improvement expected. He half cocked an ear at the wind blustering against the Red Lion's sturdy walls and the faint rattling of tiles above his head. Periodically the fire sizzled and smoked as, through some vagary of the chimney, a spatter of rain was driven down against the updraught.

He wriggled his toes again, content: in Harwich there was a chambermaid in the Three Cups who was worth the effort, despite the weather, for Annie Davis had taken a shine to him on a previous visit and would share his bed for a florin.

The easterly gale which had begun that morning threatened to blow for a week, a wind which, despite its ferocity, would once have had every Tom, Dick and Harry on the coast fearing invasion. Those days were over, thank heaven. The French were on the defensive now, hard pressed by Great Britain's Continental allies. News had arrived of the check administered by the Emperor Napoleon to Schwarzenburg's Austrians; but the two Prussian armies had achieved success. One under Blücher, had surprised Marshal Macdonald on the Katzbach River and had routed him with the loss of 20,000 Frenchmen and over 100 cannon; while the second, commanded by von Bülow, had caught Marshal Oudinot south of Potsdam, and had defeated him at Gross Beeren. Moreover, all the while, knocking at the back door of France Lord Wellington's Anglo-Portuguese army steadily advanced across the Pyrenees out of Spain.

Sparkman yawned and cast a glance at the dank leather satchels hung across the back of the room's other chair, dripping darkly over the floorboards. He thought of the report he should have been writing on the sea defences along the coast of the Wallet. It seemed a rather small and trivial task, set against this vast ebb and flow of soldiers marching and counter-marching across war-weary Europe.

Well, so be it. To the devil with his report! He would write it when he arrived at Harwich, after he had had a look at the redoubt there (and taken his pleasure on the plump but enthusiastic body of Annie Davis). The Martello towers from Point Clear to Clacton were sound enough, even if their garrisons were tucked up in Weeley barracks, a good hour or two's march from their posts.

'There's a manned battery at Chevaux-de-Frise Point,' Sparkman muttered to himself, easing his conscience, 'and no damned radeaux will put to sea without the free-trade fraternity knowing about it, never mind an invasion fleet.'

The wind boomed in the chimney and rattled the small window, emphasizing the drowsy snugness of his room under the thatch. He recalled an old woman who had passed the time of day with him in a lane that morning. Pointing to the proliferation of wayside berries, she had croaked that it would be a hard winter; perhaps the crone had been right. He continued to toast his feet and look forward to a chat with the landlord, a beef pie and clean sheets all in due time, teasing himself with anticipation at parting Annie's white thighs.

He was dozing when the landlord burst in. An uncivil clatter of boots followed him on the wooden stair. It was clear his host's abrupt entry had precious little social about it.

'Mr Sparkman, sir, Cap'n Clarke is here demanding to speak with you.'

For a moment the tired Sparkman was confused, the rum having drugged him. He woke fully to an ill-tempered resentment, irritated that men such as Clarke should call themselves 'Captain'. The upstart was no more than Master of a smuggling lugger.

'I don't know a *Captain* Clarke . . .' he began, and then Clarke himself was crowding into the room, with two ruffianly seamen in tarpaulins and a fantastically bewhiskered and cloaked officer whose moustaches curled extravagantly beneath a long nose. The quartet were soaked, their clothes running with water, which rapidly darkened the floor, mixing with the mud from their boots.

'Oh, yes you do, Sparkman,' Clarke said grinning, 'we need no introductions. But I have brought someone you haven't met yet.' Clarke drew off his low beaver and threw out an arm with a mock theatrical gesture. 'Colonel . . .'

The grotesque apparition threw back his cloak with a flourish that showered Sparkman with water, to reveal a scarlet plastron fronting a white tunic laced with silver.

'Colonel Bardolini, Captain,' the stranger announced in good English, shrugging himself free of the restraining seamen and flicking his extended wrist at Clarke in dismissal. 'I am come on an embassy to the English government. You are a naval officer, yes?'

'Rummest cargo I ever lifted, Mr Sparkman,' Clarke put in, ignoring the foreign officer.

'I daresay he paid you well,' retorted Sparkman, who had recovered something of his wits at this damp invasion. With wry amusement he observed that this Bardolini shared his own opinion of Clarke. 'You were ever one to drive a hard bargain,' he added obliquely, referring to a past transaction over some bottles of genever.

'This is different,' Clarke said darkly, ''e ain't French, 'e's Italian.'

'I am Neapolitan,' said Bardolini, firing his sentences like shot. 'I am in the service of King Joachim. I have papers for your government. I am a person of some importance.'

'Are you now,' said Sparkman 'and what proof . . .?'

But Bardolini had anticipated resistance and whipped a heavily sealed paper from the ample cuff of his white leather gauntlet.

'My passport.' He held the document out. 'I have plenipotentiary powers,' he declared impressively.

Sparkman had only the vaguest understanding of the Neapolitan's claim, but a respect for the panoply of administrative office bade him be cautious. He slit the seal and with a crackle opened the paper.

'Signor, please, these men . . .'

Sparkman looked up and nodded to the smuggler.

'Tell your men to be off, Clarke,' he ordered and then, as the seamen retreated, clumping down the stairs, he asked, 'Where did you pick this fellow up?'

'At Flushing. I was told take a passenger . . .'

'Told?' Sparkman asked. 'By whom?' and, seeing Clarke's hesitation, 'Come on, Clarke, you've no need to haver. If I read you aright, you've brought live cargo over before, have you not?'

'A man has to feed his family, Sparkman, and these are hard times . . .'

'Never mind your damned excuses. Who approached you?'

'A man who has arranged this kind of business before.'

'Very well. And what were you contracted to do with this fine gentleman?' Sparkman indicated the Neapolitan who was about to speak. 'A moment, sir,' Sparkman cut him short. 'Go on, Clarke.'

'To deliver him to a government officer. When I heard you had been inspecting the coast . . .'

'You were damned lucky I was about, then, and that it wasn't an Exciseman or a Riding Officer you bumped into.'

'I wouldn't call it luck, Sparkman,' Clarke countered darkly, alluding to the intelligence system the so-called 'free-traders' possessed.

'I suppose you'd have left him to walk the Gunfleet Sands until the tide covered him?'

'I usually do what I'm told in these circumstances, Sparkman . . .'

'Aye, and avoid the gallows by it!'

'I'd advise you to do the same, Sparkman. The gentlemen at Colchester are in my pocket too,' Clarke said, his grin sinister with implication.

'Why you impertinent . . .' The reference to the army officers of the local garrison irritated him.

'Are you a naval officer?' Bardolini snapped, breaking into the row fomenting between the two men, which it was clear he understood perfectly. 'You have my passport. Please be good enough to read it.'

Sparkman turned his attention on the colonel. He was about to retort, but the gleam in Bardolini's eye persuaded him otherwise. He shrugged and looked at the paper the Neapolitan held out. It was in French and English, that much he could see, but his sight was poor and with only the light of the fire he could make out little more than the formula 'allow to pass without let or hindrance, the bearer, Colonel Umberto Bardolini of the Neapolitan Service on a mission to the Court of St James's'. There was a string of legal mumbo-jumbo in which the words 'plenipotentiary. . . . authorized to act on behalf of . . . is of my mind and fully conversant with my innermost thoughts', seemed sufficiently portentous to confirm Lieutenant Sparkman in the wisdom of his caution. At the bottom, above another seal, was a scrawl that may or may not have spelled out the name 'Joachim', but in fact used the Italian form 'Giacomo'.

Sparkman looked up at the bristling moustaches. 'Colonel, my apologies. Welcome to Great Britain.' He held out his hand, but Bardolini ignored it and bowed stiffly from the waist.

Sparkman was aware of Clarke grinning diabolically in the firelight at this slight.

'Who are you?' Bardolini asked peremptorily and for the third time.

'Shall I get you some vittals, Lieutenant Sparkman?' put in the landlord who had remained silent until a commercial opportunity offered.

'No, damn you,' Sparkman snapped, 'tell your boy I want my horse again, and get me another for this fellow to ride.' He handed the passport back to Bardolini. 'I am Lieutenant Sparkman of His Britannic Majesty's Royal Navy, Colonel.' Then he sat and pulled on his boots.

'What are you going to do with him?' asked Clarke.

'I shan't be taking any chances, God rot you,' said Sparkman, standing and stamping his feet into the boots, then casting about the room for his belongings, muttering about the lack of candles.

'D'you wish for a candle, sir?' enquired the landlord. 'It will take but a moment . . .'

'I want a quiet evening before the fire,' Sparkman muttered through clenched teeth.

'Aye, sir, 'tis a bad night, and . . .'

'Be so good as to stand aside!' Sparkman exploded.

'What about payment for the room?'

Bardolini shuffled round as Sparkman seized his damp cloak from the bed and drew it about his shoulders. The wet collar rasped against his neck, reminding him of the weather outside and the comfort he was forsaking. He threw the landlord a handful of silver.

'You will take me to see the General Officer commanding at Colchester?' the Neapolitan asked, obviously well-informed.

'No, sir, 'tis too far. I will take you to Harwich for tonight. Tomorrow we will see about Colchester.' Sparkman turned on Clarke who barred his exit. 'You must have had a bad passage, Clarke.'

Clarke grinned and jerked his head at Bardolini, at the same time holding out his hand and preventing anyone from leaving the room. 'He certainly did.'

With an extravagant sigh, Bardolini drew a purse from his belt. Sparkman heard the chink of coin as he passed it to the smuggler.

'I wish you good-night, gentlemen,' said Clarke, standing aside and bowing with an ironic exaggeration.

Sparkman threw the wet satchel over his shoulder and picked up a pair of pistol holsters. 'Be so kind as to bring my baggage, landlord,' he ordered, nodding at his portmanteau, then he stepped forward, through the slime his visitors had left by the door.

As he passed, Clarke muttered sarcastically, 'I took his pistols while he was vomiting over the rail. He won't give you too much trouble.'

'I am much obliged to you, Clarke,' Sparkman retorted with equal incivility.

'*Captain* Clarke, Mr Sparkman.'

'Damn you for an insolent dog, Clarke . . .'

Clarke laughed and held up the jingling purse under Sparkman's nose. 'There's more than you make in a year in here, Sparkman . . .'

'God help England when money purchases rank, Clarke! You're a dog and always will be a dog, and no amount of gold, no, nor putting your betters in your pocket, can make you a gentleman! Come, Colonel.'

'What pretty notions you do have, Sparkman,' Clarke called after them, laughing as they clattered down the stairs.

Sparkman had to put his shoulder to the outer door

as a gust of wind eddied round the yard. Rain lashed him in the twilight as Bardolini emerged, attempting to put a crazy, square-topped shako on to his head. Then Sparkman was struggling with his reluctant horse and taking the reins from a wretched little stable-boy. Satchel, portmanteau and saddle-bags were finally settled on the fractious animal and then Sparkman hoisted himself aloft.

Bardolini was already mounted, smoothing his curvetting horse's neck with a gloved and practised hand. The sight irritated Sparkman; but for this effete Italian he might, at that moment, be tucking into a beef pie.

'Come on, then, damn you!' he roared and put spurs to his tired horse, which jerked him forward into the rain and wind.

1 A Lucky Chance
September 1813

Captain Nathaniel Drinkwater read the paragraph for the fourth time, aware that he had not understood a word of it. The handwriting was crabbed, the spelling idiosyncratic and the ink smudged. He began again. The lines forming the words seemed to uncoil from the paper into a thin trail of smoke. He was aware he had fallen asleep, his mind dulled with a torpor he found difficult to shake off.

'God's bones,' he muttered, tossing the paper on to the pile which covered the green baize on the desktop and standing up with such violence that his chair overturned and, for a moment, he had to clutch at the desk to stop himself from falling.

The dizziness passed, but left his brow clammy with sweat. He ran a forefinger round his neck, tugging at the constriction of his stock, swearing beneath his breath with forceful eloquence. He went to the window and leaned his head upon the cool glass. The sash vibrated slightly to the gale blowing outside, and rain fell upon the glass panes with a patter which occasionally grew to a vicious tattoo in the gusts. It was almost dark and he told himself it was the dusk which had brought on his tiredness, nothing more.

He turned and, leaning against the shutter, stared back into the room. It was small, containing the baize-covered desk, his chair and a wicker basket which stood on a square of carpet to keep his feet from the draught that blew between the wide deal floorboards. The window was flanked on one side by a tall cabinet whose glazed doors covered shelves of guard books, on the other by a low chest whose upper surface was a plane table. It had a trough for pencil and dividers, beneath which a series of shallow drawers contained several folios of charts. On its top was a long wooden box containing a single deep and narrow drawer.

The only other article of furniture in the room was a small, rickety, half-moon table set against the wall beside the door. Upon it were a pair of decanters, a biscuit barrel and four glasses. One contained a residual teaspoonful of madeira.

On the wall opposite the window, above the grate and mantelpiece, hung a gilt-framed canvas depicting a moonlit frigate action. It had been commissioned by Drinkwater and painted by the ageing Nicholas Pocock, whose house in Great George Street was hard by Storey's Gate into St James's Park. The painting showed the frigate *Patrician* overhauling and engaging the French National frigate *Sybille* and Drinkwater had described the canvas to his wife Elizabeth as 'a last vanity, m'dear. I shan't fight again, now that I've swallowed the anchor.'

The recollection made him turn to the window again, and stare down into the darkening street. Despite the weather, Whitehall was full of the evening's traffic: a foot patrol of guardsmen, a pair of doxies in a doorway cozening the grenadiers, whose bearskins lost their military air in the rain, a dog pissing against a porter's rest, and a handful of pathetic loiterers huddling out of the rain in the sparse and inadequate clothing of the indigent. Carriages came and went across his field of view, but he saw none of this. It depressed him; after the broad sweep of the distant horizon seen from the pristine standpoint of a frigate's quarterdeck, the horse turds and grime of Whitehall were a mockery.

He turned and, as abruptly as he had risen, closed the shutters against the night. Then he righted his capsized Windsor chair and sat in it. Picking up the paper he twisted round, held it to the flickering firelight and began to read out loud, as if by enunciating the ill-written words he would keep himself awake enough to assimilate their content.

'Sir, further to my communications of December last and May of this year, in which there was little of an unusual nature to report, it is now common knowledge here . . .' Drinkwater had forgotten the origin of the paper and looked at the heading. 'Ah, yes,' he murmured, 'from Helgoland . . . last month, no, July . . .'

He read on, 'that a considerable quantity of arms for equipping troops have lately arrived in Hamburg and in expectation of their shipment, have been placed in a warehouse which is guarded by . . .'

There was a knock at the door and Drinkwater paused. 'Enter,' he called.

A slim, pinch-faced man with prematurely thinning hair appeared. He wore a black, waisted and high-collared coat. The points of his shirt poked up

15

either side of his face, and a tight cravat in dark, watered silk frothed beneath a sharp, blue chin. The figure was elegant and, though daylight would have betrayed the threadbare nature of his dress, the candelabra he bore only enhanced the ascetic architecture of his skull.

'Ah, Templeton, about time you brought candles.'

'My apologies, Captain, I was delayed in the copy room . . .'

'Scuttlebutt, I suppose.'

'I wish it were only gossip, sir, but I fear the worst.' Templeton's words were so full of foreboding that Drinkwater was compelled to look up. Templeton's head was bent askew in such a way that, though he stood, his eyes must of necessity look under his brow so that his whole demeanour bespoke grave concern.

'Which touches me, Mr Templeton?'

'Indeed, sir, I fear so.' A brief smirk passed across Templeton's features, the merest hint of satisfaction at having conveyed the full import of his meaning with such admirable economy. It would have passed a less intuitive man than Drinkwater unnoticed.

'Is this a secret of state, or merely one which is denied the Secret Department, Mr Templeton?' Drinkwater asked with heavy irony.

'The latter, Captain Drinkwater,' Templeton replied, the corners of his thin mouth creeping outwards in a smile, hinting at the possession of superior knowledge.

'Well, then, I am waiting. What is this gossip in the clerks' office?'

'I am afraid, sir, 'tis said this department is to be discontinued.'

A feeling of something akin to relief flooded through Drinkwater. There were times in a man's life when to submit to the inevitable meant avoiding disagreeable concomitances. He could never have explained to Elizabeth how constricted his soul was, cooped up in this tiny Admiralty office. He had accepted his appointment, half out of loyalty to his late predecessor, Lord Dungarth, half out of a sense of necessity.

This necessity was harder to define, exposing as it did the infirmities of his character. A believer in Providence, he knew his posting to this obscure office was only partly the result of Dungarth's dying wish. Fate had consigned him to it in expiation of his unfaithfulness to his wife, for his *affaire* with the Widow Shaw.*

Now Templeton, his obsequious but able cipher clerk, a man steeped in the clandestine doings of the Secret Department, who possessed encyclopaedic knowledge of the letters pasted in the guard books resting behind the glass doors of the cabinet, brought him release from this imprisonment.

'I see you are shocked, Captain Drinkwater.'

'I am certainly surprised,' Drinkwater dissimulated. 'Upon what logic is this based?'

'Cost, I believe,' Templeton replied and added, rolling his eyes with lugubrious emphasis and pointing his right index finger upwards, though Drinkwater knew nothing but the attics were there, 'and a certain feeling among those whose business it is to attend to such matters, that our continued existence is no longer necessary.'

---

* See *The Flying Squadron*.

'The war is not yet over, Templeton.'

'I entirely agree, sir.'

Drinkwater realized Templeton awaited his reply as a matter of some importance. Indeed the clerk had confided in Drinkwater in order to rouse him to a defence of the Secret Department, not so much to contribute to ending the war by its continued existence, but to preserve Templeton's unique position within the Admiralty's bureaucratic hierarchy. Templeton was not the first to assume, quite wrongly, that Nathaniel Drinkwater was a man of influence. How else had he inherited this post of Head of the Secret Department?

How indeed? It was a conundrum which obsessed Drinkwater himself. He knew no more than that he had received a letter signed by the Second Secretary to the Board of Admiralty, John Barrow, appointing him, and a visit from the Earl of Moira explaining that it had been the dying wish of Lord Dungarth that Drinkwater should take over the office.

'Johnnie said you were the only man capable of doin' the job, Captain, the only man with the *nous*. He was emphatic upon the point, wanted me to tell you about a bookseller fellow in Paris, and a Madame de Santon, or some such, but he slipped away, poor devil. He was in a deuce of a lot of pain at the end, despite the paregoric.'

Moira had given him the key to the desk at which he now sat, striving for some temporizing reaction to Templeton's news.

'Barrow has not mentioned the matter . . .'

'It was only decided at Board this morning . . .'

'You're damned quick with your intelligence,'

Drinkwater snapped sharply. 'So much for the confidentiality of the copy room!'

'I believe Mr Barrow wished it to be known, sir, in this roundabout way.'

'How obligin' of him,' Drinkwater muttered, knowing that in the past he had once crossed the Second Secretary and done himself no favour thereby. 'You had better pour us both a glass, Templeton.'

Drinkwater rose, aware that he had still not thoroughly read the dispatch from Helgoland. He moved towards the little half-moon table where the clerk poured the rich madeira. He caught sight of himself reflected in the glass doors of the cabinet. The bottle-green coat did not suit him, and was at odd variance with his old-fashioned queue with its clump of black ribbon nestling at the nape of his neck. He looked a damn fool!

Templeton handed him the glass. 'What are we to do, Templeton?' he asked. 'D'you have any bright ideas? If they want for money, we've no means of raisin' revenue, and if they want value for what little they allow us, how in heaven's name do we give it to 'em?'

He was half-hearted in his complaint, but Templeton did not seem to notice. The truth was, the intelligence reports processed by the two of them contained little of significance now that the naval war on the coast of Europe was reduced to the tedious matter of blockade. There were the lists of Yankee ships slipping in and out of French ports, but as many were doing the same in Spain and the British were purchasing the supplies they brought to keep Wellington's Anglo-Portuguese army in the field. As for the matter of their own funds, Drinkwater had learned that Dungarth had himself underwritten most of the department's expenses, squandering his modest inheritance to the distress of his Irish tenants. His own finances would not extend so far.

In so far as the Secret Department had achieved anything recently, Drinkwater could recollect only his pressing the Board to increase the strength of the blockade on the eastern coast of the United States. He had written an appreciation of the matter born out of his own experience of Yankee privateers rather than the coded missives of spies.

'We appear to be redundant, Mr Templeton,' he said with an air of finality.

'I fear that may well be the case, Captain Drinkwater,' Templeton said, sipping his wine unhappily.

'You will retain a position within the Admiralty, surely.'

'Oh, I daresay, sir, but not one of such gravity, sir, not one with such, er, such opportunities.'

The emphasis on the last word reminded Drinkwater of the vital perquisites of office among these black-garbed jobbers. There were expenses to be written off, bribes to be paid and spies to be funded. Everything was reduced to money and everyone had their price, women as well as men.

He thought of Moira's 'Madame de Santon, or some such'. Drinkwater knew her better as Hortense Santhonax, née Montholon. Dungarth's key had revealed his secret dossier on Hortense and the small pension she received to keep open communications with the Emperor Napoleon's former Foreign Minister, Talleyrand. He concentrated on the present.

There was Liepmann in Hamburg, Van Ouden in Flushing and Vlieghere at Antwerp.

'Well, Templeton, what have we received recently? There was the letter from Carlscrona reporting eleven of the line in ordinary . . .'

'From the Master of the *Lady Erskine*, sir.'

'Quite so . . .'

'And the message from Antwerp about the current state of new building there, four ships and a frigate. A routine report, to be sure, but one which demonstrates the continuing ability and determination of the French and their allies to build men o' war.'

'Yes, and the encrypted dispatch from Helgoland spoke of arms being stored at Hamburg. There does not seem much of significance in that.'

'No, no,' Templeton agreed quickly, 'Hamburg is a French fortress. Cavalry remounts, recruits, stores and so forth are all assembled there. The French Army Corps in North Germany draw their reinforcements from the Hamburg depot.'

'And yet Liepmann thought it worth letting them know in Helgoland,' Drinkwater reflected, adding, 'Liepmann is in our pay, not that of the Foreign Office.'

'You have great faith in Herr Liepmann, sir,' said Templeton obliquely, knowing that Drinkwater had once met the Jewish merchant.

'It would not surprise me if these arms are locked away in one of our Hebrew friend's warehouses, Templeton. If so, he has probably learned of their purpose. Don't you think it odd they may be secured in a warehouse, rather than in the possession of the French military authorities?'

'That is mere conjecture,' Templeton said dismissively.

'True.' Drinkwater was content to leave the matter there. He knew Templeton set great store by the intelligence from Antwerp. It was a regular dispatch, a long message in the cipher it was Templeton's peculiar skill to disentangle and he had a proprietorial air towards it.

But Templeton had become wary of his new master. The ageing post captain with his outmoded queue, lopsided shoulders and thin sword scar down his left cheek was a contrast after the huge, dropsical bulk of the one-legged Lord Dungarth. But, Templeton had come to learn, both had an uncanny knack of nosing out the obscure from the obfusc. The talent made Templeton nervous.

'Your meaning is unclear, sir,' Templeton prompted.

'Mmm? You mean the significance of my conjecture is unclear?' Drinkwater asked wryly.

'Exactly so.'

'Well, you are right. It is only conjecture, but Liepmann finds it necessary to tell us a quantity of arms has arrived at Hamburg. There is nothing unusual in that, we conclude, except that Herr Liepmann knows of it. Now I'll warrant that there is nothin' significant in replacement equipment arriving in Hamburg in the normal run of things, eh? Nor would one expect Liepmann to know of it. But Liepmann does know, and considers it worth lettin' us know.'

'But if the fact was of real significance then surely he would have amplified the matter. The message is in cipher. If these arms, whatever they consist of, are in his own warehouses, he would have given us more details. I don't see it signifies anything.'

'You have a point, Templeton. Perhaps my assumption was foolish. But suppose they are in the custody of a friend, an associate. Liepmann perhaps smells a rat. He sends us the information thinking it may be a piece of a larger puzzle.'

'Well, it isn't.'

'You are not convinced.' Drinkwater's tone was flat, a statement, not a question. He shrugged, drained his glass and sighed. 'So be it. Come, it is gettin' late. It is time you went home.'

Templeton put his empty glass down on the half-moon table. 'Good-night, sir,' he said, but he seemed reluctant to leave.

'Good-night.' Drinkwater turned to his desk, gathering the scattered papers, waiting for Templeton to go. When the clerk had finally gone, he locked them away. He turned then to the shutters and opened them. Throughout his interview with Templeton he had been aware of their faint but persistent rattle.

He peered again through the window. For a moment, the full moon appeared from behind flying cloud and he thought of the strong spring tides its influence would produce and the ferocious seas which would be running in the Channel.

'God help sailors on a night like this,' he muttered to himself in a pious incantation. The brilliant moonlight and a clatter below briefly attracted his attention. He caught a glimpse of a horseman turning in off the street and entering through Nash's screen wall, his mount striking sparks off the wet cobbles. Messengers

23

were something of a rarity nowadays, he reflected, so sophisticated had the semaphore telegraph system become. It was capable of transmitting news with great speed from the standard on the Admiralty roof, along half a dozen arteries to the great seaports of Britain, even to such exposed outposts as Yarmouth Road, on the coast of East Anglia. He wondered idly where the rider's dispatches originated, then dismissed the thought and closed the shutters.

Drinkwater succumbed to the temptation to pour another glass and sat again, turning his chair so that it faced the dying fire. He was in no mood to return to a house empty of all except its staff. Bending, he stoked the fire into a final flaring, listening awhile to the boom of the gale across the massed chimney pots on the roof above while the tiny flames licked round the glowing coals, then subsided into a dull, ruby coruscation.

He brooded on his predicament. He was supposed to be a puppet-master, pulling strings at the extremities of which several score of agents danced, ceaselessly gleaning information for the British Admiralty. Templeton, his confidential cipher clerk, decoded their messages and entered their dispatches in the guard books. He was a genius of sorts, a man whose mind could disinter a hidden fact, cross-refer it to some other seemingly unrelated circumstance and draw a thread of logic from the process. Except, of course, when he disagreed, as at present. Then he could be monstrously stubborn. Drinkwater sometimes marvelled at the obscure man's abilities, quite oblivious of his own part in these deliberations and the confidence his personal imprimatur gave

Templeton. He was more likely to see himself as a fish out of water, an ageing and foppish extravagant in his bottle-green coat and his increasingly affected mode of speaking. It seemed to him that he had reached this point in his life without quite knowing how he had got there, carried, like a piece of wood on the tide, into some shallow backwater and left grounded in a creek.

He had fondly supposed that he would see something of his wife, but Elizabeth and the children were almost a hundred miles away, in Suffolk, while he vegetated in the capital, choking on smoke and falling victim to the blue devils and every quinsy and ague coughed over him by London's denizens! Moira had implied he might mastermind a *coup*, insisting Dungarth knew him capable of executing some brilliant feat. But while Drinkwater had pored in fascination over the papers pasted in the guard books, prompted by a natural curiosity concerning the fate of Madame Santhonax, whose husband Drinkwater had killed in action, he had come to realize all such opportunities seemed to reside firmly in the past, and the distant past at that.[*]

His present duties seemed to entail nothing more than reading endless reports and dispatches, many of no apparent meaning, still less of significance, until he dozed over them, half asleep with inertia.

'God's bones,' he had snapped at Templeton one morning, 'what am I to make of this catalogue of stupefying facts? If they conceal some great truth then it passes over my head.'

[*] See *Baltic Mission*.

'Patience, sir,' Templeton had soothed, 'gold is never found in great quantities.'

'Damn you for your philosophical cant, Templeton! Did Lord Dungarth never venture abroad, eh? Send himself on some mission to rouse his blood?'

'Yes, sir, indeed he did, and lost a leg if you recall, when his carriage was mined by Bonaparte's police.'

'You are altogether too *reasonable* for your own good, Templeton. If you were on my quarterdeck I should mast-head you for your impudence.'

'You are not on your quarterdeck, Captain Drinkwater,' Templeton had replied coolly, with that fastidious detachment which could either annoy or amuse Drinkwater.

'More's the damned pity,' Drinkwater had flung back, irritated on this occasion and aware that here, in the Admiralty, he was bereft of the trappings of pomp he had become so used to. It reduced the bottle-green coat to the uniform of a kind of servitude and his clipped speech to a pompous mannerism acquired at sea through the isolation of command. Neither consideration brought him much comfort, for the one reminded him of what he had relinquished, the other of what he had become.

Nevertheless, Drinkwater mused, leaning back in his chair and staring into the fire's dying embers, it seemed enough for Templeton methodically to unscramble the reports of spies while Drinkwater himself ached for something useful to do, instead of this tedious seeking of windmills to tilt at.

He was fast asleep when Templeton knocked on the door and he woke with a start as the clerk urgently shook his shoulder. Templeton's thin visage hung over him like a spectre.

'Captain Drinkwater, sir, wake up!'

'What the devil . . .?' Drinkwater's heart pounded with alarm, for there was something wild in Templeton's eye.

'I have just received a message from Harwich, sir. Sent up post-haste by a Lieutenant Sparkman.'

'Who the devil is he?' Drinkwater asked testily, his eye catching sight of a folded paper in Templeton's hand.

'An Inspector of Fencibles . . .'

'Well?'

'He is holding a prisoner there, sir, a man claiming to be a colonel in the service of the King of Naples.'

'The King of Naples? Marshal Murat?'

'The same . . .'

'Let me see, damn it!' Drinkwater shot out his hand, took the hurriedly offered note and read:

Sir, I have the Honour to Acquaint Their Lordships that I am just Arrived at Harwich and have in My Custody a Man just lately Arrived upon the Coast and claiming to be a Colonel Bardolini, in the Service of the King of Naples and Invested with Special Powers. I have Lodged him in the Redoubt here and Await your Instructions at the Three Cups Inn.

Sparkman, Lieutenant and Inspector of Sea Fencibles

Drinkwater turned the letter over and read the superscription with a frown.

'This is addressed to the Secretary . . .'

'Mr Croker is at Downing Street, Captain

Drinkwater, and Mr Barrow is paying his respects to Mr Murray, the publisher.'

A wry and rather mischievous expression crossed Templeton's face. 'And it is getting rather late.' Templeton paused. 'I was alone in the copy room when the messenger was brought in . . .' The clerk let the sentence hang unfinished between them.

'A *coup de hasard*, is it, Mr Templeton?'

'Better than the *coup de grâce* for the Department, sir.'

'Perhaps.' Drinkwater paused. 'What d'you think it means? I recollect it was Murat's men who approached Colonel . . . damn me, what was his name . . .?'

'Colonel Coffin, sir, he was commanding Ponza and received overtures from Naples to Lord William Bentinck at Palermo,' said Templeton, already moving across the room to the long wooden box on the table from which he pulled an equally long drawer. It contained a well-thumbed card index and Templeton's thin fingers manipulated the contents with practised ease. After a moment he drew out a small, white rectangle covered with his own meticulous script. Holding it up to the candles he read aloud: 'Joachim Murat, born Lot 1767, trooper 1787, commissioned 1792, Italy, Egypt, assisted Bonaparte in his *coup d'état*, commanded Consular Guard, fought at Marengo and in operations against King Ferdinand of the Two Sicilies . . .'

'Whom he has now despoiled of half his kingdom,' put in Drinkwater, 'and not in the manner of a fairy tale.'

'No, indeed,' Templeton coughed and resumed the

card's details. 'Marshal of France 1804, occupied Vienna 1805, Grand Duke of Berg and Cleves 1808, Jena, Eylau, Madrid, King of Naples 1808. Commanded cavalry of Grande Armée in Russia, succeeded Bonaparte as C-in-C. Married to Caroline Bonaparte . . .' Templeton paused, continuing to read in silence for a moment. Then he looked up, smiling.

'In addition to the communication opened with Coffin and Lord William, we have several references to him from captains of men-of-war off the Calabrian coast.'

Drinkwater knew that the card index, with its potted biographies, was but an index to the volumes of guard books, and the references to which Templeton referred were intelligence reports concerning Marshal Murat, husband of Caroline Bonaparte and puppet King of Naples.

'I think we have an emissary of the Emperor's brother-in-law on our hands, sir.'

'Then it is a *coup de main*, is it not, Templeton?' Drinkwater jested, but his clerk wanted none of the pun. 'The question is, does he act on his own or Bonaparte's behalf?'

'Captain Drinkwater,' Templeton said in an urgent whisper as if he feared the very walls would betray him, 'if Mr Croker had received that letter he would pass it to the Foreign Secretary.'

'What letter?' asked Drinkwater, letting the missive go. It fluttered from his hand, slid sideways into the draught drawn into the chimney, hovered a moment above the glowing coals, then began to sink, shrivelling, charring and then touching down in a little upsurge of yellow flame before it turned to black ash,

29

with a curl of grey smoke, and subsided among the clinkers in the grate. Drinkwater looked up, expecting outrage at this high-handed action, but was disappointed to see Templeton's face bore a look of such inscrutability that it crossed Drinkwater's mind that the clerk was pleased.

'I shall go to Harwich, Mr Templeton.'

'Tonight, sir?'

'Of course. Be so kind as to pass word for a chaise and let Williams know my portmanteau is to be made ready . . .'

'At once, at once . . .'

Templeton scuttled from the room and Drinkwater had the impression that he was actually running along the corridor outside. 'A rum fellow,' Drinkwater muttered, dismissively.

He rose from his chair, poured himself another glass of wine and took it to the window. He opened the shutters again. The moon had vanished and the night was black. Rain still drove on the panes, and the gusting wind rattled the sash incessantly.

'What a deuced dreadful night to go a-travelling,' he muttered to himself, but the window reflected a lop-sided grin above the rim of the wine glass.

2 A Secret from the South

September 1813

Lieutenant Sparkman dozed over the mulled wine, one booted leg stretched out on the wooden settle. Curled at his feet lay a brindled mongrel cur of menacing size. Periodically it came to frantic life, a hind leg vigorously clawing at a hidden flea, before it subsided again.

Having discommoded himself of the Neapolitan officer, he had not had much sleep in the arms of the energetic Annie. He was no longer a young man and the excesses of the night dissuaded him from taking too much of an interest in his report. He felt as weary that morning in the empty tap-room of the Three Cups at Harwich as he had at the Red Lion at Kirby-le-Soken the previous evening. He looked up as the latch of the door lifted and Annie, smiling at him above her unlaced stays and white breasts, led a stranger into the room.

'Tell your master that I want new horses in three hours and a dinner in two,' the stranger said, turning his back on Sparkman as he took off his tricorn and a heavy cloak and threw them on a wooden chair on the opposite side of the fireplace. The newcomer wore a suit of bottle-green which sat awkwardly on asymmetrical shoulders down which fell his hair in an old-fashioned queue set off with a black ribbon.

'New horses, sir, an' a dinner, aye, sir . . .' Annie bobbed and pouted at the newcomer and Sparkman felt a mean resentment at the intrusion, at the bossing of Annie Davis, at the little whore's attitude.

'Put some more coal on the fire,' Sparkman commanded, 'and get me a pipe and baccy while you're about it.'

Annie flashed him a quick, pleading look which spoke of obligations and priorities not purchased with his single florin.

'A glass of black-strap, if you please,' said the stranger, re-engaging Annie's attention, and she curtsied again, to Sparkman's intense irritation. But before he could add to the catalogue of Annie's chores, the man turned.

He was about fifty with a high forehead from which his grey-brown hair was drawn back severely. His face was lined and weatherbeaten, though a faint, pallid sword scar ran down his left cheek. His mouth, circumscribed by deep furrows, was expressive of contempt as he regarded the dishevelled Sparkman from stern grey eyes.

Sparkman's irritation withered under the stranger's scrutiny. He felt uncomfortably conscious of his dirty neck linen and the mud-stained boot outstretched on the settle seat. He lowered his eyes, raised the tankard to his lips. The fellow had no business with him and could go to the devil!

Drinkwater stared at the slovenly figure, noting the blue coat of naval undress uniform.

'Lieutenant Sparkman?'

Sparkman coughed with surprise, spluttering into his mulled wine in an infuriating indignity which he disguised in anger. 'And who the deuce wants to know?'

'You are Lieutenant Sparkman, Inspector of Sea Fencibles, are you not?' Drinkwater persisted coolly, drawing a paper from his breast pocket and shaking it so that the heavy seal fell, and unfolded it for Sparkman to read.

'I am Captain Nathaniel Drinkwater, from the Admiralty, Mr Sparkman. You wrote to their Lordships about a Colonel Bardolini.'

Sparkman's mouth fell open; he put his tankard down, wiped his hands upon his stained breeches and took Drinkwater's identification paper, looking at Drinkwater as he sat up straight.

'I beg pardon, sir . . .' He read the pass and handed it back. 'I beg pardon, sir, I had no idea . . . I wasn't expectin' . . .'

'No matter, Mr Sparkman, no matter.' Captain Drinkwater took the paper, refolded it and tucked it inside his coat.

'Where is this fellow Bardolini? In the Redoubt, I think you said.'

'Yes, sir, I thought it best . . .'

Annie Davis came back into the room with a glass of black-strap on a tray. 'Here you'm be, sir.'

'Obliged.' Drinkwater swallowed hard. 'No doubt you did think it for the best, Mr Sparkman, but I doubt Colonel Bardolini will be of so sanguine an opinion. Does he speak English?'

'Yes, very well.'

'Good. Where is this Redoubt?'

'You passed it, sir, just before you came to the main gate . . .'

'Ah yes, the glacis, I recollect it. Shall we go then?' Drinkwater tossed off the glass and swept up his cloak and hat. 'A dinner in two hours, my girl, and no later; a hot meat pie will do very well.'

Apart from its flagstaff, the Redoubt was as well hidden from sight as from cannon shot, nestling below a glacis which rose fifty feet above the level of the country. This slope terminated on the edge of a vertical counterscarp, and the brick bulk of the circular fort rose on the far side of a wide ditch. This was crossed by a drawbridge which led directly to the rampart, which was pierced by embrasures each housing a huge, black 24-pounder. Under the iron arch with its empty sconce, which marked the inconspicuous gateway to this military wonder, they were challenged halfheartedly by a blue-coated artilleryman on sentry duty. He had spied them walking out through the town's main gate and he had summoned a lieutenant who hurried up to greet them. For the second time in an hour, Drinkwater produced his identification.

'Your servant, sir,' the artillery officer said with a good deal more *savoir-faire* than Sparkman had mustered, handing back the paper. 'Lieutenant Patmore, sir, at your service. I've made the Italian officer as comfortable as possible, sir . . .' Patmore paused and shot a look at Sparkman, 'but I'm afraid he's frightfully touchy about his honour.'

Drinkwater regarded Sparkman and raised an

eyebrow. 'You may announce me, Mr Sparkman. Lead on, Mr Patmore.'

They turned left and for a moment Drinkwater caught a glimpse of the open sea to the south-east, then the opposing salient of Landguard Point with its much older fortification, a shingle distal which formed a breakwater to the Harwich Shelf whereon a dozen merchantmen, collier brigs for the most part, rode out the last of the gale. To the north the River Orwell disappeared beyond a pair of Martello towers, winding through woodland to the port of Ipswich. Somewhere, beyond those tree-tops, lay Gantley Hall beneath the roof of which dwelt his wife Elizabeth, his children Amelia and Richard, and all his worldly desires.

Closer, behind the roofs of Harwich itself, the River Stour stretched westward to Manningtree, where he had had his final change of horses prior to traversing its banks that very forenoon.

'Your batteries command the harbour very well, Mr Patmore. Have you been stationed here long?'

'I came with the guns, sir, from Woolwich, three years ago.'

They passed a stiffly rigid bombardier and two gunners, then turned suddenly, out of the wind and down through a stepped tunnel, descending rapidly to the level of the bottom of the dry moat, emerging within the wall's circumference on to a parade ground almost ninety feet across. Walking quickly round its edge they passed a number of wooden doors, some open, betraying a kitchen, a guardroom and the garrison's quarters, then stopped beside one which Sparkman unlocked.

Inside the casemate, wooden stalls formed the fort's prison, and at the opening of the door the inmate of the nearer leapt to his feet and Drinkwater saw the blazing dark eyes and fierce moustaches of the Neapolitan officer.

'This is an outrage! I demand you release me at once! I am invested with plenipotentiary powers by King Joachim Napoleon of Naples! An insult to me is an insult to the King my master! You have taken my sword and with my sword my honour! I wish to be taken to London . . .'

As this tirade burst upon them, Drinkwater turned to Patmore and, putting up a hand to the artillery officer's ear, asked, 'Do you have a room I could use? Somewhere you could serve some bread and meat, and perhaps a conciliatory bottle?'

Patmore nodded.

'Would you oblige me by attending to the matter?'

'Of course, sir. I advised Sparkman against this line of conduct.'

'Leave the matter to me, Mr Patmore.'

'Of course, sir. If you'll excuse me . . .' Patmore turned away, obviously glad to be out of the embarrassing din which echoed about the chamber.

'I give myself up to you, Signor Sparkman, in honour, in friendship, in trust. I have plenipotentiary powers . . .'

'Will you hold your damned tongue!' Sparkman cried, his efforts to expostulate having failed under Bardolini's verbal barrage. Bardolini grew quiet, seeing Drinkwater properly for the first time as he moved away from the door and ceased to be in silhouette to a man who had spent fifteen hours in the dark.

'This is Captain Drinkwater, Colonel, from London . . .'

'A *captain*,' Bardolini sneered, 'a *captain*? I am a colonel in the light cavalry of the Royal Life Guard! Am I to be met by a *captain*?'

'I am a captain in His Britannic Majesty's Royal Navy, Colonel Bardolini,' Drinkwater said, stepping forward and edging Sparkman to one side. 'I believe us to be equal in rank, sir,' he added with a hint of sarcasm which, he noted, was lost on Bardolini. 'Do you release our guest, Mr Sparkman.'

'I, er, I don't have the key, sir. Mr Patmore . . .'

'Then run and get it,' Drinkwater snapped. As soon as they were alone, he turned to Bardolini. 'I beg you to forgive the inconvenience to which you have been put, Colonel. You must appreciate the dangers of accepting everyone arriving from Europe at face value. Our orders are quite specific and to men of Lieutenant Sparkman's stamp, essential. D'you understand?'

'What is *stamp*?'

'Character . . .'

'Ah, *si*. Not so clever, eh?'

'Indeed, yes.' Drinkwater smiled. The untruthful but reassuring little collusion between two senior officers mollified Bardolini, and then Sparkman was back with a key and they led the Neapolitan out into a watery sunshine which showed the breaking up of the scud and foretold a shift in the wind. On the far side of the parade, Patmore stood beside an open door and Drinkwater began to walk towards him.

Behind him Bardolini stopped and looked up at the circle of sky above them, stretching ostentatiously. He ran a finger round his stock, then put on the hat which he had tucked under his arm. Drinkwater was amazed at the splendour of the man. He wore the tight *kurtka* deriving from the Polish lancers of the Grande Armée, a white jacket with a scarlet plastron and silver epaulettes. His long cavalry overalls were scarlet, trimmed with twin rows of silver lace, while his headdress also echoed the Polish fashion, a *czapka* with its peak and tall, square top, braided with silver and magnificently plumed in white. Colonel Bardolini was turned out in *la grande tenue* of parade dress and wanted only a shave to complete the impression of military perfection.

'Come, Colonel. I have ordered some meat and wine for you, and if you wish we can send for hot water for you to shave . . .'

'Good!' snapped Bardolini and crossed the parade.

Patmore led them into another casemate which served as the officers' mess. It was simply furnished with a table, chairs, a sideboard and some plate. Another artillery lieutenant lounged over a glass and bottle, already well down the latter for his welcome was heartily indulgent.

'Please sit down, gentlemen. Henry Courtney *à votre service*. Here, sir,' he said to Bardolini, 'your breakfast.' A gunner in shirt-sleeves brought in a platter of sliced meat and bread. Courtney poured wine into a second glass. Bardolini hesitated, then sat and fell ravenously upon the plate.

'Mr Courtney,' Drinkwater said as Bardolini devoured the food, 'would you do me the courtesy of allowing me a few moments of privacy with our guest?'

'Oh, I say, I've not finished . . .'

'Harry!'

Courtney turned and caught the severe look in Patmore's eye. 'Oh, very well,' he said unconvincingly, and rose with a certain display of languid condescension, 'as you wish.'

Drinkwater helped himself to a glass of wine as the door closed. The shirt-sleeved gunner looked in and Drinkwater dismissed him, closing the door behind him. Then he walked back to the table, drew the identification paper from his breast yet again and laid it before Bardolini. The Neapolitan read it, still chewing vigorously. Then he stopped and looked up.

'My own papers, they are with my sword and sabretache! I do not have them!'

'Calm yourself, my dear Colonel,' Drinkwater said and sat down opposite Bardolini. 'We can attend to the formalities on our way back to London. At the moment I wish only to know the purpose of your visit.'

'I have plenipotentiary powers, Captain. They are, with respect to yourself, for the ears of King George's ministers. I have a letter of introduction to Lord Castlereagh . . .'

'You speak excellent English, Colonel, where did you learn?' Drinkwater adroitly changed the subject.

'I worked for many years in the counting-house of an English merchant in Napoli. He taught it to all his clerks.'

'You were a clerk then, once upon a time?'

'But a republican always,' Bardolini flared.

'Yet you represent a king, and seek the ministers of a king. That is curious, is it not?'

'King Joachim is a soldier. He is a republican at heart, himself the son of an inn-keeper. He is a benevolent monarch, one who wishes to unite Italy and be a new Julius Caesar.'

'I thought Caesar refused a crown . . .'

'King Joachim is not a king as you understand it, Captain. Believe me, I lived under the rule of that despot Ferdinand and his Austrian bitch. They are filth, perhaps as mad as they say your own king is, but certainly filth, not worthy to eat the shit that ran out of the sewers of their own palazzo.'

'And yet I have to ask what King Joachim would say to the mad King George's ministers?'

'I cannot tell you.'

'I cannot take you to London.'

'You would not dare to refuse!' Bardolini's eyes blazed.

'Colonel, the ocean is wide, deep and cold. The men who have seen you today will have forgotten you in a month. Why do you think I have come here today? Do you think I myself do not have special powers, eh?' Drinkwater paused, letting his words sink in. 'Come, sir, telling me what you have come here for is likely to have little effect on matters if I am a man of no account. On the other hand, going forward to London on my recommendation will ensure your mission is swiftly accomplished.'

Bardolini remained silent.

'Let me guess, then. You are here in order to open secret negotiations to preserve the throne of Naples in the name of King Joachim Napoleon. You speak very good English and have plenipotentiary powers in case it becomes possible, in the course of your discussions, to conclude a formal accommodation, or even a full treaty of alliance, in which the British government guarantee Naples for the King your master who, though he remains a Marshal of France and Grand Admiral of the Empire, lost his French citizenship on succeeding to the crown of Naples.' Drinkwater paused, aware that he had Bardolini's full attention.

'You have, moreover, a difficult game to play because, on the one hand, King Joachim does not want his brother-in-law, the Emperor Napoleon, to know of this action. Nor does he wish the Austrians to learn of it, for while they may well toy with King Joachim, his desire to unite the Italian republicans and then the whole peninsula is inimical to their own interests. Moreover, it will cause deep offence to King Ferdinand, whose wife, Queen Maria Carolina, is not only the sister of the late Queen of France, Marie Antoinette, but was also born an Austrian arch-duchess and who, though ruling still in Sicily, has been deprived of the Italian portion of his kingdom by conquest. King Ferdinand regards your King Joachim as an usurper.

'Nevertheless, Prince Cariati at Vienna is assidu-ously pressing King Joachim's suit to the Austrian ministry. So your master must play a double game, for the Emperor Napoleon works to detach the Austrian Emperor from his alliance with us, thinking his own new wife, the Empress Marie-Louise, yet another Austrian archduchess, possesses influence to succeed in this endeavour, being daughter to the Emperor Francis himself.'

Drinkwater paused. Bardolini had ceased chewing and his jaw lay unpleasantly open so that half-

41

masticated food was exposed upon his tongue. Drinkwater poured another glass of wine and looked away.

'Now, Colonel, do you have anything to add to this?'

Bardolini shut his mouth, chewed rapidly and swallowed prematurely. He lunged at his glass and gulped at the claret, wiping his mouth on the scarlet turn-back of his cuff.

'*Sympatico*, Captain, we are of one mind!'

'Perhaps. But King George's ministers will be less easy to oblige than you imagine, Colonel. Consider. Your master has already communicated with us through his Minister of Police, the Duke of Campochiaro, who sent one of his agents, a certain Signor Cerculi, to discuss with Colonel Coffin at Ponza matters of trade and an easement of the naval blockade of Calabria. Is that not true? And after these negotiations had been concluded, Cerculi let it be known that King Joachim and his brother-in-law had fallen out, indeed, that they were frequently at odds. King Joachim wants to rule in his own name and Napoleon wants him as no more than a tributary-king, a puppet – a marionette. Is this not so?'

'How do you know all this?' Bardolini looked genuinely puzzled.

'Because', Drinkwater said, leaning forward and lowering his voice, 'Colonel Coffin reported the matter back to the Sicilian court at Palermo, and from there it was passed to London.'

Such a torrent of detail clearly surprised Bardolini. He was astonished at the knowledge possessed by this strange Englishman. He did not know that Coffin had regaled the British frigate captain with the whole story and he, bored with the tedium of blockade, had confided all the details to his routine report of proceedings. This, in turn, had crossed Drinkwater's desk within two months, at the same time that the confidential diplomatic dispatch from Sicily had reached the office of the Foreign Secretary.

'But therein lies our dilemma, Colonel,' Drinkwater continued relentlessly. 'King Ferdinand has been assured that the British government wants to see the King of the Two Sicilies restored to his rightful place in his palace at Naples. How, then, can His Britannic Majesty's government take King Joachim seriously?'

It was, Drinkwater thought wryly, a fair question. Napoleon Bonaparte, having driven Ferdinand across the Strait of Messina, placed his brother Joseph on the vacant throne at Naples, leaving Ferdinand and Maria Carolina to vegetate under British protection at Palermo. Then, when he deceived the King of Spain and took him prisoner, Napoleon transferred Joseph to Madrid, installing him as king there, and sent Marshal Murat to Naples as King Joachim. It was rather a tawdry and expedient proceeding.

'Ferdinand is not important. He fled in English ships to Palermo. You support him there, without English ships he is powerless. Your government can abandon Ferdinand. Lord William Bentinck, your former minister at Palermo, has already been recalled by Lord Castlereagh.'

'But what has King Joachim to offer us in exchange for our protection? Can he guarantee that, if we maintain the dignity of his throne, the people of Naples, let alone of the whole of Italy, will acknowledge him as king?'

'*Si!* Yes! He is most popular! Without your ships, Ferdinand would be lost and Sicily would join all of Italy. Would that not be better for England? To have a friendly power in the Mediterranean? You would like a naval port at Livorno, or La Spezia.'

'Perhaps. Are you empowered to offer us a naval port?'

Bardolini shrugged again and looked about him. 'This is not the place . . .'

Drinkwater grinned. 'You may have to content yourself with such a place, Colonel,' he said dryly, 'you are in my hands now,' and his expression and tone of voice, strained by tiredness, appeared to Bardolini to be full of menace.

In fact Drinkwater was disappointed. The Neapolitan had nothing to offer. Joachim Murat was hedging his bets fantastically. It would be an act of humanity to send this candy-stick officer back to Flushing by the first available boat, but perhaps he would play the charade for just a little longer.

'Well, Colonel,' he said with an air of finality, stirring as though to rise and call Patmore and Sparkman, 'is King Joachim to be trusted? He is married to Caroline Bonaparte, the Emperor's sister. If he commits himself to coming over to the Allied cause like Bernadotte, his position must be unassailable. He courts Austria, which has her own deep interest in Tuscany and the Papal States, and would rather an accommodation with Ferdinand of the Two Sicilies than the adventurer and parvenu King Joachim . . .'

'Captain! You should not call him that! He is brave,

44

and true! And devoted to his people and the Rights of Man!'

The sincerity of Bardolini's florid passion was genuine, though he had looked angry at Drinkwater's reference to Bernadotte. They were getting nowhere. For all the confidence of his exposition, Drinkwater was exhausted. The overnight journey jolting in a chaise, turning over and over in his mind the likely outcome of this queer meeting; the memorizing of the notes he had scribbled from a quick rereading of the guard books; the rehearsal of facts; the guessing at motives and the building in his own mind of a convincing, watertight reason for this singular, strange invasion, had left him weary. He had wanted to rage at the imbecile Sparkman, so obviously raddled by a night of dissolution, yet the lieutenant's inhumane treatment of Bardolini had left the man indignant for his own honour, and unguarded about his master's.

Drinkwater mustered his wits for one last argument. The drink had made him dopey and he forced himself to his feet, leaning forward for emphasis, his hands spread on the table before him. Again he managed a thin smile at Bardolini.

'There is one last point that we must consider, Colonel Bardolini. Where is the King of Naples now?'

The question caught Bardolini off guard. 'He is at Dresden.'

'With his Emperor?'

'With the Emperor of the French, yes.'

'As a Marshal of France, commanding the cavalry of the Grande Armée.'

Bardolini nodded, frowning.

'Yet he must be on the winning side, must he not?

And to preserve his integrity it must never be known that he treated with the other. Is that not so?'

'You are an intelligent man, Captain. The King is married to the Emperor's sister. They correspond. There could be no absolute secrets between them . . .'

'No!' snapped Drinkwater with sudden vehemence. 'Bonaparte is a cynic; he will overlook base ingratitude, even treason if it serves his purpose, but do you think the Emperor Francis of Austria will be so tolerant? He is not so *republican* a king.'

Bardolini shrugged, missing the sarcasm. 'The Emperor Francis will bow if England is in alliance with the King of Napoli. A man who will declare war on the husband of his daughter will do anything.'

The cogency of the argument was impressive; and Bardolini's diplomatic ability was clear. Drinkwater fought to retain control of the dialogue.

'But, Colonel Bardolini, even as we speak Marshal Murat is in the field alongside his imperial brother-in-law. At least Bernadotte has repudiated his former master and is at the head of his Swedish troops and in command of an Allied army. His victory over his old friend Marshal Oudinot at Gross Beeren can hardly be called equivocating. Moreover, Colonel, on the sixth of this month, this same *ci-devant* republican soldier of France beat another old friend, Michel Ney, at Dennewitz. You did not know that, eh?' Drinkwater paused to let the import of the news sink in, then added, 'but your master has no such earnest of good faith to offer from his headquarters at Dresden, does he, eh? He behaves as he is, a tributary king, a puppy fawning on the hand that feeds him.'

Drinkwater finished his diatribe. Tiredness lent a

menace to his final words and Bardolini was visibly upset by the torrent of logic poured upon him by this apparently scornful Englishman. He remained silent as Drinkwater straightened up, contemplating the evaporation of his hopes.

'Come, sir. We will summon your sword and sabretache. You shall accompany me to an inn where my chaise will be ready. You may shave there while I eat. I can promise you nothing, but we will proceed to London.'

Bardolini looked relieved as he stood and reached for his ornate *czapka*.

'By the way, Colonel, we do not need an Italian port as long as we have Malta. Besides, how long could we trust a king who was married to a Bonaparte princess, eh? Tell me that if you can.'

Suddenly, in the ill-lit casemate, the beplumed Neapolitan looked ridiculously crestfallen.

The wind, which had veered in the night and brought a cold forenoon of bright sunshine, backed against the sun as it westered, so that the sky clouded and it began to rain long before they reached Colchester. Drinkwater was tempted to stop and spend the night there, but the steak-and-kidney pie Annie Davis had served him at the Three Cups put him into a doze so that inertia dissuaded him from making a decision and the chaise rumbled on westward.

He had no thought now but to disencumber himself of Bardolini as soon as they reached London, and when he woke briefly as they changed horses he felt only an intense irritation that he could not have turned north at Manningtree, crossed the Stour and taken the Ipswich road towards Gantley Hall and his wife Elizabeth's bed.

The recent weather had turned the road into a quagmire. Every rut had become a ditch, the horses were muddied to their bellies and the wheels spun arcs of filth behind them. The chaise lurched over this morass and bucked and rocked in the gusts of wind, the rain drummed on the hood and he heard Bardolini cursing, though whether it was the weather or his predicament that most discommoded the Neapolitan, Drinkwater neither knew nor cared. At about eleven that night it stopped raining. On the open road the going improved and they reached Kelvedon before midnight. Both men got out to stretch their legs and visit the necessary at the post-house. A draught of flip restored Drinkwater to a lucid state of mind. The stimulus of the alcohol and the irregular motion of the chaise when they drove forward again continued to make sleep impossible. Bardolini, sitting opposite, was equally unable to doze off and in the intermittent moonlight that peeped from behind the torn and ragged cumulus, Drinkwater was aware of the fierce glitter of the Neapolitan officer's eyes.

Initially Drinkwater expected sudden attack, an instinctive if illogical fear of treacherous assault. But then he realized Bardolini was caught in a reverie and his eyes merely sought the future. Or perhaps the past, Drinkwater mused, which might be full of disappointments, but was at least inhabited by certainties. As he had found so often at sea, the light doze he had enjoyed earlier had restored him, and he felt an indulgence towards his fellow-traveller.

'Colonel,' he said, as they passed through a patch

of brilliant moonlight and he could see Bardolini's face in stark tones, 'I do not hold out much hope for your mission. *Entre nous*, the idea of a republican king is something of a contradiction in terms. Your reception in London is not likely to be, what do you say? *Sympatico?*'

'I have plenipotentiary powers, Captain. I am on diplomatic service. I expect the normal courtesies . . .'

'I do not wish to alarm you unduly, Colonel, but I am not aware that we recognize the government of King Joachim. Only your uniform prevents your arrest as a spy. That, and my company.'

'But you will take me to Lord Castlereagh, Captain?' Bardolini asked with a plaintive anxiety.

'I will send word to the Foreign Secretary that you are in London, but . . .' Drinkwater left the conjunction hanging in the darkness that now engulfed the two men. The unspoken cláuse was ominous and, unknown to Drinkwater, had the effect on the Neapolitan of causing him to come to a decision.

Upon landing in England, Colonel Bardolini had expected to be quickly picked up by the police, to be whisked to London with the Napoleonic thoroughness by which such things were managed in the French Empire and those states under its influence. He had not expected to stumble upon the discreditable Sparkman and then be locked up like a common criminal. Protestations about his honour, his plenipotentiary status and offers of his parole had fallen upon deaf ears. Now Drinkwater's assertions clothed this outrage with a chilling logic. The English were, just as he had been led to believe, barbarians.

Notwithstanding these considerations, Bardolini

had not anticipated this strange English naval officer would possess such a commanding knowledge of the situation in Napoli; it was uncanny. Indeed, such was the extent of the captain's familiarity with the plight of his master, King Joachim, that Bardolini suspected treachery. His imprisonment was consonant with such a hypothesis and he believed he was, even now, on his way to a more secure incarceration.

The only thing which Bardolini *had* expected was the violence of the sea passage and the weather which now assailed the chaise and deterred him from any rash ideas of escape. Not that he had abandoned them altogether; he carried a stiletto inside his right boot, but to reach it beneath his tight cavalryman's overalls was well-nigh impossible, and his sword was secured to his portmanteau. Besides, there were other considerations. Though he spoke English well, he could hardly melt inconspicuously into the countryside! Besides, if he stole a horse, he would only be returned the faster to the shores of that damnable sea.

As the dismal hours succeeded one another, he resolved on the one course of action he had reserved for Lord Castlereagh alone, in the hope that this naval officer, whose grasp of diplomatic affairs seemed so inexplicably comprehensive, would favourably influence his request for an interview with the British Foreign Minister. Now, as Drinkwater hinted so forbiddingly at the hostility of his reception, Bardolini played his trump card and spoke out of the darkness.

'Captain Drinkwater, I believe you to be a man of honour. You are clearly a person of some influence, your knowledge of affairs of state makes that quite clear. It is possible you are a police agent . . . If that is so, I ask only that what I am about to confide in you, you report to your superiors . . .'

'I am not a police agent, Colonel. We have not yet adopted all your Continental fashions. I am what I told you.'

'Perhaps,' Bardolini acknowledged doubtfully, 'but your word, please, that what I tell you will be treated with the confidence it deserves and be passed to Lord Castlereagh himself.'

'Are you about to give me a pledge of your master's good faith?'

'*Si.*'

'Very well. You have my word.'

'You are at war with the Americans, are you not?'

'You know that very well.'

'I also know that there are men in America who would rule Canada, and Frenchmen in Canada who would welcome American assistance to separate them from your country, even if it meant joining the United States.'

'That is not a very great secret, Colonel.'

'No. But King Joachim wishes to make known to your government that the Americans have negotiated a secret treaty of mutual assistance with the Emperor Napoleon, a treaty which, in exchange for American attacks on British ships and a quantity of gold, guarantees a large shipment of arms, powder and shot. These are to be used for raising a revolution in Quebec. The Quebecois will join up with an American army marching north from New York next spring.'

'Go on, Colonel, you have my full attention.'

'During the winter bad weather, American ships will arrive in the waters of Norway . . .'

51

'Where in Norway?' Drinkwater cut in.

'A place called the Vikkenfiord.'

'Go on, Colonel.'

'Secretly, the arms and munitions will be taken to them by the Danes. The Americans will also stop supplying your army in the Iberian Peninsula. The Emperor believes that with rebellion in Canada, your government will no longer be able to support the Spanish insurrection, will withdraw Wellington's army and transport it to North America. Great Britain will retreat behind its traditional defence, the sea. It will not be able to expend its treasure on maintaining Austrian, Prussian and Russian armies in the field. Your country's alliance will die and the Emperor of Austria will accept King Joachim as the sovereign of Italy.'

But Drinkwater was no longer listening; he was thinking of Herr Liepmann's dispatch and the shipment of arms lying somewhere in Hamburg.

3   Arrivals
September 1813

There was a clever simplicity in Bardolini's revelations. Not only was their substance of crucial importance to the survival of Great Britain, but the plan was cunning in its construction, satisfying both political and economic needs. For while raising rebellion and absorbing Canada in the Union would placate the war-hawks in the American Congress, it would also compensate the United States' treasury for the loss of British gold now paid for the grain being sent to Wellington's army in Spain. For Britain herself, the loss of American supplies was more important than the saving to her exchequer. It was well known that the Americans were happy to export to both contending parties in the great war in Europe, and that they sold wheat to the British with whom they were themselves at war! But a greater irony existed if the arms they were to buy from the French were paid for with gold sent to the United States by Great Britain in the first place.

This vast and complex circulation wormed its way into Drinkwater's tired brain as the buffeted chaise passed Chelmsford and rumbled on towards London.

He mused on the tortuous yet simple logic, aware from his own experience with Yankee privateers that American ambition was as resourceful as it was boundless. There was, moreover, an insidious and personal reflection in his train of thought. In all the weary months he had spent at the Admiralty's Secret Department, he had hoped for some news like Bardolini's. He had not the slightest doubt that the Neapolitan colonel had been delivered into his hands by Providence itself, nor that it was not Joachim Murat's secret overtures that were the most important feature of Bardolini's intelligence.

The fantastical image of Napoleon's great cavalry leader was a tragi-comic figure in Drinkwater's perception, a man raised to such heights of pomp and pride that violent descent could be its only consequence. The very weakness of the parvenu king's position, his desire to maintain friends on both sides of the fence, so that when he tumbled from it there would be waiting arms to save him, was too ridiculous to be treated seriously.

King Joachim's secret earnest of good faith, the revelation of the bargain struck between the French Emperor and the Americans, was clever enough, for it was invaluable to Great Britain, but its defeat, if the British chose to act, left King Joachim untouched and would hurt his brother-in-law enough to incline fate to favour the Allied cause. Nor was its betrayal a serious enough treachery to deprive Murat of his kingdom if Napoleon defeated his enemies in detail. The French Emperor was not a man to deprive the husband of his favourite sister of his crown for a mere peccadillo!

Nor could Drinkwater ignore the consequences of

success for Napoleon himself. If the Emperor of the French did succeed in forcing the British to withdraw Wellington's army for service in America or Canada, such a move would not only remove the threat to southern France, it would also release battle-hardened troops under his most experienced marshals to reinforce the ranks of the green 'Marie-Louises' now opposing the combined might of Russia, Prussia and Austria.

As Drinkwater nursed an aching head and the beginnings of yet another quinsy, as he slipped in and out of conscious thought, nodding opposite the now sleeping Bardolini, his resolve hardened round the central thought that this was without doubt the event for which Lord Dungarth had named Nathaniel Drinkwater his successor in the Secret Department of the British Admiralty.

In his tired and half-conscious state, Drinkwater found nothing incongruous in attributing Dungarth with such prescience. The earl had possessed a keen and analytical brain and had been quite capable of sensing some innate ability in his ageing protégé. But for Drinkwater it was to prove a dangerously deluded piece of self-conceit.

Drinkwater was at his desk by three o'clock that afternoon. When they changed horses at Brentwood he had instructed the post boy to take them directly to his home in Lord North Street. Both he and Bardolini were jerked rudely awake when the chaise finally stopped outside the terraced house.

The place had been left to Drinkwater by Lord Dungarth with a pitifully small legacy for its upkeep and the continued maintenance of its staff. It was a modest house, the austere earl's only London establishment, which had become home for Drinkwater now that his new post detained him so much in the capital. Ideas of a convenient *pied-à-terre* for Captain and Mistress Drinkwater had proved impractical. Elizabeth, never entirely at ease in town, had almost conceded defeat, and contented herself with running the small Suffolk estate, while Drinkwater led his own miserable and unhappy existence dragging daily to Whitehall.

He had done nothing to the interior of the house and it remained as it had been when Dungarth occupied it. He had even ordered Williams, Dungarth's manservant, who had performed the joint offices of butler, valet and occasional secretary to the earl, to retain the black crêpe drapes over the full-length portrait of Dungarth's long-dead countess which hung above the fireplace in the withdrawing-room. The gesture had earned Williams's approval and the transfer of loyalty to Captain Drinkwater had thereafter been total.

'He's very like his Lordship in many ways,' Williams had confided to his common-law wife who, as cook and housekeeper, formed the remainder of the staff.

'Yes, he's a gennelman all right,' she agreed.

'Not *quite* in the same way as Lord John was,' Williams added, his notion of the finer distinctions of society more acute than that of his spouse, his terminology uttered with an unassailable familiarity, 'but inclining that way, to be sure.'

'To be sure,' agreed his wife docilely, aware that her own status was as much a matter of delicate uncertainty as Captain Drinkwater's, and always anxious to avoid the slightest disturbance to her husband's tranquillity of mind which, he had long ago assured her, was of the utmost importance in their relationship.

Williams now met Drinkwater and took his instructions. The strange colonel was to be given every comfort; a meal, a bath and, if he wished, an immediate bed after his long and tedious journey.

Williams's long service had conditioned him to odd arrivals and departures. He was well aware of the nature of the business of his employers, past and present, and the moustachioed figure was but one of a succession of ill-assorted 'guests' that he had accommodated. Having instructed Williams, Drinkwater turned to Bardolini.

'My dear Colonel, please accept my hospitality without my presence. Williams here will see to your wants. You must, as we say, make yourself at home.' He smiled at Bardolini who, as he removed his cloak, looked round with an air of curiosity, then gravely bowed a courtly acknowledgement. He looked every inch the plenipotentiary in his scarlet, white and silver.

'Thank you, Captain.'

'I shall leave you for a matter of a few hours. We will dine together tonight, when I hope to have news for you. In the meantime I will announce your arrival.'

'You wish to see my accreditation?' asked Bardolini, recovering his dangling sabretache on its silver-laced straps.

'Indeed, I do.'

'I am trusting you, Captain, with my life,' Bardolini

said solemnly, handing over the heavily sealed paper which Drinkwater opened and scanned briefly.

'It is not misplaced, I assure you,' said Drinkwater, turning to Williams. 'See Colonel Bardolini wants for nothing, if you please, Williams. I shall be back for dinner at eight.'

Thus Captain Drinkwater was at the Admiralty before the clock at the Horse Guards struck three hours after noon.

Templeton met him as the Admiralty porter stirred himself from his chair.

'Good to have you return, sir,' said Templeton with a curtness that drew Drinkwater's attention to the fixed and unhappy expression on his face. 'Shall we go up directly?'

'As you please, Templeton,' said Drinkwater, somewhat nonplussed by his clerk's obvious discomfiture.

'What the devil's the matter?' Drinkwater asked, the moment they were inside his room. They had met but one other clerk upon the stairs and he had drawn aside with an unusual display of deference as Templeton had sped past, so that Drinkwater became alarmed at what news had broken in his absence.

'Barrow is the matter, sir. He has closed us down without further ado and in your absence. The matter is most improper.' Templeton fidgeted with an unhappy agitation, his face pale and anxious. 'The guard books are to be transferred to the Second Secretary's office, sir, and I,' Templeton's voice cracked with emotion, 'I am to be returned to the general copy room.'

It was not the worst fate that could befall an

Englishman, Drinkwater thought, Templeton could be press-ganged, but he forbore from pointing this out. Nevertheless, it was clear that this humiliation had hurt the clerk, for news of the projected closure had come as no surprise. The thought sowed a seed in Drinkwater's over-stimulated brain but, for the moment, he confined himself to a sympathetic concern.

'My dear fellow, that is bad news, but don't despair, perhaps . . .'

Templeton shook his head. 'I have remonstrated with Barrow, sir. He is adamant that our activities can be subsumed by his own office and that my own personal expertise is of little consequence.' Templeton paused to master his bitterness, adding, with a touch of venom, 'I think he is jealous of our independence.'

'I shouldn't wonder,' Drinkwater temporized, pondering on how best to further matters in so far as Bardolini's news was concerned.

'I assured him that, notwithstanding our lack of recent progress, there were indications that matters of importance would shortly come to a head and that your own absence testified to this.' Templeton fell ominously silent. There was obviously an element of deep and significant drama, at least as far as Templeton was concerned, in this exchange.

'What did Mr Barrow say to that?' Drinkwater prompted with a tolerant patience he was far from feeling.

'He said', Templeton began with an evasive air, as if he found the admission distasteful, 'that it did not seem to much matter these days whether you were in or out, sir, but that on balance your achievements in the past had proved rather more effective in the public service when you were out, preferably at sea, sir.'

Drinkwater suppressed an outburst of laughter with a snort that Templeton construed as indignation. In all justice Drinkwater could not find much flaw in Barrow's decision, given that Barrow knew nothing of the events of the last two days, but in consideration of Templeton's feelings, he kept his face straight.

'It is my fault, I'm afraid, Barrow has never liked me . . .'

'I find it difficult to see why, sir.'

'Thank you, but we disagreed some years ago and I think he has seen my installation here as something to be terminated when the opportunity arose. I do not believe he wanted the department to outlive Lord Dungarth. Anyway, I think it is no matter now . . .'

'Oh, yes . . . forgive me, Captain Drinkwater, I have been so unseated by this unpleasant matter . . .'

'Of course, Templeton, of course. I take it you do not wish to return to the copy room?'

'The loss of emolument, sir . . .' Templeton looked aghast.

'How attached *are* you to my person, Templeton? Sufficient to go a-voyaging?'

'To sea, sir?' Templeton asked incredulously.

'That is the purpose of Admiralty,' Drinkwater replied drily.

'Well yes, sir, I understand, but my widowed mother . . .' Templeton was deathly pale.

'Never mind, then,' Drinkwater said brusquely, 'go at once and inform Mr Barrow of my return and my desire to speak with Mr Croker. Then, if you please, find out for me the ships and vessels currently at anchor in roadsteads on the east coast, from the Downs to Leith. A list of guardships and convoy escorts, that sort of thing, do you understand?'

'Perfectly.' The clerk's voice was not above a whisper.

'Good, then bring that to me, wherever I am in the building.'

Barrow received Drinkwater in his spacious office. Neither man had alluded to their disagreement some six years earlier.* Indeed Drinkwater supposed Barrow had long ago forgotten about it, for it was Drinkwater himself who had been the more angered by their unfortunate encounter. Nevertheless, since his posting to the Secret Department, memory of the matter had disinclined Drinkwater to force his presence on the Second Secretary and he had preferred to rely upon written memoranda to communicate with the Board.

'Pray sit down, Captain Drinkwater. Mr Croker has taken his seat in the House today and I have therefore taken the liberty of asking you to see me. I think I know why you wish to speak with the First Secretary and I apologize for the manner in which you learned of our decision to incorporate Lord Dungarth's old office with my own. I am sure you can see the logic . . .'

'I perfectly understand the logic, Mr Barrow,' Drinkwater broke in, 'and it is *not* what I have come to discuss with either Mr Croker or yourself.'

'Oh, I see, then what may I ask . . . ?'

* See *Baltic Mission*.

'Templeton is somewhat anxious about his future as, I admit, I am for my own.'

Barrow was immediately deceived by Drinkwater's opening. He was used to self-seeking, whether it was that of clerks or sea-officers, but it was crucial to Drinkwater that he should know whether or not the Admiralty had any plans for himself.

'We thought perhaps some furlough; you have not had the opportunity to spend much time on your estate, nor to enjoy the society of your wife and family.'

'You have no plans for me to have a ship?'

'Not immediately, Captain, no. There are Edwardes and Milne both clamouring for release from the American blockade, and when Green returns from the West Indies . . .'

'I am not anxious for a seventy-four.'

'No, quite, blockade is a confoundedly tedious business, I'm told.' Barrow smiled. 'Since you're too old for a frigate,' he added with a laugh, 'it looks as if your Suffolk acres will have to serve you for a quarterdeck.'

Drinkwater ignored the mockery and changed the subject. 'I have been away, Mr Barrow, and I desire you to communicate a matter of some importance to the Foreign Secretary directly.'

'And what is that?' Barrow asked with unfeigned surprise.

'I have, in my custody, a Colonel Bardolini of the household cavalry of King Joachim of Naples. The King, if that is what he is, wishes to secure a guarantee from His Britannic Majesty's government that, irrespective of the fate of the Emperor of the French,

Joachim Napoleon will remain King of Naples.'

'But King Ferdinand . . .'

'I have explained *all* the ramifications attaching to the matter,' Drinkwater said wearily, drawing from his breast pocket Bardolini's diplomatic accreditation and laying it on the desk before Barrow. 'Moreover, I am of the opinion that King Joachim is a reed awaiting the stronger breeze. Nevertheless, Bardolini has been invested with plenipotentiary powers and sent here on a mission to the Court of St James's.'

Barrow leaned forward and drew the document towards him. 'Murat,' he murmured, reading the paper, 'well, well.'

'There is another matter, Mr Barrow,' Drinkwater began, but he was interrupted by a knock at the door.

'Come,' Barrow called, without looking up from Bardolini's paper.

Templeton approached across the carpet and held out a sheet of paper. Drinkwater took it and stared at it. Templeton had written: *The Downs*, *The Nore*, *Ho'sley Bay*, *Yarmouth*, *The Humber*, *Tyne*, *Leith*, and under each the names of one or two ships.

'What is that? What do you want, Templeton?' Barrow looked up, frowning at the intrusion.

'My fault, Mr Barrow,' Drinkwater put in quickly, 'I asked Templeton to bring me a list of ships in the ports of the east coast . . .'

'What on earth for . . . ?'

'Thank you, Templeton, kindly wait for me in my room.'

'Very well, sir.' Reluctance was in every step of the clerk's retreat.

'Captain, if you please, explain . . .'

'Of course, Mr Barrow, of course. There is another matter arising out of this approach from Marshal Murat . . .'

'I presume this other matter touches us . . . I mean their Lordships, rather than the Foreign Secretary?'

'You are an astute man, Mr Barrow.'

Drinkwater explained, repeating Bardolini's revelation and adding the corroborative evidence from Herr Liepmann at Hamburg sent through the British-held island of Helgoland. When he had finished, Barrow was silent for a moment. 'I recollect', he said gravely, 'your report on the destruction of the American privateers, and the concomitant matters you raised.' Barrow frowned, deep in thought. 'You are uniquely placed to understand the importance of this intelligence, are you not?'

'Hence this paper, Mr Barrow.'

'The paper?' Barrow frowned again, but this time with incomprehension.

'I want two things, Mr Barrow . . .'

'You *want* . . . ?'

'You give my office a brief stay of execution and you give me', he looked down at the paper Templeton had brought to where his thumb lay adjacent to the note *Leith*, 'the frigate *Andromeda*.'

'But I . . .'

'Come, come, I have been here long enough to know Lord Melville will put his name to anything you recommend, as will Mr Croker . . .'

Barrow grunted, fell silent, then said, 'But is one frigate enough, Captain? You had a flying squadron at your disposal before.'

'Another thing I have learned is that we have few

enough ships to protect our own trade, Mr Barrow. How many can you spare me? The cutter *Kestrel* used to be at Lord Dungarth's disposal, but she has long since . . .'

'No, no, you may have her, if you wish, as a tender or dispatch vessel.'

'And I may write my own orders?'

'You may *draft* your own orders, Captain,' said Barrow smiling, 'and you may retain Templeton to do it . . .'

'I was thinking of taking him to sea.'

'A capital idea.'

'I think their Lordships might permit me the luxury of a secretary.'

'I think they might be persuaded.' Relief at having the problem of Templeton so neatly resolved delighted Barrow.

Drinkwater rose. 'What of Bardolini? He is safe enough with me for a few days and I shall want a week to make my preparations, but after that he will be an encumbrance.'

'Give me a day or two, Captain Drinkwater, and I will let you know – by, say, Thursday?'

Drinkwater nodded. 'What d'you think Castlereagh will do?'

'I would imagine almost anything to string Murat along and prevent him giving his wholehearted support to Bonaparte.'

'So we will send Bardolini back with a diplomatic humbug?'

'It is not for me to say, but I would imagine so.'

'Poor fellow.'

'*C'est la guerre, n'est-ce pas?* You may send him to

Helgoland in the *Kestrel*. He may then be landed near Hamburg and rejoin his master at Dresden.'

Drinkwater nodded. 'Very well. I shall hear from you by Thursday?'

'Of course.'

Whether or not Barrow recalled their past disagreement, Drinkwater had forgotten it as he left the room.

Templeton was not in his room when Drinkwater returned to it, and he sat and contemplated the papers on his desk. A dozen dispatches and reports had come in in his absence, an unusual amount for two days and ironic in the light of the imminent demise of his office. The sheets were neatly minuted in Templeton's impeccable script and, where necessary, additional sheets of paper were pinned to the originals, decryptions of enciphered text.

He riffled through them. They were tediously routine: a deciphered message from a Chouan agent in Brittany recounting the numbers of French warships in Brest which would serve merely to corroborate the sightings of the blockading frigates off Ushant; a report from St Helier in the Channel Islands about a small convoy which would have reached its destination by now; and a report from Exeter concerning the escape of a score of American prisoners-of-war from a working detail sent out from Dartmoor prison.

Templeton entered the room at that moment. 'I'm sorry, sir, I . . .'

Drinkwater waved aside the man's apology. 'No matter. How do we come to receive this? This is a matter for the civil authorities.' He indicated the report concerning the American prisoners.

'They were seamen, sir, and therefore we were noti-fied. We usually inform the Regulating Captains . . .'

'And they try and pick them up for service in our own fleet, eh?'

'I believe so, sir. They are more productive serving His Majesty at sea, rather than being detained at His Majesty's pleasure ashore!'

'A vicious habit, Templeton, which don't make the life of a sea-officer at all comfortable, and a pretty extremity to be driven to.' Drinkwater pulled himself up short. Templeton was not to blame for such matters, though it would do him good to see something of life's realities. 'Besides,' he added, 'they were not idle when they escaped, they were building dry-stone walls.'

'Yes, sir,' Templeton said resignedly, leaning for-ward and drawing a last letter to Drinkwater's attention. 'There is a *post scriptum* to the affair.'

Drinkwater took the letter and read it. 'So they melted into the countryside. Does the fact seem the least remarkable to you, Templeton? Wouldn't you have done the same?'

'It is customary to have a few reports of sightings.'

Drinkwater dropped the letter. 'Pass these to Mr Barrow's people. We have other work to do. Do you draft orders, in the usual form, to the officer com-manding HMS *Andromeda* . . .'

'He is not on board, sir, having been lately called to Parliament . . .'

'Then that is his damned bad luck, who is he?'

'Captain Pardoe. He is the Member for Eyesham.'

'Well, so much the better for Eyesham. An order for his replacement, my commission . . . where is *Kestrel*?'

'*Kestrel*, sir? Er, she is a cutter . . .'

'I know *what* she is, I want to know *where* she is.'

'Laid up, I think,' said Templeton frowning, 'at Chatham, I believe.'

'Find out. Let me know. Now I shall write to my wife. We have less than a week before we leave London, Templeton.'

'*We*, sir?'

'Yes. You are appointed my secretary.'

Templeton stared blankly at Drinkwater and opened his mouth to protest. It had gone dry and he found it difficult to speak, managing only a little gasp before Drinkwater's glare dissuaded him from the matter and he fled. To lose all hope of elevation and suffer the ignominy of virtual demotion was enough for one day, but to be a pressed man as well was more than flesh and blood could stand. Templeton reeled out into the corridor dashing the tears from his eyes.

He left behind a chuckling Drinkwater who drew a clean sheet of paper towards him, picked up his pen and flipped open the inkwell.

My Darling Wife . . . he began to write and, for a few moments, all thoughts of the war left him. As he finished the letter he looked up. It was almost dark and the unlit room allowed his eyes to focus on the deep blue of the cloudless evening sky. The first stars twinkled dimly, increasing in brilliance as he watched, marvelling.

He would soon see again not merely those four circumscribed rectangles, but the entire, majestic firmament.

It was almost a cruelty to bring Elizabeth to London

for a mere three days, but two in the society of Bardolini, who insisted on continually badgering his host for news, was a trial to Drinkwater for whom the wait, with little to do beyond a brief daily attendance at the Admiralty, was tedious enough.

Difficulties began to crowd him within an hour of his wife's arrival. Bardolini insisted upon paying her elaborate court, depriving her husband of even the chilliest formality of a greeting, but then a more serious arrival in the shape of the young Captain Pardoe threatened to upset Drinkwater's humour still further.

'I understand, sir, that it is largely upon your intervention that I have been deprived of my command,' Pardoe had expostulated on the doorstep.

'Whereas I understand the demands of party expect you in Westminster, sir, where, happily, you are,' Drinkwater replied coolly.

'Damn it, sir, by what right do you . . . ?'

'You are making a fool of yourself, Captain Pardoe, pray come inside . . .' Pardoe was admitted and confronted with the uniformed splendour of Colonel Bardolini. Introductions were effected to both the Neapolitan and Elizabeth, hushing Pardoe. At an opportune moment, Drinkwater was able to draw him aside and whisper, 'Colonel Bardolini is an important diplomatic envoy. Your ship is wanted for a mission of some delicacy, such that an officer of my seniority must assume command. It was thought better all round by the ministry that you should take your seat, I believe you are warm in the government's cause, and I should take command.'

Drinkwater's dark dissimulation appeared to have

a swiftly mollifying effect. 'I see,' said Pardoe. 'Of course, if that is the case, I am naturally happy to oblige.'

'We knew you would be, Pardoe,' Drinkwater smiled, hoping Pardoe connected all the insinuations and believed *Andromeda* to be bound for the Mediterranean.

'D'you care for some tea, Captain?' asked Elizabeth soothingly, and the awkward incident passed, dissolving into the inconsequential small-talk of the moment. Elizabeth delighted in talking to a man who seemed to be at the heart of affairs and Drinkwater unobtrusively observed the pleasure she took in the company of Pardoe and Bardolini.

When, at last, they were alone together in their bedroom and Elizabeth had unburdened herself of news of the farms and the well-being of family and tenantry, he asked, 'Have you seen James Quilhampton recently?'

'Yes. He was dandling his son on his knee,' Elizabeth said pointedly.

'But was anxious for employment?'

'He did not say.'

'Bess, I . . .'

'You said you would not be going to sea again, not that it matters much since I think I would rather you were as sea than languishing in this gloomy place.'

'I thought you liked this house?'

'When it was Lord Dungarth's, I did; as your London establishment, I don't care for it at all.

'Johnnie died in this room, didn't he?' His wife's familiar reference to the dead Dungarth discomfited Drinkwater. She had been as fond of him as he of her, and the difference between the sexes had led to an easing of the formalities that bound her husband. He changed the subject.

'I have to go, Bess . . .'

'I know, affairs of state,' she sighed, then resumed, 'though I wonder what important matters demand the presence of so obscure an officer as my husband.'

'Perhaps I am not so obscure,' he said, in a poor attempt to jest, or to boast.

'Try persuading me otherwise, Nathaniel.'

'There is Colonel Bardolini.'

'He is pathetic and rather frightened.'

'Frightened? Why do you say that?' Drinkwater asked with sudden interest.

Elizabeth shrugged. 'I don't know; he just gives that impression.'

'Well, he's safe enough here and, for the few days we have, you can look after him.'

'Thank you, kind sir,' she said. 'But you have changed the subject. I want to know more of this proposed voyage. I suppose you wish me to carry orders to James when I return in the same way that I carried your sea-kit up to London.'

'You rumble me damned easily, Elizabeth.'

'You shouldn't be so transparent. I suppose you cannot or will not confide in me.'

'It is not . . .'

'A woman's business, I know.'

'I was about to say, it is not easy to explain.'

'Try.'

And when he had finished Elizabeth said, 'I hate you going, my darling, but knowing why makes it bearable. I know I shall never have you to myself until

71

this war is over and anything that brings peace nearer is to be welcomed. I can only pray that God will spare you.'

He bent and kissed her, but she yielded only a little, pushing him gently away. 'Must you take James? Catriona has waited so long for him and you summoned him before, then left her to bear the child alone.'

'Bess, you know James has no means of support beyond his half-pay; he yearns for a ship . . .'

'You promised him his swab, Nathaniel, yet he remains on the lieutenants' list.'

'You know I recommended him, but . . .'

'The matter proved only your obscurity,' Elizabeth was quick to point out.

'*Touché*,' he muttered. 'Well, I can't guarantee him his swab, but I can put him in a good position to earn it. He can have the *Kestrel*, d'you remember her?'

'She's only a little cutter, isn't she?'

'Yes, but she provides him with an opportunity,' countered Drinkwater, increasingly desperate. 'You know too damned much about naval affairs, Elizabeth,' he said, rising from the bed and tearing testily at his stock.

And though they lay in each other's arms until dawn, they were unable to find the satisfaction true lovers expect of one another.

4 Departures
October 1813

On the last Thursday in September, Drinkwater rose before dawn. Elizabeth, as used to the regime of the byre as her husband was to that of a ship, was astir equally early. She was to leave for Gantley Hall after breakfast, though without orders for James Quilhampton who had been sent to Chatham the instant Drinkwater learned the cutter *Kestrel* was mastless.

'My dear, I have to go to the Admiralty. I shall have the coach brought round for you.'

'As you wish.'

Bardolini, in shirt and overalls, caught him on the landing as he prepared to leave.

'Captain, please, today . . .'

'Colonel, today I promise. I told you not to expect a response until Thursday, and you shall have your answer today.'

'But I have yet to meet Lord Castlereagh . . .'

'Lord Castlereagh has been informed of your arrival. Now do be a good fellow and be patient. I shall send for you before this evening, rest assured upon the matter.'

'This evening? But, Captain . . .'

Drinkwater hurried on down the stairs and met Williams in the hall. 'Williams, be so kind as to send word for the coach. My wife's portmanteau is almost ready to come down.'

Elizabeth, in grey travelling dress and boots, her bonnet in her hand, joined him for coffee. He nodded at the sunlight streaming in through the window.

'Well, my dear, you should have a pleasant enough run. D'you have something to read?'

'You know I have trouble reading in a coach, Nathaniel.'

'I'm sorry. I had forgotten. You used to . . .'

'We *used* to do a lot of things,' she said quietly, and the words stung him with reproach.

'The Colonel will have to break his fast alone this morning,' she continued. 'It is curious, but I always thought soldiers were early afoot.'

'I think not Neapolitan soldiers,' he said, smiling, grateful for the change of subject and the lifeline she had thrown him.

'He is a strange fellow, though well enough educated. He reads English books. I found him reading your copy of Prince Eugène's *Memoirs* yesterday, but he seemed distracted. Has he been out since his arrival?'

'I cautioned him not to venture far and not to be absent for more than half an hour. His uniform is somewhat distinctive, even when he wears a cloak.'

'At least he doesn't wear his hat.'

'No,' Drinkwater laughed, 'though there are so many foreign corps in our service today that I doubt one more fantastic uniform among so many peacocks will turn any heads. Have you seen what they have done to our light dragoons? They've turned them into hussars with pelisses and more frogging than ratlines on a first-rate's mainmast. How the poor devils are supposed to campaign, let alone fight in such ridiculous clothes, I'm damned if I know.'

Williams looked in to announce the coach.

'Well, my dear, looks like goodbye.' He stood as she dabbed at her lips with a napkin and rose, picking up her bonnet. He took it from her and kissed her. He felt her yield and stirred in reaction to her softness.

'Oh Bess, my darling, don't think too ill of me.'

'I should be used to you by now,' she murmured, but both knew it was the unfamiliar and uncertain future that lay between them.

At the Admiralty Drinkwater called upon Barrow and received the orders he had drafted. 'God speed and good fortune, Captain. Lord Castlereagh will receive Bardolini this evening.'

'Thank you, Mr Barrow.'

In his office he removed Pocock's painting and asked for a porter to take it to Lord North Street, then sent for Templeton.

'D'you have all your dunnage, Templeton?'

'I believe so, sir.' Templeton's tone was, Drinkwater thought, one of miserable and reluctant martyrdom.

'You have done as I asked?'

'To the letter, sir.'

'Good. That is a sound principle.'

'The papers you were anxious about are secured in oilcloth in the corner.' Templeton pointed to a brown parcel secured with string and sealing wax.

'Very well, I shall take them myself.' Drinkwater looked round the room. The bookcase which had contained Templeton's meticulously maintained guard books was empty.

'This is a damnable place,' Drinkwater said curtly. Templeton sniffed disagreement. 'It is better to be pleased to leave a place than to mope over it,' Drinkwater added.

'It is a matter of opinion, sir,' Templeton grumbled.

Drinkwater grunted and picked up the parcel. 'Come, sir, let us be gone.'

The clock at the Horse Guards was chiming eleven as he walked back to Lord North Street to take his final departure. Williams greeted him and Drinkwater asked that his sea-chest be made ready.

'Mrs Williams is ironing the last of the shirts, sir.'

'Very good. Where is the Colonel?'

'He left an hour ago, sir.'

'What, for a walk?'

'No, sir, a gentleman called for him. He seemed to be expected.'

Drinkwater frowned. 'Expected? What d'you mean?'

'The man said he had called for Colonel Bardolini. I asked him to come into the hall and wait. When I brought the Colonel into the hall, he asked the gentleman whether he had come from Lord Castlereagh. The gentleman said he had, and Bardolini left immediately.'

'You are quite certain it was Bardolini who mentioned Lord Castlereagh?'

'Positive upon the point, sir. I could not have been

mistaken. If you'll forgive my saying so, sir, I could not . . .'

'No, no, of course not, Williams, I just need to be certain upon the matter.'

'Is something amiss, sir?'

Drinkwater shrugged. 'I'm not sure. Perhaps not . . . Come, I must gather the last of my traps together, or I shall leave something vital behind.' And so, in the pressing needs of the everyday, Drinkwater submerged a primitive foreboding.

At four in the afternoon an under-secretary on Lord Castlereagh's staff arrived in a barouche to convey Bardolini to his Lordship's presence.

Drinkwater met the young man in the withdrawing-room. 'Is the Colonel not with his Lordship already?'

'Not that I am aware of,' said the under-secretary with a degree of hauteur. Drinkwater, in grubby shirt-sleeves as he finished preparing his sea-kit after so long in London, felt a spurt of anger along with a sense of alarm.

'But I understand one of his Lordship's *flunkeys* called for him this morning.'

'Mr Barrow was told that Colonel Bardolini would not be received before noon, very probably not before evening. His Lordship has rearranged his schedule to accommodate the Colonel, not to mention Captain, er, Drink . . .'

'Drinkwater. I am Captain Drinkwater and I am obliged to his Lordship, but I fear the worst. It would appear that the Colonel has been carried off by an impostor.'

'An impostor? How is that?'

'Come, sir,' said Drinkwater sharply, 'there are French agents in London, are there not?'

'I really have no idea.'

'I am sure Lord Castlereagh is aware of their presence.'

'How very unfortunate,' said the under-secretary. 'I had better inform his Lordship.'

'A moment. I'd be obliged if you would take me to the Admiralty.'

Drinkwater was fortunate that Barrow had not yet left. 'This is a damnable business,' he concluded.

'I do not think Lord Castlereagh will trouble himself overmuch, Captain.'

'No, probably not,' Drinkwater said, 'until Canada catches fire.'

Drinkwater returned to Lord North Street for the second time that day. He was in an ill humour and full of a sense of foreboding. He put this down to Bardolini's disappearance and Elizabeth's departure, and these circumstances undoubtedly made him nervously susceptible to a curious sensation of being followed. He could see no one in the gathering darkness and dismissed the idea as ludicrous.

But the moment he turned the corner he knew instinctively that something was wrong. He broke into a run and found his front door ajar. In the hall Williams was distraught; not half an hour earlier a carriage with drawn blinds had pulled up and a heavily cloaked figure had knocked at the door. Williams had opened it and had immediately been dashed aside. Thereafter two masked accomplices had appeared, forcing their way into the house and ransacking it.

'I thought it was the Colonel or yourself coming back, sir,' a shaken Williams confessed, his tranquillity of mind banished.

'Did you hear them speak?' Drinkwater asked, handing Williams a glass of wine.

'No, sir, but they weren't Frenchmen.'

'How d'you know?'

'I'd have smelled them, sir, no doubt about it. Besides, I think I heard one of them say something in English. He was quickly hushed up, but I am almost certain of it.'

'What did he say?'

'Oh, "nothing in here," something to that effect. They had just turned over the withdrawing-room.'

A faint wail came from below stairs. 'Did they molest your wife?'

'No, sir, but she is badly frightened. They were looking for papers . . .'

'Were they, by God!'

'They broke into the strong-room.'

'They took everything?'

'Everything.'

Drinkwater closed his eyes. 'God's bones!' he blasphemed.

He waited upon Mr Barrow at nine the following morning. Curiously, the Second Secretary was not surprised to see him. 'You have heard, then?' he said, waving Drinkwater to a chair.

'Heard?'

'The body of your guest was found in an alley last

evening. He had been severely beaten about the head and was unrecognizable but for the remnants of his uniform. Oddly enough I was with Murray last evening when Canning arrived with the news. It crossed my mind then that it might be our friend and I instituted enquiries.'

'You did not think to send me word . . .'

'Come, come, Captain, the man was an opportunist, like his master. He played for high stakes, and he lost. As for yourself, you would have insisted on viewing the corpse and drawing attention to your connection with the man.'

'Opportunist or not, he had placed himself under my protection.' Drinkwater remembered Elizabeth's assertion that Bardolini was a frightened man. 'Whoever killed Bardolini ransacked my house. I have spent half the night pacifying my housekeeper.'

'Did they, by heaven? D'you know why?'

'I think they were after papers. I have no idea what, apart from his accreditation, Bardolini carried. Whatever it was he did not take it to what he supposed to be a meeting with Lord Castlereagh.'

'Then they left empty-handed?' asked Barrow.

'More or less. I had some private papers . . .'

'Ahhh. How distressing for you . . . Still, someone knew who he was and where he was in London.'

'That argues against your hope of keeping me out of the affair.'

'Damn it, yes,' Barrow frowned. 'And we must also assume they knew why he was here.'

'Exactly so.'

'I should not delay in your own departure, Captain Drinkwater. Would you like me to pass word to the commander of the *Kestrel* to proceed? At least you have no need to divert to Helgoland now.'

'No. I'd be obliged if you would order Lieutenant Quilhampton to Leith without delay.'

'Consider it done.'

After the hectic activity of the past fortnight, there was a vast and wonderful pleasure in the day of the departure of HMS *Andromeda* from Leith Road that early October forenoon. The grey waters of the Firth of Forth were driven ahead of the ship by the fresh westerly breeze, quartered by fulmars and gannets whose colonies had whitened with their droppings the Bass Rock to the southward. Ahead of them lay the greener wedge of the Isle of May with its square stone light-tower and its antediluvian coal chauffer. To the north, clad in dying bracken, lay the dun coast of the ancient kingdom of Fife, a title whose pretentiousness reminded Drinkwater briefly of the sunburnt coast of Calabria and the compromised claims of the pretender to its tottering throne.

He had not realized how much he had missed the independence, even the solitariness, of command, or the sheer unalloyed pleasure of the thing. There was a purposeful simplicity in the way of life, for which, he admitted a little ruefully, his existence had fitted him at the expense of much else. It was, God knew, not the rollicking life of a sailor, or the seductiveness of sea-breezes that the British public thought all their ill-assorted and maltreated tars thrived upon.

If it had been, he would have enjoyed the passage north in the Leith packet which had stormed up the English coast from the Pool of London on the last dregs of the gale. As it was the heavily sparred and over-canvassed cutter with its crowded accommodation and puking passengers contained all the misery of seafaring. True, he had enjoyed the company of Captain McCrindle, a burly and bewhiskered Scot whose sole preoccupations were wind and tide, and who, when asked if he ever feared interception by a French corsair, had replied he 'would be verra much afeared, if there was the slightest chance of being overtaken by one!'

The old seaman's indignation made Drinkwater smile even now, but he threw the recollection aside as quickly as it had occurred for Lieutenant Mosse was claiming his attention.

'If you please, sir, she will lay a course clear of Fife Ness for the Bell Rock.'

'By all means, Mr Mosse, pray carry on.'

'Aye, aye, sir.'

Drinkwater watched the young second lieutenant. He was something of a dandy, a sharp contrast to the first luff, a more seasoned man who, like James Quilhampton aboard the cutter *Kestrel* dancing in their wake, was of an age to be at least a commander, if not made post. Drinkwater had yet to make up his mind about Lieutenant Huke, though he appeared a most competent officer, for there seemed about him a withdrawn quality that concealed a suspicion which made Drinkwater feel uneasy.

As for the other officers, apart from the master, a middle-aged man named Birkbeck, he had seen little of them since coming aboard three days earlier.

The crew seemed willing enough, moving about their duties with quiet purpose and a minimum degree of starting from the bosun's mates. The boat's crew which had met him had been commanded by a dapper midshipman named Fisher who, if he was setting out to make a good impression upon his new captain, had succeeded.

He could have wished for a heavier frigate, his old *Patrician*, perhaps, or at least *Antigone* with her 18-pounders, but *Andromeda* handled well, and if she was not the fastest or most weatherly class of frigate possessed by the Royal Navy, the ageing thirty-six gun, 12-pounder ships were known for their endurance and sea-kindliness.

She bore along now, hurrying before the westerly wind and following sea, her weatherbeaten topgallants set above her deep topsails, the forecourse straining and flogging in its bunt and clewlines as it was lowered from the yards on the order 'Let fall!'

'Sheet home!'

The ungainly bulging canvas, constrained by the controlling ropes, was now tamed by the sheets which, with the tacks, were secured from its lower corners and transmitted its driving power to the speeding hull. With the low note of the quartering wind sounding in the taut stays, the frigate ran to the east-north-east.

A moment or two later the topmen, left aloft to make up the gaskets after overhauling the gear and ensuring the large sail was set without mishap, lowered themselves hand over hand to the deck by way of the backstays. Standing by the starboard hance, Drinkwater concluded that he had, like those simian jacks, fallen on his feet.

Evening found them passing the Bell Rock lighthouse, a marvel of modern engineering built as it was upon a tide-washed rock. The brilliance of its reflected light far outclassed the obsolete coal chauffer of the Isle of May, and Birkbeck confidently took his departure bearing from it when it bore well astern.

Having assured himself of the presence of *Kestrel*, Drinkwater went below. His quarters were small compared to those he had enjoyed on board *Patrician*, but admirably snug, he told himself, for a voyage to the Norwegian Sea with winter approaching. He settled in his cot with a degree of contentment that might have worried a less elated man. But that day of departure had been, in any case, a day of seduction; if Captain Drinkwater failed to notice any of the many faults that encumbered his command, it was because he had been too long ashore, too long kept from contact with the sea.

And the sea was too indifferent to the fates of men to keep him long in such a placid state of grace.

PART TWO

A Portion of Madness

'A portion of madness is a necessary ingredient in the character of an English seaman.'

LORD HOWARD OF EFFINGHAM

5   A Most Prejudicial Circumstance
October 1813

'Pray sit down, Mr Huke.'

Huke threw out his coat-tails and sat on the edge of the chair bolt upright with his hands upon his knees and his elbows inclined slightly outwards. It was not a posture to put either of the two men at ease.

'I was much taken up with the urgency of departure and communicating the purpose of this voyage to Lieutenant Quilhampton of the *Kestrel*.' If Drinkwater had expected Huke to look from his captain to the cutter, which could be glimpsed through the stern windows when both vessels rode the crest of the wave simultaneously, he was mistaken. Mr Huke's eyes remained disconcertingly upon Drinkwater who wondered, in parenthesis, if the man ever blinked.

'Sir,' said Huke in monosyllabic acknowledgement.

'It is proper that I explain something of the matter to you.' Huke merely nodded, which irritated Drinkwater. He felt like the interloper he was, in a borrowed ship and a borrowed cabin, and that this was the light in which this strange man regarded him. He considered offering Huke a glass, but the fellow was so damnably unbending that he would seem to be currying favour if he did. 'Before I do confide in you,'

Drinkwater went on pointedly, regretting the necessity of revealing anything to Huke, 'perhaps you will be kind enough to answer a few questions about the ship.'

'Sir.'

'You are up to complement?'

'Within a score of hands, aye.'

'Is that not unusual?'

'We took aboard near twenty men during the last week off Leith. All seamen. Took most of 'em out of a merchantman.'

'Very well. Now the Master reports the stores will hold for three months more . . .'

'And our magazines are full; we have scarce fired a shot.'

'Did Captain Pardoe not exercise the guns?'

'Oh, aye, sir.'

'I don't follow . . .'

'Captain Pardoe was not often aboard, sir.'

'Not often aboard?' Drinkwater frowned; he was genuinely puzzled and Huke's evasive answers, though understandable, were confoundedly irritating.

He rose with a sudden impatience, just as the ship lurched and heaved. A huge sea ran up under her quarter, then on beneath her. As he staggered to maintain his equilibrium, Drinkwater's chair crashed backwards and he scrabbled at the beam above his head. From the adjacent pantry came a crash of crockery and a cry of anger. So violent was the movement of the frigate that the perching Huke tumbled from his seat. For a moment the first lieutenant's arms flailed, then his chair upset and he fell awkwardly, his skinny shanks kicking out incongruously. Hanging over the table, Drinkwater noticed the hole worn in the sole of his first lieutenant's right shoe.

He was round the far side of the table and offering the other his hand the moment the ship steadied. 'Here, let me help . . . there . . . I think a glass to settle us both, eh?'

He was gratified to see a spark of appreciation in Huke's eyes.

'Frampton!'

Pardoe's harassed servant appeared and Drinkwater ordered a bottle and two glasses.

'We'll have a blow by nightfall,' Drinkwater remarked, as they wedged themselves as best they could; and while they waited for Frampton, Drinkwater filled the silence with a reminiscence.

'This is not the first ship I have joined in a hurry, Mr Huke. I took command of the sloop *Melusine* in circumstances not dissimilar to this. The captain had become embroiled in a ridiculous affair of honour and left me to make a voyage to the Greenland Sea in a ship I knew nothing of, with officers I did not know. You can doubtless imagine my sentiments then.'*

'When was that?' Huke asked, curiosity about his new commander emerging for the first time.

'At the termination of the last peace, the spring of the year three.'

'I was promoted lieutenant that year.'

'Mr Huke,' Drinkwater began, then Frampton appeared and they concentrated on the wine and glasses. 'Did you lose much just now, in the pantry?'

'Aye, sir, two cups and a glass.'

* See *The Corvette*.

'Oh, a pity.'

'Aye, sir.'

'You were saying, sir?' Huke prompted expectantly.

Drinkwater felt suddenly meanly disobliging. 'I forget,' he said, ''twas no matter.'

Huke's face fell, relapsing into its disinterested expression. There was a predictability about the man, Drinkwater thought, to say nothing of a dullness.

'Anyway, your health.' Huke mumbled a reply before his beak of a nose dipped into the glass.

'Ah, I recall, I was asking about Captain Pardoe, his exercising of the crew. They seem reasonably proficient.'

'Aye, they are.'

'Thanks to you?'

'Yes, in part.'

'Well come, Mr Huke,' said Drinkwater, a note of asperity creeping into his voice. 'Do I attribute your lack of respect to your not being unduly used to having an officer superior to yourself on board?'

Drinkwater caught the swift appraising glance of Huke's eyes and knew he had struck home. It had not entirely been guesswork, for in addition to Huke's hints had come a somewhat belated realization that it was odd that Pardoe had turned up on his London doorstep so promptly after Barrow had indicated that the *Andromeda* could be made available.

'I thought the regulations were quite specific upon the point, expressly forbidding captains to sleep out of their ships . . .'

Huke gave a great sigh. 'Very well, since you'll not be content, *sir*, until you have dredged the bottom of the matter, Pardoe has no interest in the ship and we are cousins. I made up the ship's books and the rest of the officers and crew thought he was detained on parliamentary business. He is the Member for Eyesham . . .'

'So *you* maintained the fiction?'

'That is right,' Huke said wearily. 'And in return I was allowed an emolument . . .'

'An emolument?'

'A portion of Captain Pardoe's pay went to my sister who lives with my widowed mother and has no other means of subsistence.'

'And will Captain Pardoe continue with this arrangement?'

Huke gave a thin and chilly smile. 'Would you, Captain Drinkwater, if there was no reason to?'

No wonder, thought Drinkwater, Pardoe had been so keen to relinquish his ship once it was clear that the interests of party had been served by his obliging the ministry. The captain's protests had been all sham. He would make an excellent politician, Drinkwater privately concluded.

'If he told you he regretted handing over command, sir, it was a lie. He is a man who seeks ease at all times, and even when aboard never took the conn or put himself to the least trouble. He is a great dissembler; any man would be fooled by him as would be any woman.'

Huke broke off. He did not reveal that his sister had been dishonoured by Pardoe, and had borne him a bastard, acknowledged only because of the ties of blood. The child had died of smallpox eighteen months earlier, so Pardoe could cynically drop the old commitment.

'I'm sorry, Mr Huke. I had no wish to pry. Pray, help yourself.'

'It's been difficult, sir,' Huke said, the wine loosening his tongue. 'It was not in Captain Pardoe's interest to see me advanced . . .'

'No, I can see that,' Drinkwater frowned. 'My presence here is hardly welcome then?'

'I could not expect promotion because of Captain Pardoe's removal, sir, but, yes, at least under the previous arrangements I had a free hand on board and my dependants cared for.'

'Damn it, Huke, 'tis outrageous! We must do something about it!'

Huke looked up sharply. 'No, sir! Thank you, but you would oblige me if you would leave the matter alone. It was inevitable that it would end one day . . .'

'Well, what did Pardoe think would happen when I joined?'

'That I would simply carry on as any first lieutenant.'

'I don't want a resentful first lieutenant, Mr Huke, damn me, I don't, but I'm confounded glad you have told me your circumstances. What's your Christian name?'

'Thomas, sir.'

'D'you answer to Tom?'

Something of a smile appeared on Huke's weatherbeaten face. 'I haven't for some time, sir.'

Drinkwater smiled. This was better; he felt they were making progress. 'Very well, then let us to business.' Drinkwater pulled a rolled chart from a brass tube lashed to the table leg and was gratified that Huke helped spread it and quickly located the lead weights to hold it down upon the table. He indicated its salient points:

'To the west Orkney and Shetland, to the east the Skaw of Denmark, the Naze of Norway and here,' his finger traced the Norwegian coast due east of Orkney, 'Utsira.' Beside the offshore island of Utsira the ragged outline of the coast became more deeply indented, fissured with re-entrant inlets, long tapering fiords that bit far into the mountainous terrain, separating ridge from ridge where the sea exploited every glacial valley to thrust into the interior. Each fiord was guarded by rocks, islets and islands of every conceivable shape and size, their number, like the leaves upon a tree, inconceivable.

The names upon the chart were long and unpronounceable, the headwaters of the inlets faded into dotted conjecture, the hachured mountains rose ever vaguer into the wild hinterland.

'It is a Danish chart, Tom, incomplete and probably poorly surveyed. It is the best the British Admiralty could come up with. The Hydrographer himself, Captain Hurd, sent it . . .'

Huke straightened up and looked Drinkwater squarely in the eye. 'There is something out of the ordinary in this business, then,' he said quietly.

Drinkwater nodded. 'Yes, very. Is it only the chart that has made you think this?'

'And the manner of your arrival, sir.'

'Ah. In what way?'

'I had heard of you, sir. Your name is not unfamiliar.'

'I had no idea,' Drinkwater said, genuinely surprised.

'You mentioned the *Melusine* and a Greenland

voyage. And did you not take a Russian seventy-four in the Pacific?' There was a strained tone of bitterness in Huke's words.

'Luck has a great deal to do with success, Tom . . .'

'As does a lack of it with what others are pleased to call failure.'

'Indeed, but look, see that little fellow doing a dido on the quarter?' They stared across the mile of grey, windswept wilderness that separated the diminutive cutter *Kestrel* from her larger consort. 'Her commander is a mere lieutenant, like yourself, an *élève* of mine, God help him, a bold and brave fellow who lost a hand when a mere midshipman before the fortress of Kosseir on the Red Sea.* I have been striving to get a swab for him for years, so do not conceive great expectations; by which I do not mean I will not strive to advance any officer worth his salt.'

'I shall concede him the precedence,' Huke said, adding, 'he has independent command in any case.'

'I shall do my best for both of you, but James Quilhampton is a good fellow.'

'I have not yet met him . . .'

'No, had we had more time, I should have dined all of you. I hope that we shall yet have that pleasure, but for now rest assured that if we are successful in our enterprise, then I will move heaven and earth to have those officers who distinguish themselves given a step in rank.'

'And what *is* this enterprise?'

'Blowin' great guns, sir!'

* See *A Brig of War*.

Lieutenant Mosse was a dark blur in the blackness.

'Indeed it is.' Drinkwater put a hand to his hat and felt the wind tear at his cloak as he leaned into it, seeking the vertical on the wildly gyrating deck. Above his head the wind shrieked in the rigging, its note subtly changing to a booming roar in the gusts which had the almost painful though short-lived effect of applying pressure on the ears. The ship seemed to stagger under these periodic onslaughts, and around them the hiss and thunder of tumbling seas broke in looming chaos beyond the safety of the wooden bulwarks.

As he struggled past the wheel and peeped momentarily into the dimly lit binnacle, the quartermaster shouted, 'Course dead nor' east, sir.'

He tried looking upwards at the tell-tales in the thrumming shrouds but he could see nothing but the pale blur of a scrap of canvas somewhere forward.

'Wind's sou' by east, sir, more or less, been backing an' filling a bit, but tending to veer all the time.'

'Thank you. What's your name?'

'Collier, sir.'

'Very well, Collier, and thank you.'

He passed from the feeble light of the binnacle into the manic darkness. The moving deck beneath his feet dropped, leaving him weightless. He felt the wild thrust of the storm as *Andromeda* dipped her stern and a sea ran beneath her. Then the next wave was upon them, hissing and roaring at them, its crest tumbling in a pale, sub-luminous glow that lay above the line of the taffrail. The frigate felt the uplifting buoyancy of its front, she pressed her decks insistently against the soles of Drinkwater's shoes and he was saved from blowing overboard. He reached for and grasped the lanyard of an after mizen backstay, pulling himself into the security of the pinrail where he looped a bight of downhaul round his waist and settled his cloak in a warm cocoon, feeling still the forces of nature through the vibrating rigging.

He had not forgotten the knack, though he had certainly lost his sea-legs in his months ashore. It was preferable to be up here than cooped in his cabin, for he could not sleep. He was too restless, his mind too active to compose himself, and even lying in the cot had failed to lull him. The ship was noisy as she strained under the onslaught of the sea. Her complex fabric groaned whilst she alternately hogged and sagged as the following waves lifted her and thrust her forward, then passed under her and she fell back off each crest, into the succeeding trough.

Added to this ceaseless cycle of stresses was the resonance produced in the hull by the deep boom of the storm in the spars and rigging, that terrible noise that lay above the adolescent howl of a mere gale and sounded like nothing so much as the great guns of Mosse's phrase. And for Drinkwater and the officers quartered in the stern of the ship, there was the grind of the rudder stock, the clink of chains, and the curious noise made by the stretching of white hemp under extreme tension as the tiller ropes flexed from the heavy tiller through their sheaves to the wheel above, where Collier and his four helmsmen struggled to keep *Andromeda* on her course.

Secure and familiar now with the pattern of the ship's motion, Drinkwater took stock. They had struck the topgallant masts before sunset, and sent the upper yards down. Only the small triangle of the fore topmast staysail and the clews of the heavy fore-course remained set above the forecastle, yet even this small area of sail, combined as it was with the mighty thrust of the wind in the standing masts, spars and rigging, sent *Andromeda* down wind at a spanking six or seven knots.

This, Drinkwater consoled himself, was what frigates of her class were renowned for, this seaworthiness which, provided everything was done in due and proper form, engendered a sense of security. Then a thought struck him with as much violence as the storm.

'Mr Mosse!' he bellowed, 'Mr Mosse!' He began to unravel himself, but then the lieutenant appeared at his elbow.

'Sir?'

'The lantern! Did I not leave orders for the lantern to be left burning for *Kestrel* to keep station by?'

'Aye, sir. But it has proved impossible to keep it alight. I sent young Pearce below to set a new wick in it. He should be back soon.'

'When did you last see the cutter?'

'I haven't seen her at all, sir, not this watch.' Mosse continued to stand expectantly, waiting for Drinkwater to speak, but there was nothing he could say.

'Very well, Mr Mosse, chase the midshipman up.'

A few minutes later Drinkwater was aware of figures going aft with a gunner's lantern to transfer the light. They knelt in the lee of the taffrail and struggled for a quarter of an hour before, with a muffled cheer, Pearce succeeded in coaxing the flame to burn from the new wick and the stern lantern was shut with a triumphant snap.

Its dim glow, masked forward, threw just enough light for Drinkwater to see the muffled figure of the marine sentry posted by the lifebuoy at the starboard quarter. Neither vigilant sentry nor lifebuoy would do any poor devil the least good if he fell overboard tonight, Drinkwater thought, feeling for poor Quilhampton in his unfamiliar and tiny little ship.

No, that was ridiculous, James was as pleased as punch with his toy command and had made a brilliant passage from the Chapman light to Leith Road in four days, comparable to the best of the Leith packets and certainly faster then the passage Drinkwater had himself made with Captain McCrindle.

'She's a damned sight handier than the old *Tracker*,' Quilhampton had crowed, as he entertained Drinkwater to dinner in the cabin of the cutter aboard which Drinkwater himself had once served. He had proudly related how he had overhauled one of the packets off the Dudgeon light vessel.*

The recollection alarmed Drinkwater. He had so often witnessed pride coming before a fall, and, moreover, he was acutely aware that history had a humiliating habit of repeating itself. He recalled a storm off Helgoland when he had lost contact with his friend aboard the gun-brig *Tracker*. He had later been overwhelmed by Danish gun-boats, wounded and compelled to surrender, and the ship in which Drinkwater sailed had been wrecked upon the reefs off Helgoland itself.†

He discarded the unpleasant memory, choking off

* See *A King's Cutter*.
† See *Under False Colours*.

the train of reminiscence as it threatened to overwhelm him. The past was past and could not, in truth, be reproduced or resurrected. He stared out into the hideously noisy darkness, aware that the motion of the ship had changed. The sea no longer roared up astern in precipitous and tumbling ridges from which *Andromeda* flew headlong. Now the crests had gone and, as he craned his head round, he felt the stinging impact of sodden air, the dissolution of those very wavetops into an aqueous vapour that filled the air they breathed.

Looking up he saw the night was not so dark: a pallid, spectral mist flew about them, streaming down wind with the velocity of a pistol shot, it seemed, so that the masts and rigging were discernibly black again, yet limned in with a faint and tenuous chiaroscuro. For a moment he thought it was St Elmo's fire, but there was no luminosity in it – it was merely the effect of salt water torn from the surface of the sea and carried along by the extreme violence of the wind.

A man could not face this onslaught, for it excoriated the skin and stung even squinting eyes. It not only made manifest the frigate's top-hamper, it also carried moisture into every corner. Running before even so severe a storm, *Andromeda*'s decks had remained dry. Hardly a patter of spray had hissed over the rail, but now, in the back eddies and arabesque fantasies of air rushing over the irregularities of her upperworks and deck fittings, the sodden air flew everywhere. In minutes Drinkwater's cloak was soaked, as though he had been deluged with a green sea; and while hitherto the wind had not seemed excessively cold, there now struck a numbing chill.

He tried to imagine what it would be like for Quilhampton aboard *Kestrel*. The cutter's low free-board and counter-stern would have made her prey to a pooping sea. If she still swam out there somewhere astern, Quilhampton would have hove her to, he was sure of that. She hove to fairly comfortably, Drinkwater remembered.

Somewhere, distant in the booming night, the ship's bell tolled the passing hours. The incongruity of the faultless practice of naval routine in such primeval conditions struck no one on the deck of the labouring British frigate. Such routine formed their lifeline to sanity, to the world of order and purpose, of politics and war, and so it went on in its own inexorable way as did the watch changes. The blear-eyed, shivering men emerged on to the wet deck to relieve their soaked and tired shipmates who slid below in the futile hope that some small comfort awaited them in their hammocks. Watch change followed watch change as the routine plodded through the appalling night and, in the end, triumphed.

For dawn brought respite, and a steady easing of the wind, and found Drinkwater asleep, unrested, half severed by the downhaul. He staggered and gasped as he woke and Huke gave him his hand.

'God's bones!' he groaned. The furrow caused by the lashing had bruised his ribs and he gasped as he drew breath.

'Are you able to stand, sir?' Huke's expression of concern was clear in the dawn's light. Even as return-ing circulation caused him a slow agony and brought tears to Drinkwater's eyes, he found some satisfaction in the knowledge. He had won Huke over.

'Damn stupid thing to do,' Drinkwater managed, gradually mastering himself as the pain eased. 'How's the ship?'

'When I heard you had been up all night I came to report. I've had a look round. She's tight enough, four feet of water in the well, but the watch are dealing with that now. One seaman sprained an ankle, but he'll mend.'

'Is the surgeon competent?' Drinkwater asked.

'It would appear so, by all accounts. He's a young fellow, by the name of Kennedy. Scuttlebutt has it that he had to leave Bath in a hurry. Something about a jealous husband. He's full of fashionable cant and thinks himself the equal of a physician, but he does well enough. At least Bath taught him plenty about clap and the lues.' Huke dismissed the world of the *ton* with contempt. Drinkwater liked him the more. He began to pace the deck, Huke falling in alongside of him. Every moment the light grew stronger.

'Odd, ain't it, that hurricane last night knocked the sea down so fast, there'll be little swell today if the wind continues to drop.'

'Did you look at the glass this morning?' Drinkwater asked.

'Steadied up.'

'Good. I'm concerned about the *Kestrel*.'

'She'll fetch the rendezvous at Utsira. We're almost certainly bound to be there before her.'

'Yes, you are very probably right.' There was a reassuring conviction in Huke's words. 'Yes, you're right. Nevertheless . . .'

'Don't concern yourself, sir. I'll have the t'gallant masts sent up again after breakfast and a lookout posted aloft.'

'Very well.' They walked on a little. Then Drinkwater remarked, 'She's a lot easier now.'

It was relative, of course. The ship still scended and the dying sea surged alongside her hurrying hull.

'Shall I let fall the forecourse and set the tops'ls?'

'No, let us wait for full daylight and assure ourselves that *Kestrel* ain't in sight before we crack on sail.'

Drinkwater felt much better with a bellyful of burgoo and a pot of hot coffee inside him. Huke, he had learned during their morning walk, prescribed hot chocolate for the wardroom, said it gave the young layabouts a 'fizzing start to the day'. Apparently the idea originated with Kennedy, but Huke had tried it and endorsed it, to the disgust of several of the younger officers. Drinkwater had promised he would try it himself, but not this morning. After so miserable and worrying a night, he wanted the comfort of the familiar and had, in any case, brought a quantity of good coffee aboard in his otherwise meagre and hastily purchased cabin stores.

Mr Templeton joined him for a cup as he finished breakfast. The poor man looked terrible and stared unhappily at the rapid rise and fall of the sea astern, visible now that Drinkwater had had the shutters lowered. Templeton had been prostrated by sea-sickness before they passed the Isle of May, and last night had reduced him to a shadow.

'If it is any consolation, Mr Templeton,' Drinkwater

said, waving him to a chair, 'the storm last night was one of the most severe I have experienced, certainly for the violence of the wind.'

'I scarcely feel much better for the news, sir, but thank you for your encouragement.' And, seeing Drinkwater smile, he added, 'I never imagined . . . never imagined . . .'

'Well, buck up,' Drinkwater said with a cheeriness he did not truly feel. 'We have lost contact with the *Kestrel*, but perhaps we shall have news of her before nightfall. Just thank your lucky stars that it was over so soon; I've known weather like that last for a week. Today promises to be different.' Drinkwater grabbed the table as *Andromeda* heeled to leeward and drove her bowsprit at the sea-bed.

'You mean *this* is a moderation?'

'Oh my goodness, yes! Why, you should have been in the old *Patrician* with me when we fell foul of a typhoon in the China Sea . . .'

But Drinkwater's consoling reminiscence was cut short by a short, sharp rumble that was itself terminated by a shuddering crash.

Drinkwater knew instantly what the noise was, for it was followed by a further rumbling and crash as *Andromeda* rolled easily back to starboard. He was out of his chair and halfway to the door before Templeton had recovered from this further shock.

'Gun adrift!' snapped Drinkwater by way of explanation as he flung open the cabin door and the noise of turmoil flooded in further to assault the already affronted Templeton. Rising unsteadily, he followed the captain, but waited on the cabin threshold. Beside

103

him the marine sentry fidgeted uncomfortably.

'Number seven gun,' he muttered confidentially to the captain's clerk. The significance of the remark, if it had any, was lost on Templeton. He did not know that the guns in the starboard battery were, by convention, numbered oddly. Moreover, the perspective of the gun deck allowed him to see little. The receding twin rows of bulky black cannon breeches, with their accompanying ropework, blocks, shot garlands and overhead rammers, worms and sponges, looked much as normal. It was always a crowded space, and if there were more men loitering about than usual, a cause was not obvious. His view, it was true, was obscured by the masts, the capstans, stanchions, and so forth, but the marine's confident assertion meant nothing to him and gave him no clue.

And then the tableau before him dissolved. The frigate's lazy counter-roll scattered the group of men. With shouts and cries they spread asunder, leaping clear of something which, Templeton could see now, was indeed a loose cannon. The lashings which normally held it tight, with its muzzle elevated and lodged against the lintel of its gun-port, seemed to have given way and parted.

This had caused the gun to roll inboard, as though recoiling beyond the constraints of its breechings. It had fetched up against one of the stanchions, a heavy vertical timber supporting the deck above. Here it had slewed, perhaps due to one of its training tackles fouling, but this had caused it to swing from right angles to the ship's fore and aft axis, thus giving it greater range to trundle threateningly up and down. Its two tons of avoirdupois had already destroyed a lifted grating, splintered half a dozen mess kids, buckets and benches, and split the heavy vertical timber of the after bitts.

As *Andromeda* heaved over a sea, the malevolent mass began to move aft, gaining a steady momentum that caused Templeton, well out of its line of advance, to flinch involuntarily. As the deck rocked, this slowed and then went into reverse, but by now the forces of order were mustered. Templeton could see Captain Drinkwater and Lieutenant Huke (a dour but competent soul, Templeton thought), the marine sergeant and Greer, an active boatswain's mate who had befriended Templeton in an odd kind of way and seemed willing to answer any of Templeton's technical questions. He had asked them at first of Mosse, but that dapper young officer did not conceive his duty to be the instructing of a mere clerk. Greer had overheard the exchange, made in Leith Road before the onset of sea-sickness, and volunteered himself as a 'sea-daddy'.

Templeton watched fascinated as ropes appeared, sinuous lines of seamen running to keep them clear of fouling as, in a moment of temporary equilibrium, someone shouted:

'Now!'

And the errant gun was miraculously and suddenly overwhelmed. A knot of officers remained round the gun, Drinkwater among them. Templeton was childishly gleeful. He felt less queasy, slightly happier with his lot. The swift, corporate response had impressed him. Men drew back grinning with satisfaction, and although the 12-pounder stared the length of the gun deck, it was held unmoving in a web of rope, even when *Andromeda* tested the skill of her company by kicking her stern in the air and then plunging it into the abyss.

'Like Gulliver upon the Lilliputian beach,' he muttered to himself.

'Like 'oo, sir?' the marine beside him asked.

'Like Gulliver . . .' he repeated, before seeing the ludicrous waste of the remark.

From behind him came the crash of crockery. He turned and looked back into the cabin. Coffee pot, cups and saucers lay smashed on the chequer-painted canvas saveall.

'Cap'n's china, sir,' said the marine unnecessarily.

'Oh dear . . .'

Templeton retreated into the cabin and stood irresolute above the slopping mess, then Frampton, the captain's servant, with much clucking of his tongue, appeared with a cloth.

'I don't know what Cap'n Pardoe'll say. We've only the pewter pot left,' he grumbled.

'Get out!' Templeton swung round to find Drinkwater in the doorway. The captain's face was strangely set. He shut the door and strode aft, putting his right hand on the aftermost beam, resting his head on his arm and staring astern. The servant swiftly vanished and Templeton himself hesitated; but it was clear the captain did not mean him. Templeton averted his eyes from the heave and suck of the wake and turned his gaze inboard. He admired again the rather fine painting of Mrs Drinkwater which the captain had hung the previous afternoon. He felt a return of his nausea and fought to occupy his mind with something else.

'Is . . . is something the matter, sir? I, um, thought the taming of the gun accomplished most expertly, sir.'

Drinkwater remained unmoving, braced against the ship's motion. 'Did you now; how very condescending of you.' Templeton considered the captain might have been speaking through clenched teeth. Was this another sea-mystery? Was the captain himself suffering from *mal de mer*?

Templeton had reached this fascinating conclusion when the door opened once more and Huke strode in. He was carrying a short length of thick brown rope.

'Well?' Drinkwater turned. 'What d'you think?'

Huke held the rope out. 'There's no doubt, sir. Cut two-thirds through and the rest left to nature. Thank God it didn't part six hours earlier.'

And it slowly dawned upon Mr Templeton that the breaking adrift of the cannon had been no accident, but a deliberate act of sabotage.

'That is', he said, intruding into the exchange of looks of his two superiors, 'a most prejudicial circumstance, is it not?'

6 Typhus
October 1813

'We must not make our concern too obvious,'
Drinkwater said, after a pause during which
Templeton blushed in acknowledgement that he had
spoken out of turn. 'If the sabotage was merely mali-
cious, a detestation at having been sent so abruptly on
foreign service, or some such, vigilance may be all
that is necessary. Do you, Mr Huke, have a discreet
word with all of the other officers on those lines.'

'Aye, aye, sir. You want any other construction
played down, I assume.' Huke looked significantly at
the captain's secretary.

'Templeton is party to everything, Mr Huke. He
was lately a cipher clerk at the Admiralty.'

'I see,' said Huke, who did nothing of the kind.

'But yes, play it down, just the same,' Drinkwater
said, and Huke nodded. 'And I think I will let the
marine officer know exactly what is going on. Is he a
sound man, Mr Huke?'

'Mr Walsh is reliable enough, but unimaginative
and not given to using his initiative. He is somewhat
talkative but steady under fire.' Huke paused. 'If I
might presume to advise you, sir . . .'

'Yes, of course. You think him liable to be indiscreet?'

Huke nodded again. 'I should tell him only that we are bound upon a special service. It is not necessary to say more. He will be as vigilant as Old Harry if he thinks there's the merest whiff of mutiny attached to this business.'

'So be it.' Drinkwater looked from one to the other. 'Are there any questions?'

'Do you think it is possible to identify the culprits?'

Drinkwater and Huke stared incredulously at the clerk who, for the third time that morning, wished he had kept his mouth shut.

'These things are managed by men who take every precaution to ensure no officer ever gets to hear how they happen,' Drinkwater explained. 'These men are not stupid, Mr Templeton, even when they lack the advantages of knowledge or education.'

'And one or two', added Huke with heavy emphasis, 'are not wanting in either.'

Drinkwater spoke to Lieutenant Walsh shortly afterwards. 'The gun that broke loose was partially cut adrift, Mr Walsh. Have you had much of this sort of thing in the ship before?'

Walsh whistled through his teeth at the intelligence, then shook his head. He was a thick-set, middle-aged man whose prospects looked exceedingly dim. He should have reached the rank of major long before, and have been commanding the marine detachment aboard a flagship. He had a high colour, and Drinkwater suspected his loquacity might be proportional to his intake of black-strap.

'Nothing, sir, of much significance. The odd out-break of thievery and so forth, but nothing *organized*.'

'Well, I want you to keep your eyes open – and your mouth shut if you find anything out. I want to be the first to know *anything*; any scuttlebutt, any evidence of combinations, any mutterings in odd corners. D'you understand?'

'Yes, sir.'

'But I don't want a hornet's nest stirred up. I don't want your men ferreting and fossicking through the ship so that even a blind fiddler can see we're concerned.' Walsh frowned. 'The point is, Mr Walsh, and this is strictly confidential, we are engaged upon a special service and delay of any kind would be most unfortunate. Do I make myself clear?'

'You want me to keep my eyes and ears open, sir, but not to let on too much, and to let you know immediately if I get wind of anything.'

'You have it in a nutshell.'

Drinkwater went on deck after terminating his interview with the red-coated marine. The topgallant masts were already aloft again, the order to refid them having just been given. Drinkwater paced the quarterdeck, watching the men as they set up the rigging. From time to time he fished in his tail pocket and levelled his glass at the horizon, sweeping it in arcs, hoping to see the angular peak of *Kestrel's* mainsail breaking its uniformity.

The wind was down to a stiff breeze from the south-east and *Andromeda* bowled along, her topsail yards braced round to catch it, the deep-cut sails straining in their bolt-ropes.

As they went about their tasks under the supervision of Mr Birkbeck, the boatswain and his mates, the men frequently cast their eyes in Drinkwater's direction. If he caught their glance they swiftly looked away. This was no admission of guilt, or even caginess. Their curiosity would have been natural enough in any circumstances, given his recent arrival on board, for the captain of a man-of-war held autocratic powers over his unfortunate crew. Indeed, Drinkwater recalled incidents of flogging for 'dumb insolence' if a man so much as stared fixedly at his commander, so he attached no importance to this phenomenon. There would be no one on the frigate who did not know by now of the incident of the cannon, for it remained where it had been lashed. How their new captain reacted was of general interest. If his restless scourings of the horizon with his glass conveyed the impression of a greater anxiety for Quilhampton's *Kestrel*, it would not have been far from the truth.

At one point he thought he saw her. A blurred image swam past the telescope's lenses. Unaccountably the cutter had somehow worked ahead of them. He moved smartly forward, along the gangway on to the forecastle. Here, the boatswain, Mr Hardy, was about to sway up the fore topgallant yard.

'Carry on, Mr Hardy,' he said as the petty officer touched his hat.

'Aye, aye, sir.'

Reaching the foremast shrouds, Drinkwater levelled his glass. He carefully traversed the horizon. It was blank. He worked carefully backwards from right to left. Again, nothing.

'T'garn yardmen to the top!' Hardy bawled almost in his ear as he conned the horizon yet again, convinced that he had seen something and waiting for the ship to lift to a wave on each small sector again.

'Send down the yard ropes!'

The yard, its sail furled along it, rose from the boat booms and began its journey aloft.

'High enough! Rig the yardarms!'

The men on the forecastle waited for their colleagues aloft to finish their preparatory work.

'Taking their bloody time . . .' a man grumbled quietly.

'Shut up, Hopkins, the cap'n's over there . . .'

'Hold your blethering tongues!' Hardy said as he stared aloft, where some difficulty was being experienced. Drinkwater barely noticed these *sotto voce* remarks. He was concentrating on the business of seeking a second glimpse of that distant sail.

Hardy and the men aloft held a brief exchange. A call came down that all was now well. 'Sway higher . . . avast! Tend lifts and braces!' Men shuffled across the deck, more ropes were cast off belaying pins, their coils flung out for quick running and tailed on to by the seamen, chivvied by Greer.

'That's well there. Stand by! Now . . . sway across!'

Hitched properly the topgallant yard left the vertical and assumed its more natural horizontal position. 'Bend the gear!'

It was secured in its parrel and the mast slushed. Those on deck cleared up, recoiling the ropes and preparing to move aft to the mainmast. If the southeasterly wind continued to fall away, they would be setting those sails before they were piped to dinner.

'Lay down from aloft!'

The topmen swarmed down the backstays, hand

over hand, saw the captain and ceased their chaffing with hissed cautions. Drinkwater shut his glass with a snap and walked aft. He must have been mistaken. There was no sign of *Kestrel*.

Halfway along the gangway a thought struck him with such force that he stopped beside the men now mustering round the mainmast. The man who had been called Hopkins caught his eye.

'You there!' he called. 'That man, Mr Hardy, beside the larboard pinrail, d'you know his name?'

The boatswain looked round. 'That's Hopkins, sir.'

'Hopkins, come here.'

The men had stopped work. Lieutenant Huke and the master, Mr Birkbeck, came towards him, uncertain of what was happening. With obvious reluctance the man identified as Hopkins approached and stood before Drinkwater.

'Have I sailed with you before, Hopkins?' Drinkwater asked. His tone of voice was pleasant, deliberately relaxed, as though wanting to make an impression by this mock familiarity.

'No, sir.'

'I'm certain we've sailed together before. D'you have a twin?'

'No, sir.'

'You were on the *Antigone*, or was it the *Patrician*?'

'No, sir.'

'Where are you from, Hopkins, eh?' Drinkwater went on, probing for something longer than these monosyllabic words. Watching his quarry, Drinkwater saw the eyes flicker uncertainly. 'Where were you born?'

'London, sir.'

'What part of London?'

Hopkins shrugged. 'Just London, sir.'

'And you say you've never sailed with me before?' Sweat was standing out on Hopkins's brow.

'No, sir.'

'Well stap me, Hopkins, I'd have laid money on the fact!' Drinkwater smiled. 'Very well, then, carry on. Carry on, Mr Hardy, let's have the men at it again. I want those t'gallants set.'

'Aye, aye, sir.'

Hopkins turned and escaped. Odd looks were exchanged between officers and men alike as they went back to their tasks. Drinkwater continued aft, with Huke and Birkbeck staring after him.

'Odd cove,' remarked the master, looking at Drinkwater who had continued to the taffrail and stood staring astern, his hands clasping the brass tube of the Dollond glass behind his back.

'Yes,' replied Huke doubtfully. 'Carry on, will you, Mr Birkbeck.'

Huke walked aft himself and stood next to Drinkwater. After a moment Drinkwater said, without turning his head, 'That man Hopkins, have you had him aboard long?'

'No, sir. Pressed him out of that merchantman I mentioned.'

'Ah, yes, I recall . . .'

Huke waited for more, but Drinkwater continued to stare astern.

'I cannot imagine what has happened to Quilhampton,' he said with a faint air of abstraction.

'Sir, d'you mind if I ask . . . ?'

'No, Mr Huke, I don't mind you asking.' Drinkwater swung round and looked at his first

114

lieutenant. 'But perhaps you'll answer my question first. How many more men that you pressed from that same merchantman are Yankees?'

It was far from a comforting thought, and it would not leave Drinkwater alone throughout that worrying day. Huke had hurried off and returned after a few moments with the assurance that, although most of the men out of the merchantmen had American accents, when challenged, all had claimed to have been of loyalist descent.

'Very fine and dandy, if it's true, which I doubt.'

'But why should it not be true? If they had been Americans, they would not have submitted without protesting at being pressed.'

'Indeed. But that doesn't prove they are what they say they are. Did they submit to being placed on board docilely?'

'No, of course not, sir, but they said they were owed money, that they had not received their wages or slops and they were dressed in filthy rags. I ordered them fitted out.' Huke's explanation petered out, then, as if summoning himself, he added, 'Sir, if I might say so, I think you are concerning yourself over-much. You had little sleep last night.' Huke stopped as the spark of anger kindled in Drinkwater's eye.

'Damn it, sir . . . !'

'I mean no impertinence, Captain Drinkwater.' Huke stood his ground. Several thoughts flashed through Drinkwater's mind. He was tired, it was true, but all was far from well and he felt he had touched something. The man Hopkins had been deliberately evasive. Not merely unwilling to answer the captain's questions, but suspecting something when asked, persistently, if he had sailed with Drinkwater before. Moreover, no Londoner would be content not to refer to his natal quarter of the capital.

If Drinkwater was right, doubts had been sowed in Hopkins's mind as much as in Drinkwater's, and he might move again, and soon. The reflections calmed Drinkwater.

'You are right, Tom, forgive me.' He smiled and Huke reciprocated.

'Of course, sir.'

'Just humour an old fool and keep a damned close eye, as unobtrusively as possible, on that man. Make a particular note of his cronies.'

'Very well, sir, I'll see to that.'

'I think I shall take a nap then. Be so good as to see the t'gallants set and have me called at six bells in the afternoon watch.'

'Of course, sir.'

'And round up Walsh, Birkbeck, Templeton and, what did you say the Bones's name was?'

'Kennedy.'

'Him and a couple of the midshipmen, to join me at dinner. I'll tell Frampton to have a pig killed.'

'I'll do that, sir.'

'Very good of you, Tom.'

The wind held steady from the south-east, but continued to fall away during the afternoon so that as the officers assembled for dinner, *Andromeda* slipped easily through the water.

Circulating among them, Drinkwater sought to draw his guests in turn. Walsh proved as talkative a

116

fellow as the first lieutenant had suggested, battering Drinkwater with a torrent of inconsequences he quite failed to understand so that Walsh followed when he stepped forward to meet the two midshipmen, one of whom was no more than a child.

'You are Mr Fisher, are you not?' Drinkwater quizzed, as the boy nervously entered the cabin in the company of a much taller, out-at-elbows young man Drinkwater recognized as Pearce.

'Yes, sir,' the boy squeaked. 'My name is Richard Fisher.'

'How old are you, Mr Fisher?'

'Eleven, sir.'

'That is very young, is it not? And how long have you been aboard this ship?'

'Three months, sir.'

'Ah, quite the old hand, eh? You commanded the gig when I came on board.'

'Yes, sir.'

The similarity of names reminded Drinkwater of his own son Richard who had once implored to be taken to sea. Drinkwater had not even entered him on a ship's books, so little did he want to encourage the lad. Now the youthful Dickon increasingly managed the modest Suffolk estate with its two farms and had forgotten his idea of following his father's footsteps into the Royal Navy.

'There's one born every minute,' Walsh remarked, and Drinkwater let the rubicund marine officer scoop up the younkers and bore them with tales of derring-do when the war and he had been young.

Drinkwater raised an eyebrow at Huke, who gave a slow, tolerant smile and shrugged.

'When will we close Utsira, Mr Birkbeck?' Drinkwater asked conversationally. 'I have somewhat neglected matters today.'

'You had a bad night of it, sir,' said Birkbeck indulgently, 'but I got a squint at the sun and reckon, all being well, noon tomorrow.'

'I think we may be able to take stellar observations at twilight tomorrow morning,' Drinkwater said.

Frampton, the captain's steward, went round and refilled the glasses, Fisher's included, and the air rapidly filled with chatter. Drinkwater looked round with a sense of some satisfaction. It was only a small portion of the complement of the wardroom, of course, but they seemed good enough fellows. He caught Frampton's eye.

'Sir?'

'Five minutes.'

'Aye, aye, sir.'

'And no more wine for Mr Fisher.'

'Aye, aye, sir.'

Drinkwater turned to Huke. 'Damn fool,' he muttered, then, 'Would you introduce me to the surgeon, Tom?'

Huke performed the introduction. 'Mr Kennedy, sir.' The curt half-bows performed, Drinkwater said, 'Glad to make your acquaintance,' and to the company at large, 'I'm sorry, gentlemen, not to have made your acquaintance earlier, but the somewhat irregular circumstances of my joining and the haste of our departure combined with last night's blow to make the matter rather difficult. I hope this evening will set matters to rights.'

'I'm sure, sir,' said Jameson, the third lieutenant, in

his thick Scotch burr. ''Twas an infernal night; ha'e ye ever known its like afore, sir?'

'Well, yes,' Drinkwater said, and told briefly of the typhoon and the storm off Helgoland before turning to the surgeon. 'You have not been long at sea, I understand, Mr Kennedy, how did you cope with the motion?'

'Somewhat miserably I fear, sir. When the physician is indisposed, there is little hope for the sick.'

'You are better now?'

'As a matter of fact, sir, I'm ravenous.'

The remark coincided with Frampton's arrival with the meat. The delicious smell of succulent roast pork filled the cabin, killing the conversation as all swung in happy anticipation to the table. The joint, the fresh vegetables, potatoes, gravy and apple sauce suggested a meal ashore, rather than one aboard a man-of-war upon an urgent cruise.

'Please take your seats, gentlemen.'

The rumble of talk resumed, joining the scraping of chairs as the officers sat and flicked their napkins into their laps. Then they fell silent, leaving only Walsh to remark to Fisher, 'You had better ask the captain, young fella.'

'What had you better ask me, Mr Fisher?'

'Why, sir, where we are going?'

Surprise at the youthful indiscretion was clear on all their faces, though it amused Drinkwater. 'What makes you think we are going anywhere particular, Mr Fisher?'

Midshipman Fisher was flushing with the realization that he was the cynosure of all eyes. 'Well, s . . . s . . . sir,' he stammered, 'I s . . . supposed we might be, sir.'

'Go on, sir,' said Drinkwater, breaking the expectation by beginning to carve.

'Well, sir, we were quietly at anchor with Captain Pardoe away in Parliament and then, sir, here you are and off we go!'

He was in his stride by the end of it and the officers laughed indulgently as Frampton went round filling their glasses.

'Well, Mr Fisher has a point, gentlemen,' Drinkwater said as he finished passing the platters of sliced meat down the table. 'We are engaged on a particular service, as some of you may know. As to what it is, it is difficult at this juncture to be absolutely certain, so shall we say we are engaged on a reconnaissance?' He handed a plate to Huke and looked at Fisher. 'Well now, Mr Fisher, do you know the course?'

'North-east, sir?'

'And what do you suppose lies to the nor' east of Leith Road, eh?'

'Norway, sir?'

'Indeed, Mr Fisher, Norway. In the next few days we shall take a look into a fiord or two and see what we can find . . .'

'In the way of an enemy, sir?' asked Fisher, pot-valiant.

'Possibly, Mr Fisher. Mr Walsh, do see that Mr Fisher has enough potatoes.'

'Oh, yes sir, of course.'

'Tae stop his gob,' Jameson muttered.

The general babble recommenced with indulgent grins bestowed on the blushing midshipman. After the pork, a duff appeared and when the cloth had been drawn and the loyal toast drunk, Walsh lit a cheroot and hogged the decanter.

'A fair wind, if you please, Walsh,' prompted Huke, and the evening passed into a pleasant blur.

When it was over Drinkwater invited Huke to take a turn on deck to clear their heads. It was not quite dark. Thin tendrils of high cloud partially veiled some of the stars, but a dull red glow hung in the northern sky.

'It looks like a misplaced sunset,' Huke remarked, puzzled.

'Aurora borealis,' Drinkwater said, and they paused to stare at it for a moment. The crimson glow seemed to pulse gently, increasing in brilliance, then dying again, like coals that are almost extinguished. 'It can take on the most incredible forms,' Drinkwater remarked, and they began walking again.

Andromeda ghosted through the water, for the wind had gone down with the sun.

'I wish to God we knew the whereabouts of the *Kestrel*.'

'Yes. Perhaps he'll head back to Leith, the wind's been fair.'

'Sir?' A figure loomed in the darkness. It was not Mosse, the officer of the watch.

'Is that you, Mr Kennedy?'

'Yes, sir. I'm afraid I've some rather bad news.'

'Then keep your voice down, man,' hissed Huke.

'We've a case of typhus aboard,' Kennedy whispered.

7   Utsira
October 1813

At dawn next morning the frigate was stirred to life by the marine drummer beating the ship's company to quarters. It was a grey morning, with a translucent veil of high altitude cloud spread across the sky, robbing them of the stellar observations Drinkwater and Birkbeck had hoped to secure. The horizon had not yet hardened before the stars, like distant lamps, had faded. Extinguished, Drinkwater mused to himself as he came on deck and took stock, by overly frugal angels.

The ship's company knew nothing of this disappointment. The watch on deck cast about in confusion at the sudden appearance of the captain, marine officer and first lieutenant and the rattle of the drummer's snare, for there was no obvious enemy in the offing. The watches below tumbled up, chivvied by thundering hearts and starters, and equally confused for, as they ran to their actions stations, the mystified petty officers knew only that the men were to be stopped from clearing for action and casting off the guns' breechings. Instead, they were to fall in in their messes, and the transmission of this unorthodox procedure caused further confusion. This took a few extra moments and in turn provided an adequate time-lapse to breed rumour.

There were two of these speculations forming and they spread by muttered word of mouth faster than a spark along a quick-match. How these incomplete utterances sped round the ship, how one utterly defeated the other so that, by the time the divisional officers each sent their midshipmen aft to report their men mustered, the victorious buzz had convinced thirteen score of men, is a mystery understood only by those who have experienced it.

One theory was that their proximity to the enemy coast was such that standing to in the light of dawn was a precautionary measure. It gained ground among the more experienced, but it swiftly withered when the second overwhelmed it. They had been called to account, it was asserted, for the cutting adrift of the cannon. The absence of punishment at the time had been commented upon. Neither Huke's reputation nor Drinkwater's lack of it seemed to square with inaction on the part of authority, and therefore this postponed corporate muster seemed a logical consequence. Nor did anything that happened in the next few extraordinary moments persuade the ship's company of His Britannic Majesty's frigate *Andromeda* that they were wrong.

Flanked by Huke and Walsh, Drinkwater stalked the groups of men, taking a sinister interest in several, moving close to them so that the more perceptive and less terrified said afterwards that the captain had 'sniffed them like a dog at a bitch's arse'.

This indelicacy was not so very far from the truth

and some of those subject to this personal attention were sent sheepishly aft to a waiting Kennedy, watched by the others. From time to time a muttering rose with a mutinous undertone of protest which either Huke or the divisional officer swiftly silenced. When Drinkwater's curious, shifty inspection was complete he returned to the quarterdeck.

'Very well, Mr Huke. The duty watch is to rig the washdeck pumps and the Hales's ventilators. The gunner's party is to prepare powder for burning 'tween decks. The carpenter is to take three hundred-weight of sand to the galley and the cook is to have it heated. The purser is to issue one bar of soap to every mess. The watch below is to turn up and be hosed down. After every man has been washed, he is to shift his linen and put on clean clothes. If a single man has on an item he is wearing now, I shall cover him with my cloak and flog him!'

Drinkwater gave his bizarre orders in a loud voice, and those mustered below in the gun deck who failed to hear him soon learned of his intentions. Nor was a single man under the impression that a shred of solicitude attached to Drinkwater's offer of his 'cloak'. All knew the term a euphemism for the ration of lashes permitted a post-captain under the Thirty-Sixth Article of War which he might give without reference to any higher authority. By the time Drinkwater had finished, every man jack knew that what the watch below had to endure, the duty watch would also submit to, that the ship would be scrubbed from orlop to main deck, that the ports would be opened, that a mechanically induced draught via Dr Stephen Hales's patent ventilator would join the natural air flowing reluctantly through the ship, and that hot sand and burning gunpowder would dry and purify the air between decks.

In the ensuing period the deck of the *Andromeda* assumed the grotesque appearance of a bacchanalia. Had an enemy chanced upon them at that time, it was afterwards remarked, they would have caught the *Andromeda*'s company with more than their defences down. The spurting jets of water plashed upon the naked limbs and bodies of each mess in turn, and the initial misery and humiliation of those first chosen gave way to a whooping glee as group succeeded group and the naked increased and soon outnumbered the clothed.

As each division underwent this strange, humiliating metamorphosis, their officers came aft, grinning at the men's discomfiture, grouping on the quarterdeck to be driven, as their own reserved participation in this spree, to comments of impropriety.

'My word,' rattled a red-faced Walsh, 'young Hughes is rigged like a donkey!'

An acutely embarrassed Midshipman Fisher stared wide-eyed at a small, deformed and excessively hairy man who giggled insanely and was commonly thought to be mad.

'And look at Taylor . . .'

'Good God, what a scar . . .'

Having been stripped and drenched, the ship's fiddler was set upon a forecastle carronade breech to strike up a lively jig, which prompted the most excitable to dance and skylark with even more vigour than the cold sea-water.

When the greater proportion of the watch below

cavorted in damp nudity, Drinkwater sprang a second and greater surprise upon the ship.

'Frampton!' he called, and the steward, stark naked, his hands held in front of his chill-shrivelled genitals, approached the officers. Drinkwater turned to the crescent of watching officers.

'Well, gentlemen, rank has its obligations as well as its privileges. I do not know whether it was Epictetus or Marcus Aurelius who claimed the essence of command to be example, but if this performance is to be of any benefit, then we must take part . . .'

Drinkwater stared round at the officers on whom the light of comprehension broke somewhat slowly. He began to take off his coat and held it out to the dripping and shivering Frampton who reluctantly relinquished his protective stance. Several of the officers began to move away, while the midshipmen continued to stare goggle-eyed at their commander. Drinkwater removed his neck linen, stock and shirt, kicked off his shoes and, putting his right foot on a quarterdeck carronade truck, rolled down a stocking.

'Not here, surely, sir?' queried an incredulous Walsh.

'Why not, Mr Walsh, here is as good a place as any, for we must not only take part, but be seen to take part.' Drinkwater unbuttoned his breeches.

'What is the point, sir?'

'The point, Walsh,' offered Kennedy, fast following the Captain's example, 'is prophylaxis, the prevention of disease.'

'What disease?'

'Don't bandy it about, Walsh, but ship fever, camp fever, low, slow, putrid and petechial fever, call it what you will, but do not lay yourself open to its infection . . .'

Walsh was open-mouthed, but the surgeon's words were drowned as the ship's company realized that the captain was naked and that, incredulously, the other officers were following suit, slowly at first but then faster as they were egged on by whoops of rankly insubordinate derision. Drinkwater gasped as an eager party of men turned a hose upon him, the men at the levers of the portable pumps jerking up and down, one wet with tears at the hilarity of the scene and the joy of deluging his captain with icy water.

Within moments even the sluggards were under the pumps and the tide had turned, the entire waist was filled with pink flesh and cascades of water. Buckets were cast overboard and retrieved with lanyards, their contents emptied indiscriminately.

Chaos, it seemed, reigned for a quarter of an hour, until Drinkwater, still naked, leapt up on the rail and roared for silence. Those occupants of the wardroom who afterwards deplored the anarchy were swiftly silenced by others who argued that the immediacy of the response to Drinkwater's summons to order proved them wrong.

'Very well, my lads, we are all more or less alike, I see . . .' A laugh greeted this joke, and Drinkwater, while he awaited their attention, remembered inconsequentially how, long before aboard *Patrician*, he had discovered a woman dressed and thought of for months as a man. The laughter and mutual chaffing subsided.

'Now do you pay attention. It's a change of clothing for every man jack of you, d'you hear? Then the

127

ship is to be stummed before we break our fast. After that, you are all to wash every stitch you have just removed. It looks like a drying day and you will scrub hammocks by watches. If you clear the ship by noon, we'll exercise the guns . . .'

This news raised a cheer which, half-hearted at first, soon grew in modulation, a madcap disorganized noise accompanied by grins and laughter and multiple shiverings.

'Very well, then,' Drinkwater continued after the noise had died away, 'the watches below have twenty minutes to get into fresh clothes. Then they are to relieve the watch on deck. If I see a naked man half an hour from now, he'll be in the bilboes. Pipe down the watch below!'

Drinkwater jumped down from the rail. He was shuddering from the chill and covered with goose-pimples. 'Come, gentlemen, what do you want to make of yourselves, a spectacle?'

The ship had not quite been abandoned to these cavortings, but the calm had made easier this odd business of sanitation. As the officers tumbled below to the partial privacy of the wardroom and shut the door on the berth deck beyond, they reacted according to age and temperament. The paunchy Walsh was outraged, amusingly speechless and spluttering with florid indignation. The others, even the sober Huke, were constrained to laugh, Jameson continuing to leap about, flicking a towel with aggravating accuracy at Walsh's wobbling buttocks.

'Damn you, Jameson! Don't do that, you confounded fool!'

'Come, come, Walsh, don't be an old prude, you enjoyed the bathe, don't deny it!'

The elegant Mosse had been resolutely opposed to undressing, until he realized his pride would take a bigger dent if he refused. The second lieutenant was as elegant without his uniform as when fully attired. It was, he later claimed, untrue to say clothes made the man, but that beauty only needed to be skin deep to make an impression.

In this he was disturbingly right for one member of the officers' mess. A man-of-war lodged many types but all, whether extrovert or introvert, were eventually compelled to surrender in large measure any sense of individual privilege; a mess – whether forward or aft – rubbed along together on consensus, and disagreements were usually things of small moment.

But *Andromeda*'s wardroom sheltered a misfit in Mr Templeton. As long as Templeton could haunt the captain's cabin, nursing his own secrets, he was content. But when he was compelled to associate with these bears, he felt awkward, conspicuous and a figure of ridicule. While being with them, he was not of them.

Much of this self-perception was in his own imagination, but the events of the early morning had shocked him deeply, not just as a matter of spectacle, but as a powerful and unlooked for spur to a hidden, barely acknowledged lust, which distracted him from all his other preoccupations.

Templeton had never acknowledged the proclivity that now overwhelmed him. He had spent his drab, pretentious life of genteel servitude largely occupying

129

his mind. His social life, such as it was, had revolved around that of his ageing mother and her coterie of friends. He had vaguely supposed he would at an appropriate time and when one or other of the matrons had decided the matter for him, take one or other of their plain daughters to wife. To this end, and to satisfy his ambitions, he had sought to improve his place at the Admiralty. Meddling in its intrigues and hoping to advance from lowly copying clerk, he had aspired to and achieved the post of a cipher clerk, a confidential servant of the state, whose opinion was sought first by Lord Dungarth and now by Captain Nathaniel Drinkwater.

In some ways this filled him with a heavy conceit, partially satisfying inner hungers, but from time to time he was moved to acknowledge another stirring, aware that there was about this an air of disgrace. This in turn was sublimated by classical considerations and not held to resemble, in even a distant way, the disgusting soliciting, importuning, love-struck moonings and filthy couplings of his fellow clerks with the doxies who inhabited the purlieus of Whitehall.

The morning's events had, however, brought him perilously close to a terrible exposure, for he had been physically moved by the experience, almost conspicuously aroused. He had consequently suffered the acute fear of discovery together with the agony of frustrated desire caused by the mass propinquity. Nor had it helped to see the odd individual, from an indisputably lower order of society, in a state of abandoned tumescence. That their fellows dismissed them laughingly made his own situation all the more shameful, for where this condition had occurred to him naturally, he had always banished it by occupying his mind with the diversion of a book, or some other study.

Now he hid in his flimsy cabin and wept, for it only added to his burden of fear.

The score or so of men whom Drinkwater had so disreputably sniffed out received Kennedy's especial attention. A perceptive observer would have noticed these unfortunates had in common the most wretched and ragged appearance. The surgeon took their names and ensured their washing was more than a cursory drenching, subjecting them to a thorough examination, then flinging their clothes overboard. Afterwards he sent them to the purser for new slops, brushing aside their protests that they could not afford such luxuries with the assurance that they 'would soon be able to pay out of their prize-money'.

As for the poor fellow who had caused all this to-do, he was brought on deck in a hammock and set in the pale sunshine that finally triumphed over the cloud. By mid-morning a light breeze had sprung up from the west and above the already stuffed hammock nettings, spread in the ratlines and along light lines rigged for the purpose, breeches and trousers, shirts and vests and pantaloons, cravats and neckties, scarves and bandanas, socks and stockings, aprons and breeches fluttered in the breeze.

Amid this gay and unwarlike decoration, Drinkwater paced the deck in deep confabulation with Kennedy.

'Well, sir, we have done what we can . . .'

'I'm told it is very efficacious, that the contagion is

spread by the flea and that only extreme cleanliness will extirpate it.'

Kennedy frowned. ''Tis true, sir, that the putrid fever is common to poor conditions, but to attribute it to the flea is somewhat far-fetched.' Kennedy had wanted to say 'preposterous', but in view of the captain's age and rank he forbore. Nevertheless he pressed his argument.

'If your hypothesis was right, sir, then the disease would be as prevalent among people of the better classes as among the poor; but it is the poor who are most afflicted. The flea is common to both, but dirt and misery are not.'

'*Quod erat demonstrandum*, eh, Mr Kennedy?' asked Drinkwater wryly. He was in better humour, glad that matters had passed off as well as they had and that, apart from the surplus bunting, order was now restored to the ship.

'Exactly so, sir.'

'I shall not argue the point with you. I only know what I have observed, or heard others speak of. Not all were ancient tarry-breeks.' Drinkwater smiled at his young colleague. 'Keep that fellow in a fever out of the berth deck and we may yet save others. Ah, Tom, are you better for your bath?'

'I have to say, sir, that for a moment or two, I seriously doubted the wisdom of what you were doing, but', he shrugged and looked about him, 'there seems little sign of ill-effect, beyond the adornments aloft, that is.'

They all laughed at the first lieutenant's allusion to the fluttering disorder about them.

'There'll be none, Tom,' Drinkwater said reassuringly. 'It was all taken humorously and most of 'em will know by now that it was for their own good. As for the officers, it was for their benefit too; besides, 'twas a case of *noblesse oblige*.'

'Perhaps you are right. I certainly feel better now the gunpowder is all doused. Seems a damned dangerous thing to do, to stum the ship like that.'

'But you have to dry her through, Tom; you know how oak sweats and she'd been closed down during the storm. After we've exercised the guns I want the bilges pumped dry and then have salt sprinkled into the wells . . .'

'Aye, aye, sir,' said Huke, with just a faint trace of resignation in his tone to amuse Drinkwater.

More officers joined them, and it occurred to Drinkwater that each felt a compulsion to reappear upon the quarterdeck fully accoutred, to reassert their individual status. Whatever the darker motives, they laughed and smiled, exchanging grins with the men at the wheel.

'Have you heard Jameson's joke, sir?' drawled Mosse.

'No, pray share it, Mr Jameson.'

The third lieutenant blushed, made a face at Mosse and shook his head.

'Come, Roger, or I shall steal it . . .'

'Do as you please, damn you, Stephen.'

Mosse turned insouciantly to Drinkwater and Huke. 'Jameson has some crack-pot notion that we were ridding ourselves of fleas, sir, and, having due regard to the naked disorder so recently upon our decks, likened it to an event of history, sir.'

'And what was that, Mr Mosse? As I am sure you are about to tell us.'

'Why, the Boston flea party, sir!'

Despite the misgivings of his officers, Drinkwater had known very well what he was doing. By following the mass drenching with a gunnery exercise he achieved that unity in a crew which, with a less active commander, might otherwise have taken months. He had been lucky in Huke, capitalizing on that diligent officer's hard work, but he was pleased that after noon, notwithstanding the ridiculous washing that still blew about above their heads, they had loosed three broadsides from each battery, and shot at a dahn-buoy until their ears rang with the concussions of the guns.

To crown the events of the day Drinkwater cleared the lower deck and summoned the ship's company aft.

'Well, my lads, it has been an eventful day,' he said, pausing long enough to hear a groundswell of good-natured agreement, 'and it is likely to be succeeded by a number of such eventful days. We are not far from the coast of Norway, and we are here to flush out a few privateers who have been reported lurking here-abouts. In a moment or two I am ordering the hoisting of Danish colours and we shall enter Danish waters. Next time you hear the drum beat to quarters the only surprise will be the one we will give to the enemy! Now, Mr Huke, we have disrupted the ship's routine sufficiently for one day and delayed long enough. Be so kind as to pipe up spirits!'

Drinkwater went below to a cheer; if there was opportunism, even sycophancy in it, he was unde-ceived. He had other matters to concern him.

Quilhampton was still missing, and the men who had half-severed the gun-breech were among the mob happily awaiting their daily ration of rum.

'Sir!'

Drinkwater stirred and saw Midshipman Fisher's head peering round the door. 'What is it?'

'Mr Birkbeck's compliments, sir, and we've sighted Utsira.'

'What time is it?'

'Almost six bells, sir.'

'Very well.' The boy vanished. Drinkwater roused himself, swivelled in his chair and stared through the stern windows. It was three o'clock in the afternoon and he must have dozed for over an hour.

'I am growing old,' he muttered to himself. There were not many hours of daylight left and the horizon was depressingly empty. He remembered James Quilhampton's *Kestrel* with a pang of conscience. 'Old and forgetful.' The thought, too, was depressing.

Rising stiffly, he went into his night-cabin, opened the top of his chest and poured some water into the bowl recessed there. He threw water into his face, ran the new-fangled toothbrush round his mouth and stared at himself in the mirror. He was sure there was more of his forehead visible than when he had last looked, then chid himself for a fool, for he had done his hair immediately after the morning's dousing.

On deck he became brisk and eager for a sight of the island. 'Where away, Mr Birkbeck?'

Birkbeck was standing with one of his mates, a man named Ashley. Both men lowered their glasses. 'Two points to starboard, sir.'

'Here, sir.' Ashley offered his telescope.

'Thank you, Mr Ashley.'

Drinkwater focused the lenses upon the low island that appeared blue and insubstantial, then swept the sea around it in the vain hope that the grey-white peak of *Kestrel*'s mainsail would break the bleakness of the scene.

'Not a landfall to stumble across in the dark, or the kind of weather we laboured in the other night,' remarked Birkbeck.

'No, indeed . . .' Drinkwater lowered the telescope and handed it back to the master's mate. 'Obliged, Mr Ashley.' He looked up at the spanker gaff, where the unfamiliar red swallowtail ensign with its white cross flapped bravely in the breeze.

'Handsome flag, ain't it? Last time I saw it fly in anger was at Copenhagen,' Birkbeck said.

'Which ship were you in?' Drinkwater asked attentively.

'I was with Captain Puget in *Goliath*.'

'I don't recall . . .'

'In Gambier's attack, sir, not Nelson's.'

'Ah, yes . . .'

'You were in the earlier action then?'

'Yes. I had the bomb *Virago*.'

They reminisced happily, staring at the distant island as, almost imperceptibly, it took form. Drinkwater forbore from telling Birkbeck the clandestine part he had himself played in the events that led up to the appearance of Dismal Jimmy Gambier's fleet before the spires of the Danish capital in 1807. Instead, Birkbeck wanted to know of his brief meetings with Lord Nelson, which led to the inevitable revelation that Captain Drinkwater had not only been a witness to the battle of Copenhagen in 1801, but had also, 'somewhat ignominiously', been a prisoner aboard the enemy flagship *Bucentaure* at Trafalgar.*

'I had no idea, sir,' said Birkbeck admiringly.

'It was not a post to which much glory accrued,' Drinkwater replied ruefully. 'Fate plays some odd tricks . . . I cannot begin to describe the carnage . . .'

The blue smudge hardened, grew darker and sharper, its outline more defined. Presently Huke joined them as Utsira revealed itself as a rocky, steep-sided, low island, with the surge and suck of a heavy groundswell washing its grim shoreline. Then, as the sun westered, it threw the rough and weathered surface into hostile relief.

'Nasty place,' said Huke with the true instinct of the pelagic seaman.

And then, as they watched, far beyond the island, beyond the horizon itself, the sun gleamed briefly on distant mountain peaks floating above cloud. The sight was over in a numinous moment and left them staring with wonder.

'"To Noroway, to Noroway, to Noroway, o'er the foam,"' quoted Huke in a rare and revealing aside.

'Must be thirty leagues distant,' Birkbeck said.

Drinkwater said nothing. He was reminded of the *nunataks* of Greenland which he had last seen from afar off, remembering the enchantment distance lent them, and the harshness of the landscape in reality. On that occasion he had felt relief, for it had been a moment of departure. This was the opposite, and as

* See *The Bomb Vessel* and *1805*.

the mountain summits faded, he wondered whether they had been revealed as portents and what it was that lay in wait amid their inhospitable fastnesses.

He turned his attention again to Utsira. Gone was any picturesque aspect. It was a rampart of rock, to be avoided at all costs, about which the tide ripped past.

'Put the ship about, Mr Birkbeck, and shorten down for the night. We will see whether daylight brings us the *Kestrel*.'

'Aye, aye, sir.'

Birkbeck tucked his glass away and picked up the speaking trumpet from its hook on the binnacle. He began bawling orders to the watch on deck.

'I wonder how many islands we have passed, Tom, in all our combined travels,' Drinkwater remarked idly as the helm went down and *Andromeda* swung slowly to the west, her high jibboom raking the sky.

'The Lord knows. I'm afraid I never kept count.'

'Nor me . . .' Drinkwater was thinking of the island of Juan Fernandez, with its curious rock formation, a great hole eroded through a small cape. Then he recalled the deserters, and the manhunt, and the fight in a cave below the thunder of a waterfall which had ended in the death of the runaways. One had been a gigantic Irishman, the other his lover, the girl they had all known for months as a young seaman named . . . He had forgotten. Witheredge? Witherspoon? Yes, that was it, Witherspoon.*

How one forgot, Drinkwater mused sadly, how one forgot. Again the spectre of age rose to haunt him. He shook the queer feeling off. He had remembered the

* See *In Distant Waters*.

girl's shattered and beautiful body earlier that very morning; it had stimulated the coarse joke that had bound his ship's company together. He felt a mood of awful self-loathing sweep over him. He himself had shot the girl, shot her unknowingly it was true, but had nevertheless been the agent of her death. Something of his personal disquiet must have showed on his face, for he sighed and then looked up to see Huke staring at him.

'Are you all right, sir?'

Drinkwater smiled ruefully. 'Well enough, Tom, well enough.' He brightened with an effort. 'An attack of the megrims, nothing more.' He forced a laugh. 'Too many damned islands.'

8 A Bird of Ill-omen
October 1813

The morning bore a different aspect. Drinkwater woke
to the short, jerking plunges of the creaking frigate as
she butted into a young head sea and knew the worst.
Dressing hurriedly, he went on deck to find his appre-
hensions confirmed. As he ascended to the deck, he
noticed the hammock of the sick man swinging in isolation beneath the open waist, slung between the
boat-booms. Then, as he emerged on to the quarterdeck, the near gale buffeted him, the howl of it low in
the rigging. Under topsails and a rag or two of staysails
and jibs, *Andromeda* rode a grey sea studded with paler
crests which reflected the monotone of the sky.
Curtains of rain swept eastwards some two miles away
on the lee bow, and the blurred horizon to windward
promised more. The decks were already sodden, and
much of the good work of the day before was already
undone. Staring about him he saw no sign of Utsira.

'Morning, sir.' Lieutenant Jameson touched the
forecock of his hat which, Drinkwater noted, dripped
from earlier rain as he held his head down against the
wind. 'A few squalls ha'e blown through, but she's
snug enough under this canvas, sir.'

'Yes.' Drinkwater wanted to ask if they had seen any sign of the *Kestrel*, but it would only have betrayed the extent of his anxiety, for it was obvious there was no sign of the cutter in the grey welter beyond the safety of *Andromeda*'s bulwarks. Instead he asked with almost painful inconsequence, 'Where are you from, Mr Jameson?'

'Montrose, sir.'

'And your family? Do they farm?'

'My father is an apothecary, sir,' Jameson said, with a hint of defiance, as though he was half ashamed and half daring his commander to scoff at his low birth.

'A useful calling, Mr Jameson. I wonder what he would have thought of the event of yesterday?'

'I doubt that he would ha'e seen the amusing side of it, sir.'

'And you? What did you think?'

'I, sir . . . well, I . . . I don't know . . .'

'Come, come, I never knew a lieutenant who had no opinion. I'll warrant you had one in the wardroom last night. Perhaps you did not approve?'

'No! I mean, I don't think I would ha'e done . . . I mean . . .'

'You mean you *could* not have done it, I sense. Is that not so?'

'Well, sir, perhaps,' agreed Jameson, whose chief objection had been having to jump around naked himself, though he had taken his discomfiture out on the embarrassed Walsh.

'Sometimes, Mr Jameson, it is very necessary to do things which seem, at face value, to be ridiculous. Your joke about the flea party was a good one, for, though you may have considered the proposition ridiculous, I am of the opinion that the ship-fever is caused by that annoying little parasite and that he will hop aft along the gangway and nip you as readily as he will nip those men forrard there.'

'You are very probably right, sir,' capitulated Jameson resignedly.

'Well, then, perhaps you are more resolute in what you think we should do today. What would you advise?'

Jameson shrugged. He was not used to having his opinion sought, least of all by the captain. 'Heave to, I suppose, since we are on the rendezvous.' He paused and looked at Drinkwater who said:

'Nothing more?'

'No . . . well, yes, I suppose it would be best to run back towards the island, we ha'e hauled out to the nor' west during the night.'

Drinkwater nodded. 'See to it then,' he ordered curtly and turned away, to begin pacing the deck along the line of the starboard carronades.

'Strange old cove,' Jameson muttered to himself, raising the speaking trumpet to his mouth. 'Stand by the braces, there!' he called, then lowering the trumpet towards the men at the helm, 'Larboard wheel if you please . . .'

In the cabin Drinkwater was studying the spread charts with Birkbeck when Huke knocked and entered.

'Fishing boats in sight, sir. I thought at first it was the cutter. I've told Mosse to drop down towards them.'

'What good will that do, Tom? To maintain the

fiction of being Danish we would need to speak . . .'

'We've a Dane on board, sir,' Huke interrupted, 'I meant to tell you earlier. His name is Sommer. I have instructed him to lay aft.'

'Well done. Bring him below.'

Huke disappeared and returned a few moments later with an elderly man who, from his sandy eyebrows, might once have been blond, but whose head was now devoid of hair.

'You are Sommer?'

'Yah. I am Per Sommer.'

'How long have you been in this ship?'

'Oh, long time, Captain. In *Agamemnon* before, and *Ruby* and some other ships. In King George's service long time.'

'You have no wish to go home to Denmark?'

Sommer shrugged. 'I have no family. My mother died when I was born, my father soon after. He was fisherman. I become fisherman. Then one day we have big storm, off the Hoorn's Rev. Later we see ship and I become British seaman. Now *Andromeda* my home. Not go back to Denmark. Too old.'

Drinkwater looked blankly at the elderly man. For a moment or two he was lost in contemplation at the sad biography, moved at the surrender to providence. Had fate compelled Sommer to this comfortless existence just to provide him, Captain Nathaniel Drinkwater, with an interpreter at a crucial moment?

'Lucky for us, sir,' prompted Birkbeck.

'What? Oh, yes. D'you know why we are flying the Danish flag?'

Sommer shrugged. 'Not worry very much about flags.'

'Very well. We want you to speak to the fishing boats ahead, Sommer. I want to ask them if they have seen any strange ships, big ships. American ships, in fact, Sommer. D'you understand?'

'American ships, yah, I understand.'

'What about . . . ?' began Huke, but Drinkwater had already considered the matter.

'I want you to put on my hat and cloak when you speak to them, Sommer, to look like an officer.'

'An officer . . . ?' Sommer grinned, not unwilling to enter the little conspiracy. 'Yah, I can be captain.'

And they bowed him out of the cabin with almost as much ceremony as if he were.

The two fishing boats, their grey sails almost indistinguishable against the sea, lay to leeward as the mainyards were swung aback and Sommer hoisted himself up on to the rail. There followed an exchange which, by its very nature, raised Drinkwater's spirits, for it was obvious from the Dane's question and the pointing gestures that followed that it had been positively answered.

'Give them this,' Drinkwater commanded, holding up a knotted handkerchief. Sommer took the small bundle and tossed it into the nearer boat as it wallowed below them. There were expressions of thanks and Sommer dropped down on deck, taking off the captain's cloak and hat. Drinkwater took them and, in doing so, thrust a guinea into Sommer's rough hand.

'Thank you, Sommer. What did they say?'

'Two American ships, sir, sailed into Vikkenfiord three days ago.'

'Very good. If we take them I shall rate you a quartermaster for prize money.'

'Thank you, Captain.' The Dane knuckled his forehead and shuffled forward.

'Haul the mainyards, Mr Mosse! Mr Birkbeck, the chart . . .'

They had located the Vikkenfiord as a long inlet which once, in primeval times, had been formed by the erosion of a mighty glacier. It appeared like a long finger reaching, with a slight crook in it, into the mountainous interior. Its entrance was very narrow.

'For a moment I thought it was not going to be on our chart,' Drinkwater confided.

''Twould have to be well enough known for the Americans to find, sir,' replied Birkbeck.

'Yes,' Drinkwater agreed, feeling a little foolish, for that was an obvious point and the entire ship knew by now that they were seeking Yankee privateers. 'We could do with better visibility before closing the coast, but I fear we are more likely to encounter fog.'

'Aye, I was thinking much the same. This can be a damnable spot . . .'

'Well, there is no point in dwelling on the matter. Lay us a course to Utsira. We can afford a little further delay and if the Americans were anchored three days ago, it seems unlikely they have left already . . .'

'They could have slipped out yesterday,' said Birkbeck.

'True.' Drinkwater could not tell the master why he was certain they had not left, but his own heart quickened, for he was sure they lay within the fastness of the fiord. The weather they had endured would not have encouraged the passage of a ship from Denmark with French arms, having been contrary for a passage out of the Skagerrak, for whereas the Norwegian coast north of Utsira was fissured with sheltered inland passages, the area to the south was not.

'We will pass another night on the rendezvous,' Drinkwater said firmly, 'and then, if the weather serves, we will run into this Vikkenfiord and take a look.'

Drinkwater slept well that night and woke in optimistic mood. To his unutterable joy the wind had hauled south-east and Utsira was dead astern, no more than three or four leagues distant. Such a wind shift seemed like an augury of good luck. He shaved, dressed and hurried on deck. The change in the weather had encouraged more of the local fisherfolk to venture forth, and Drinkwater saw this as additional proof of providential approval.

He had not expected to find *Kestrel* in the offing but such was his mood that he would not have been surprised had she been in sight, and he privately dared to hope that she and her company were safe.

Although it was not his watch, the master was on deck, taking bearings and hurrying below to lay them off on the chart. When he returned to the deck he approached Drinkwater.

'With your permission, sir, a course for the entrance to the fiord?'

'If you please, Mr Birkbeck.'

So they bore up and, with their yards braced to catch the steady beam breeze from the south-east,

Andromeda headed north-east again, dropping the isolated outcrop of Utsira astern and soon afterwards raising the grey ramparts of the coast of Norway.

It had escaped anyone's notice that Mr Templeton had not quitted his cabin since the morning of the great dousing. Anyone of significance, that is, for the wardroom messman was aware of the captain's secretary's 'indisposition', and catered for him until, on the morning they departed Utsira, he passed word to the surgeon.

Templeton himself had fallen victim to a conflict of emotion. Unaware of the captain's preoccupations, he was somewhat affronted that Drinkwater had not sent for him. He was also concerned, for reasons of his own, as to what Drinkwater now intended to do. On the other hand, he found himself unable to resist submitting to wild and beguiling fantasies which washed over him in waves of sensual anticipation, so that he dared not leave his cabin to confront a world of reality in which, he felt sure, his guilt would be written plain upon his face. He had not counted upon the world of reality visiting him.

Mr Kennedy knocked and immediately opened the cabin's flimsy door unannounced. 'Now what in the world is the matter with you, Templeton?'

Templeton was shocked at the intrusion. He expected his shut door to be respected as if it were that of his home. He had no concept of ship-board manners, or prerogatives, something that Kennedy had quickly assimilated. Caught off guard and guilty, he forgot his 'illness' and was merely outraged.

'How dare you come bursting in like this . . .'

147

'There's nothing wrong with you,' said Kennedy, well practised in detecting the vapours among the so-called well-to-do. 'Come, turn out! What would become of us if we all lay about in such a manner?'

'I've caught an ague from the cold water . . .'

'Rubbish! Salt water never gave a man an ague! You are malingering, sir!' Kennedy snapped, 'And I have work to do!'

'I didn't summon you,' protested Templeton, adding, as he saw the baleful look in Kennedy's eyes, 'nor has Captain Drinkwater sent for me.'

'I think he is far too busy. Do you know where we are?'

'Off Norway, I shouldn't wonder.'

'Almost *upon* it, in fact. There's talk of American ships and action before the day's done.'

'Action?' Templeton's face grew ashen.

'Aye, Templeton, action. You had better be out of bed by then, cowardice in the face of the enemy's a hanging offence! '

There were a lot of men on deck, Templeton thought, the same men he had last seen naked; men on and off duty, for the vista about them was such as to stun the dullest mind. They ran through a narrow strait in which the sea bore the colour and smoothness of a sword-blade. Upon either side rose precipitous heights, great dark cliffs, deeply fissured, their snow-capped summits wreathed in veils of cloud. As they passed the gorge, the land fell back, to reveal the fiord itself, opening ahead of them. The ground-willow and scrub of the littoral gave way to pines and firs whose dark cladding moved in waves with the breeze, accompanied by gentle susurrations. These trees climbed the slopes, finally dwindling to concede the rising ground to bare rock and, here and there, patches of scree. Above the talus, solitary snow-encrusted crags stood out against the sky, about the peaks of which an occasional eagle could be seen wheeling.

"Tis wonderful, sir,' a voice said, and Templeton turned to see his sea-mentor Greer, the boatswain's mate, standing awestruck.

'Sublime, Greer, sublime,' Templeton whispered, suddenly aware of an overpowering breathlessness.

'I've never seen nought like it, Mr Templeton, 'cept in a picture-book once, when I was a boy, like.'

The revelation of childhood wonder combined with so manly an appreciation of nature's bounty to make Templeton turn to Greer. Their eyes met and Templeton *knew* for a certainty that Greer had similar inclinations, though not a word passed between them and they regarded again the dark shores of the Vikkenfiord. Templeton felt quite deliriously free of all his cares.

A few yards away Lieutenant Mosse nudged his scarlet-clad colleague Walsh. 'There, sir, I do declare I was right and you owe me a guinea.'

'You may be right, Stephen, but that ain't proof!'

'What proof d'you want?'

'Just proof,' said Walsh enigmatically, leaving Mosse shaking his head, amused.

'You have no need to worry about the depth,' Drinkwater said to Birkbeck, 'though it will not hurt to take an occasional cast of the lead. These fiords are uncommon deep.'

'Aye, sir, but just in case . . .'

'Indeed, by all means.'

And so their progress was punctuated by low orders to the helmsmen which kept the frigate in the centre of the fiord, her yards squared to the following wind, and the desultory and unrewarded call of the labouring leadsmen of 'no botto-o-om'.

Presently the high land fell back and the gradient became less steep on the southern shore. The margins of pine forest widened to great swathes, rounding the contours of the mountains under their dark, luxuriant mantle.

'Something sinister about them damned trees,' said Huke.

'Hiding trolls and what-not, eh, Tom?' grinned Drinkwater, 'I didn't know you had a fancy for the Gothick.'

'Sir! Right ahead!' A hail from the forecastle broke into this inane conversation and Drinkwater raised his glass. Ahead of them the fiord widened considerably, having an appearance more like an English lake in Cumbria. To starboard the mountains retreated further to, perhaps, ten miles distant, while to port they remained closer, their foothills coming down in hummocks and indenting the coast, so that little bays with brief strands alternated with rocky promontories. Ahead, one such headland, more prominent than the others, gave the fiord its crooked shape. Just emerging beyond this small but impressive cape were the masts and yards of two large ships.

They were some distance off and Drinkwater could make out little of them before he was confronted by a more immediate problem. The wind, which had funnelled through the gorge, from which they had run well clear, now assumed its truer direction and swept down from the south-east and the more distant mountains to starboard. Above their heads the squared sails were all a-flutter with a dull, insistent rumble.

'Larboard braces there! Lively now! Cast off your starboard pins!'

In a few moments order was restored and, with a beam wind, *Andromeda* gathered speed. Drinkwater raised his glass again. The strange anchored ships beneath the cape were clearer now. He could see the bright spots of their ensigns and he closed his glass with a snap.

'Beat to quarters, Mr Huke, and clear for action.'

His Britannic Majesty's frigate *Andromeda* bore down upon the anchored ships at a fine clip, the deceitful swallowtail Danish ensign standing stiffly out from the peak of the spanker gaff. A British ensign awaited the order to be run aloft. Boarding parties of seamen and marines, each told off under the command of a midshipman or master's mate, waited by the quarter boats, the red and blue cutters.

It was clear that the only patch of shallow water capable of holding the flukes of an anchor lay close inshore, in the bay that, Drinkwater guessed without looking at the chart, lay just beyond the bluff. A sudden gust of wind laid the frigate over, so that she surged ahead, rapidly drawing closer to the point itself.

Beside him Huke reported the ship cleared for action. Every gun, including the runaway cannon which had been hand-spiked and shoved back into its rightful station, was loaded and shotted and every man stood ready at his post.

'We'll have the t'gallants off her and the courses clewed up. There's enough wind to handle her under the topsails.'

Huke and Birkbeck nodded their understanding. With the ship heeled and moving fast, the gunnery would be inaccurate and wild, and Drinkwater had given specific orders that he wanted little damage done to the enemies' fabric.

'Take 'em quickly by surprise, with as little damage as possible,' he had said. The thought of rich prizes gained this policy a ready co-operation and the word passed along the gun decks. A short and lucrative cruise would be dandy!

The bay beyond the bluff was just beginning to open now. They could see the two ships with boats about them, see too the stars and bars of their hostile nationality.

There was a sudden sound as of rending silk. Aloft three holes appeared in the main topsail and the twanging of parted rigging came to the astonished knot of officers on the quarterdeck. To starboard half a dozen columns of water sprung into the air.

'What the devil . . . ?'

The boom of a battery's fire rolled over the water towards them. Drinkwater saw the little clouds of smoke swiftly torn to shreds by the wind from the gun embrasures that lined the cliff-top of the bluff. Above the half-hidden but unmistakable grey line of a stone parapet, another swallowtail ensign rose upon a flagstaff.

'There's a fort there!' Birkbeck cried in sudden

comprehension, with the outraged tone of a cheat outsmarted.

'Aye,' Huke retorted, 'and he knows us for what we are.'

'He certainly ain't fooled by our colours!'

Confronted by this sudden revelation, Drinkwater had to think swiftly. He was reluctant to give up the attempt on the American ships, but the next salvo from the fort hit home, tumbling men from a forecastle gun like rag dolls. Their sudden cries rent the air, as an explosion of splinters erupted from the bulwark. Another shot ploughed up the deck and crashed through the opposite bulwark to fall, spent, into the sea alongside the starbord main-chains.

'Let fall the courses, there! Set the t'gallants!'

He must run on, then work up to windward and return under the lee of the opposite, southern shore, past the fort but out of range of the guns hidden behind those high ramparts. It was the only way he could reconnoitre the enemy position.

The discovery of the fort transformed the situation. The matter would be more difficult than he had at first anticipated, no mere tip-and-run raid, but it could be managed if he kept his head. He felt the hull shudder as more shot struck them. How far did those damned guns in the fort traverse?

Then, with the added momentum of the extra sails and without firing a shot in return, they swept out of range and Drinkwater forced himself to concentrate his attention on the two ships anchored in the bay. Both were frigate-built, large privateers, or possibly worse: perhaps naval frigates.

It was essential, then, that Drinkwater should turn

Andromeda and move her back to seaward of the enemy ships. At least he could cut them off from escape. Moreover, it was imperative that he find an anchorage, for they could not beat out through the gorge with the wind funnelling through it. The lower appearance of the southern shore suggested the sea-bed extended into the fiord at a similar gradient, affording him the shallow water he sought. He only hoped that whatever bottom the anchor flukes might strike, it would prove soft enough to hold them.

'Full and bye, Mr Birkbeck. Brace the yards sharp up. I want to claw offshore, tack ship and seek an anchorage under the lee of the farther side.' He turned to the first lieutenant. 'Secure the guns, Mr Huke.'

A buzz of disappointment greeted this order. On the gun deck Lieutenant Mosse, commanding the starboard battery, sheathed his sword and addressed his colleague in charge of the port cannon.

'He who turns and runs away, lives to fight another day, eh, Jameson?'

'A flea flees,' returned Jameson.

'You possess a shining wit, Jameson.'

'I'd sooner that than a wicked tongue.'

Andromeda came up into the wind with a clatter as the helm was put over. Her sails bellied aback as she came round and the bead-blocks aloft rattled as she bucked up into the wind.

'Mainsail haul!' The main and mizen yards were trimmed to the new course as the foreyards continued to thrust her head round on to the larboard tack.

'Let go and haul!'

The frigate settled down to claw her way across the fiord. The wind was strong now, augmented by cold

154

katabatic gusts that slid down from the distant high ground. Drinkwater regarded the enemy fort over the starboard quarter.

'The ruse with the ensign didn't pay off then, sir,' Huke said, after reporting the guns secure.

'I think, Tom,' Drinkwater replied, without taking the glass from his eye, 'that as we carried off most of the Danish fleet, what few ships they retain are well known to any Danish officer worth his salt.' –

'Even one commanding a remote fort in Norway?'

'Well, I don't think it is any coincidence,' Drinkwater said, counting the embrasures in the distant fort, 'that the Yankee ships are anchored under those guns, do you?'

'No. It's a damnably perfect rendezvous for them.'

'I think, sir,' put in Birkbeck sharply, 'they were expecting something larger!'

An urgency in Birkbeck's voice made Drinkwater lower the glass and look round. 'What the devil . . . ?'

He swung to where Birkbeck pointed. Far down the fiord, her white sails full of the following wind which had so lately wafted *Andromeda* through the narrows and which now mewed her up in the fiord, a large man-of-war was running clear of the gorge.

'Now there', said Drinkwater grimly, raising his glass, 'is a bird of exceeding ill-omen.'

9 The Wings of Nemesis
October 1813

Captain Drinkwater felt the cold grip of irresolution seize his palpitating heart. Here was the spectre of defeat, of dishonour. Retreat, he knew, merely postponed the inevitable and spawned greater reluctance; honour demanded he fight, if only to defend that of his flag. The white ensign now flew in place of the swallowtail *ruse de guerre*. He considered striking it after a few broadsides in permissible, if disreputable capitulation.

These thoughts coursed through his mind while it was yet clouding with other, more demanding preoccupations, for he saw the approaching enemy not merely as a hostile ship-of-war, but as the manifestation of something more sinister, an agent of fate itself. Here came the punishment for all his self-conceit. Sommer had served not simply his own ends, but also a greater purpose, to accomplish the destruction of Captain Nathaniel Drinkwater and his overweening pride in the obscurity of a remote Norwegian fiord.

How foolish he had been, he thought, to believe in providence as some benign deity which had taken a fancy to himself and which would cosset him personally. Blind faith proved only a blind alley, a trap.

Oh, it had sustained him, to be sure, given him a measure of protection which he, during his brief strutting moment, had transmuted into a gallant confidence, but he had outrun his allotted span, a fact which he now knew with a chilling certainty. He was old and careworn, a dog who had had his day and was masquerading in a young man's post, seduced by what . . . ?

He found, in a wave of mounting panic, that he did not know. The vaguest notion of duty swept through his perception, to be dismissed as cynical nonsense and replaced by damning self-interest. What did he hope to achieve? This enemy ship approaching them had come, undoubtedly, to transfer the arms and munitions to the waiting Yankees, as Bardolini had foretold. And if providence had, in its cosmic wisdom, decided that Canada should, like America itself, be free of King George's government, it would surely engineer the defeat of so petty a player as Nathaniel Drinkwater.

He silently cursed himself. He could have, *should* have, been at home on his Suffolk acres with Elizabeth, expiating his many sins and wickednesses. His great conceit had been to think that fate had delivered Bardolini into his hands for him to accomplish some grandiloquent design and keep Canada as a dominion of the British kingdom. If fate had wanted that, it would never have condoned the revolt of the Thirteen Colonies.

This simplistic and overwrought, though logical conclusion terminated Drinkwater's nervously self-centred train of thought. Huke, Birkbeck, Mosse and Jameson were looking at him expectantly. The hands, many belonging to the watch below, just stood down from their action stations, milled curiously in the waist. They too stared expectantly aft.

Drinkwater raised his Dollond glass again, a charade he enforced upon himself to compel his wits to return to reality. With slow deliberation he lowered the telescope.

'We will attempt to break out to seaward,' he said with what he hoped was a quiet authority. 'Send the hands back to their quarters. Starboard battery to load bar-shot and elevate high. We will exchange broadsides as we pass and do our best to cripple that fellow. Mr Birkbeck, lay me a course to pass, say, seven cables distant from him . . .'

'The wind will be foul in the narrows, sir.'

'When the wind comes ahead we will tow through. He is heavier than we are. That is a small advantage, but an advantage, none the less. You have your orders, gentlemen. We have a chance, let us exploit it!'

Drinkwater raised the glass again. Concentrating on the enemy's image occluded the closer world, left him to master himself, conspicuous upon his quarterdeck but mercifully hidden from all.

She was a big ship, a heavy frigate such as had long ago superseded the class to which *Andromeda* belonged, equal to the large American frigates which had so shocked the Royal Navy by a series of brilliant victories over British cruisers at the outbreak of the present war with the United States.

To counter this, the British had reacted by cutting down some smaller line-of-battle ships, producing *razées*, such as the *Patrician*, which Drinkwater himself had lately commanded. Had he had her at his disposal now, he would have been confident of taking on this powerful enemy, for with her he had shot to pieces the Russian seventy-four *Suvorov*. That, he reproached himself bitterly, was a past conceit, and it was for past conceits and victories that he was now to receive due retribution.

The Danish frigate, for he could tell she was such by her ensign, bore down towards them as they in turn, yards braced up, racing through the comparatively still waters of the fiord, rapidly closed the distance. Doubtless the Dane would seek to cripple *Andromeda* and, as the leeward ship, her guns would be pointing much higher. Drinkwater considered edging downwind, to give himself that advantage, but he dismissed the thought. It was just possible that the Danish commander did not know who, or what, they were, that their own ensign was masked by the mizen topsail, and he would think they were one of the American ships bearing down in welcome. No, the sooner they rushed past, the better.

At all events, the Dane stood stolidly on.

Huke came aft, his face grim. 'All ready, sir.'

'Very well.'

The first lieutenant contemplated the Danish ship. 'She's a heavy bugger.'

'Yes. Must be a new ship. I thought we'd destroyed all their power.'

'They've had time to build new. We left them numerous gun-vessels for their islands, I suppose they've built this fellow to defend the coast of Norway.'

'In which case he's doing a damnably good job.

You know, once we work ourselves past him, we could blockade those narrows . . .'

'Let us get out first,' Huke cautioned. 'Hullo, he's shortening down; the cat's fairly out of the bag now!'

Critically they watched the topgallant yards lowered and the black dots of topmen running aloft. *Andromeda* had been eight or nine miles from the Dane when they first sighted the enemy. Now less than four miles separated the two frigates as they closed at a combined speed of sixteen or seventeen knots. They would be abeam of each other in a quarter of an hour. It seemed an age.

Mr Templeton was as confused about what was happening as he was about his own, private emotions. The ship's company had run to their battle stations and the internal appearance of *Andromeda* had been transformed; bulkheads were folded up under the deckhead, and the officers' quarters on the gun deck seemed suddenly to vanish. It had all been explained to him, but he still found the reality disquieting. Then, on passing the anchorage where, it was plain even to Templeton's untutored eye, two American ships lay, they had turned away and the men had been stood easy. After what seemed to Templeton so long a voyage, with their objective at last in sight, Captain Drinkwater's present action was incomprehensible. Templeton felt a certain relief that the air was not about to be filled with cannon-balls. Some days previously, Greer had picked one out of the garlands and thrown it to him. The sudden dead weight had almost broken his wrists and Greer had explained the crude technicalities of their brutal artillery with a morbid delight.

The very obvious reversal of orders, with the men chattering excitedly as they resumed their positions, now puzzled him and he ventured to ask Lieutenant Mosse what was going on.

'There's an enemy frigate approaching,' said Mosse obliquely, drawing his hanger with a wicked rasp. 'I suggest you might go on deck and watch.' Templeton hesitated and Mosse added, 'Much safer than staying here.'

Only half-believing this lie, Templeton reluctantly made for the forward companionway. Mosse winked at Jameson.

Thus Mr Templeton made to ascend the ladder normally reserved for the crew.

'Steady there, as she goes, Mr Birkbeck.'

Drinkwater watched the approaching ship. Both frigates ran on almost exactly reciprocal courses. Birkbeck and Ashley stood beside the binnacle where three helmsmen and a quartermaster held *Andromeda* to her track. Along the bulwarks the stubby barrelled carronades of the quarterdeck battery were surrounded by their crews, the gun-captains holding the taut lanyards to the cocked flintlocks. On the forecastle a lesser number of carronades supported the long bow-chasers. Below them, a similar scene was enacted, with the larger gun-crews gathered round the heavy 12-pounders of the main batteries. At key points aboard *Andromeda* the lesser and petty officers mustered groups of men ready to board or repel the enemy, bring ammunition or fire hoses, or work the ship if she was to be manoeuvred. Other groups clustered in the tops, marines among them, to act as sharpshooters, man the light swivel guns or lay out along the yards to shorten sail.

Upon the quarterdeck Huke, the first lieutenant, assisted the captain. A trio of midshipmen waited to act as messengers or attend to signals with the yeoman and his party. Lieutenant Walsh commanded the main detachment of marines who, interspersed with the carronades, laid their long muskets on the hammocks in the nettings and drew beads on the dark heads of the approaching enemy officers.

'You may fire when your guns bear!' Drinkwater's voice rang out, clear and crisp. The moment of fearful anticipation had passed and he was as cold and as purposeful as a sword-blade. Matters would fall out as they would, come what may.

'Pass word to the lieutenants on the gun deck, Mr Fisher,' Huke said, relaying Drinkwater's instruction. The boy ran off unobserved as every man concentrated upon the enemy ship. She was much closer than the seven cables Drinkwater had intended, but Mosse had drawn all the quoins and was sanguine that his guns would elevate. Periodically Drinkwater would quiz the gun-captain at the nearest carronade whose breech-screw fulfilled the same function.

'How is she now?'

'She'll do, sir . . .'

There was a last expectant hiatus which all knew would be broken by the eruption of the first gun, the starboard bow-chaser whose position commanded a field of fire closer aligned to the *Andromeda*'s line of advance than any other. The air was filled with the subdued hiss of the sea as it curled back from *Andromeda*'s apple-bow, the steady thrum of wind in the rigging, the creak of the ship, of her hemp and canvas, of the long tiller ropes, the straining sheets and tacks, the lifts, halliards and braces that converted the energy of the wind into the advance of the frigate and her iron armament.

Then came the report of the bow-chaser, the bright flash from its muzzle and the puff of cloudy smoke which hung for a second under the lee bow before being shredded by the wind. A second report, that of the enemy's reply, coincided with the flat echo, followed by the general reverberations of a furious exchange of shots. Drinkwater marked the quickening succession of flashes rolling aft towards him as each gun bore.

Then something went terribly awry. Instead of the bearing of the enemy opening with inexorable precision as the two frigates passed each other on reciprocal courses, there was a sudden, inexplicable acceleration. The Danish ship drew aft with miraculous speed and the British guns threw their shot not at the enemy, but at the empty sea on their own starboard beam.

'What in the devil's name . . . ?'

'What the hell . . . ?'

A dozen fouler exclamatory questions stabbed the air. Drinkwater spun round, momentarily confounded and utterly confused. All he knew was that from passing the beam, the enemy was now, against all reason, crossing their stern.

'Oh, my God!'

'For what we are about to receive . . .'

Inexplicably, *Andromeda* lay in the ideal position to be raked.

*

Mr Templeton saw exactly what happened, though he did not understand it at the time. He was, however, aware that the sudden movement of a group of seamen a few moments earlier had nothing to do with the business in hand, for he had heard no orders to stimulate men who, throughout the ship, were so manifestly poised but immobile with expectation. He was ascending the forward companionway as the two ships made their final approach and before the sudden and disorientating event which so perplexed all but a few on the upper deck, when he was abruptly shoved aside. As he spun round, expecting some jibe from Mosse, he caught sight of both lieutenants bent and staring out of gun-ports at the enemy, as were most of the men clustered about the guns, oblivious to this sudden rush of others to the upper deck.

Templeton had forgotten what Greer had told him, that when the ship cleared for action, marine sentries were posted at each of the companionways throughout the ship to prevent any man from leaving his post. Thus dissuading cowardice, these sentinels let only approved persons pass them: the ship's boys, the powder-monkeys, with cartridges for the cannon, midshipmen acting as messengers, officers, stretcher parties and the walking wounded.

Now he was reminded of that rude instruction, for the marine sentry at the forward companionway had fallen almost at his feet, stretched upon the ladder, the handle of a long butcher's knife protruding from his chest. Templeton saw the man's face white with shock, his hands pulling futilely at the yellow horn handle even as death took possession of him.

So quickly and silently had the thing happened that

the sentry's musket had not clattered to the deck, but had been seized and taken by one of the men running past him. Templeton was no man of action, yet he felt shock and outrage at what had happened, knew it was impermissible, rebellious, contrary to those draconian Articles of War he had read abstractedly at the Admiralty and heard uttered by Captain Drinkwater on a windswept Sunday a few days earlier. It was this outraged impropriety, this affront to established order that propelled him upwards, after the running men; this and a horrified dread of the marine who twitched his last and had just attracted the notice of the crew of an adjacent gun.

So small a space of time had been occupied by this event that he arrived on the forecastle hard on the heels of the rebels, quite unaware that he was lucky to have escaped with his own life. He saw, looming above him and, it seemed, just beyond the stuffed hammock nettings, the rushing bowsprit, jibs, figurehead and forefoot of the passing Danish frigate.

Andromeda's starboard bow-chaser fired, the gun carriage rolled inboard and her crew leapt round it with sponge and worm, cartridge, ball and rammer. The next gun fired, and the next. Concussion was answered by concussion. The air seemed thick with great gusts of roaring wind and heated blasts that made him gasp. He was spun round, confused; he breathed with difficulty, his quarry had vanished, seemingly swallowed up in this smoky and explosive hell.

Then he saw them, clustered above the port sheet anchor lashed in the larboard forechains. A second later he also saw the fluke and stock disappear overboard.

To the buzzings and roars, cries and thumps was added an undertone he was unfamiliar with.

Unbeknown to Mr Templeton, just beneath his feet and in preparation for anchoring in the fiord if it had been necessary, the sheet anchor drew its heavy hemp cable rumbling after it to the sea-bed. In the stunning confusion of the noise and smoke, it suddenly struck him what was happening and he hesitated.

Drinkwater knew what had happened the moment he realized that the sudden acceleration of the enemy was apparent, not real, motion.

As he looked round he saw that it was the sudden swing of *Andromeda's* bow to port, manifested by the rake of the bowsprit across the distant hills, that had caused this disorientation. In the instant of comprehension, cause was of less moment than effect. From having a sporting chance at inflicting damage upon her enemy, *Andromeda* was suddenly laid helplessly supine under the enemy guns, her vulnerable stern exposed as she swung.

The Danes were not slow to exploit this chance, for the British frigate continued to turn slowly, obligingly, caught by her treacherously released larboard sheet anchor. The rebels had put wracking stoppers on the cable so that, when some fifty fathoms had run out, it jerked at the anchor, and the flukes far below bit at the deposits of moraine on the sea-bed.

Circumstances had conspired in their favour, for it so happened that, having worked across to the opposite shore, *Andromeda* was, as her captain had supposed she would be, in far shallower water than prevailed in the main body of the fiord. Her anchor, after plucking at the bottom, bit effectively. But such was her speed that, although the swinging moment was applied at her bow and she turned to expose her narrow stern to the surprised Danes, she swung through more than a neat right angle. In fact she continued to swing, turning almost back the way she had come and exposing her whole port side. Moreover, this wild turn had flung her sails aback and this caused her to slow, almost to follow her enemy as she floundered and bucked in response to the powerful tug of her hemp cable.

'Bloody anchor's shot away!' Drinkwater roared. 'We've club-hauled! Let go t'gallant halliards! Clew up tops'ls! Main and fore clew garnets!'

They scarcely felt the crash and thump of the Danish shot as it flew about. The air was full of the wind of its passing and men who had been standing one moment had vanished the next, to become a bloody pulp and then a slime as others, their eyes and attention aloft, slithered and stumbled through their remains.

Drinkwater felt a smart blow on the shoulder and the sting of something sharp across his face. His hat was torn from his head and he was vaguely aware, though he remembered this only afterwards, of something gold spinning away from him.

Walsh ran towards Drinkwater as he was consumed with anxiety for the main topgallant mast. It swayed gracefully out of the vertical, halted and swung in a web of rigging, then its broken foot pulled away from the upper hounds and it began to fall, bringing the topgallant yard and sail down with it. About twenty feet above the boats on the booms, its descent was arrested by more rigging and wreckage

167

and it hung, suspended, like the sword of Damocles above their heads, gently swaying.

Huke was already rallying men to get it lowered down on deck to salvage what they could. Drinkwater turned his attention to the departing enemy. He could not suppose the Danes would not come back and finish what they had already begun. He felt someone tugging at his clothing. It was Walsh.

'Oh, my!' the marine officer gasped, 'oh, my!' He knelt at Drinkwater's feet in a ridiculous posture, and Drinkwater looked down at him. The florid face was suffused with hurt and pain and anger, the eyes ablaze, and then the light went out of it, the shadow of death moved swiftly across it and Walsh fell full length at Drinkwater's feet. Afterwards, Drinkwater could not understand how the ball had hit the marine officer, or where it had gone, for its imprint was clear in Walsh's wrecked back.

Drinkwater stared at the mangled man for a moment, felt his gorge rise and turned away, fishing frantically in his tail pocket for the Dollond glass so that he could shut out this madness and concentrate on the neat, ordered image of the enemy frigate again.

'She's the *Odin*, sir, must be new tonnage, we burnt everything on the stocks, but I do recall timbers on the ways being marked *Odin*.' The voice of Birkbeck, calmly professional, steadied him, corroborating his earlier asides to Huke and referring to the great act of licensed arson which had followed Admiral Lord Gambier's action and the military operations of General Lord Cathcart which had culminated in the occupation of Copenhagen six years earlier.

'Thank you, Mr Birkbeck,' Drinkwater said, and

the master turned to an elderly master's mate named Beavis and remarked on the captain's coolness. 'Look at him; one epaulette shot away and taken half his cheek with it, no hat and not a word of alarm.' Birkbeck shook his head. 'I thought him half-mad t'other day when he had us all bollock-naked under the pumps, now I know he is.'

'He'll need to be,' replied Beavis, 'if we're to get out of this festering mess.'

The Danish frigate had swept past them and she too was now taking in sail. Already her topgallant yards were down and the men were aloft laying out along them to furl the sails, and her main course and forecourse were swagged up in their buntlines and clew garnets. As Drinkwater watched, he saw her turn slowly into the wind, tack neatly under topsails, spanker and jibs, and head back towards them.

On *Andromeda*'s deck order was reasserting itself. Despite being badly cut up both by the fort and the *Odin*, *Andromeda* was capable of resistance. Huke appeared at his elbow.

'Are you all right, sir?' the first lieutenant asked solicitously, seeing the blood on Drinkwater's cheek.

'Not a good moment for you to step into my shoes, Tom,' Drinkwater joked grimly.

'I meant your face.'

Drinkwater put up his hand and brought it away sticky with blood. 'Well, I'm damned; I had no idea – it's no more than a scratch.'

'You've lost your swab.'

'Ah,' Drinkwater put up his hand, 'confounded thing must have carried away. It's happened before.'

'Aye, and lacerated your cheek. Anyway, I've been

169

forward. I found Templeton up there, he saw what happened.'

'What, with the anchor?'

'Aye, it was cut away – deliberately,' Huke added, aware that Drinkwater was only half-listening, that he was concerned about the Danish frigate a mile away. He beckoned Templeton. 'Tell the Captain, Templeton.'

Templeton's face was uncertain, struggling to comprehend what had transpired.

'Go on, man! Get on with it . . . Oh, for God's sake!' Huke fumed impatiently. 'The shank painter was sliced through like that damned gun-breeching. This,' Huke gestured wildly round, 'this is no accident!'

'The devil it ain't!' Drinkwater experienced a constriction about his throat. He felt a clear sensation of being strangled and as he fought off this weakness, Templeton's expression looked oddly equivocal.

'Would you know the men who did this?' Drinkwater asked desperately.

'I don't know,' Templeton answered evasively, avoiding Drinkwater's scrutiny, 'it was all rather confusing. I could try.'

'Yes, you could,' Drinkwater snapped, his eyes cold. 'Take Walsh and a file of his men . . .' Drinkwater remembered. 'Oh, Walsh is dead.' He looked down at the red corpse. Templeton's eyes followed and saw the horror at his feet for the first time. 'Damnation!' The clerk's eyes glazed over and he crumpled in a swoon at Drinkwater's feet. 'Damnation!' Drinkwater swore again.

'Sir!' The first lieutenant's cry of warning recalled Drinkwater's attention to the *Odin*. He looked out to larboard. The Danish frigate was bearing down on them in a second attempt to rake *Andromeda* from astern. But in her approach, just for a few minutes of opportunity, she was head on to them.

'Messenger!'

'Sir?' Midshipman Fisher stood beside him. The boy was pale and fidgeted with his coat lapels.

'Are you all right, son?'

'Perfectly, sir.'

'Good, go below to the gun deck and tell . . .'

But Huke had anticipated the order and was shouting to Mosse on the gun deck below. The roar of the larboard broadside bellowed defiance at the approaching *Odin*. *Andromeda* rocked with the recoil. The men sponged and loaded and rammed, and again, then again, flung bar-shot high at the enemy's foremast. This was what Huke had trained his crew for, and if Pardoe's absence had been reprehensible, Huke had taken full advantage of the breach of regulations. The bar-shot, each comprising two hemispheres of iron joined by a rod, were flung from the gun muzzles and flailed wildly during their inaccurate, short-ranged trajectory.

The noise brought Templeton to. Drinkwater bent and shook him roughly. 'Get up!' he commanded. 'Get up and pull yourself together. I want those men rounded up.' He turned and bellowed, 'Sergeant Danks!'

'Sir?'

'A file of your men, we've work to do on board! Follow me! Quickly now!'

Drinkwater helped Templeton to his unsteady feet and thrust him forward.

'Shall I come too, sir?' It was little Fisher, still waiting for orders. Another broadside interrupted them.

'No. Do you stand by Mr Huke,' and turning to Huke, Drinkwater shouted, 'Tom, take command on the quarterdeck, d'you hear?'

'Aye, aye, sir!'

'Come, Templeton, Sergeant Danks . . .'

As he led them along the starboard gangway, Drinkwater was aware that it was already dusk, that the shadows of the surrounding mountains threw most of the water into a mysterious darkness from which the first stars were reflected. Night was almost upon them. Damnably odd that he had hardly noticed.

Since their treachery, and in anticipation of *Andromeda* being raked, the rebels had gone over the bow and concealed themselves on the heads. There, beside the pink nakedness of the carved representation of Andromeda chained to her rock, half a dozen men awaited the outcome of the battle, furiously debating their course of action, secure only for the time being, they assumed, because of the demands of the fight with the Danish ship.

As Danks's marines prodded them on to the forecastle at the point of the bayonet, they were greeted by cheers. Drinkwater forgot the matter in hand; he looked round to see the *Odin*'s foremast totter and then fall sideways.

'Secure those men in irons, Sergeant,' shouted Drinkwater, ignoring Templeton and hurrying aft towards the first lieutenant, anxiously staring at the *Odin*.

'I think we've scored a point!' Huke shouted, his words drowned in yet another discharge of Jameson's cannon.

'Well done, Tom . . .'

Both officers looked at the Dane. The *Odin* had fallen off the wind and only her bow-chasers bore; after two shots, they too fell silent. As the two men watched, the main and mizen yards were braced round; gradually the *Odin* began to make a stern-board.

'A tactical withdrawal for the night, I think,' offered Huke.

'Yes. And we shall do the same.' Drinkwater looked about him. 'God, what a shambles!' Even in the twilight, *Andromeda*'s deck bore the appearance of a slaughter-house.

Another broadside thundered out, the gun-flashes bright in the gathering gloom. 'You may cease fire now. Pipe up spirits and have the cooks get some burgoo into all hands. The men can mess at their guns, then we have work to do.' He turned to the sailing master. 'What o'clock is moonrise, Mr Birkbeck?'

'Not before three, sir.'

'We shall be gone by then.'

No one paid any attention to Templeton as he hung back until Danks had had time to secure his prisoners in the bilboes. Then he made his way hurriedly below.

10   Friends and Enemies
October 1813

The dismasting of the *Odin* brought them more than a
respite, it brought them a sense of accomplishment.
They had not achieved a victory, but they *had* beaten
off an enemy with a superior weight of metal. In his
cabin, or in the after section of the gun deck which
had formerly been his cabin, by the light of a pair of
horn-glazed battle lanterns, Drinkwater outlined his
plan to his officers. His right cheek was dark and
pocked with clotted blood.

'It is going to be a long night, gentlemen,' he concluded, 'but most of us will be able to sleep a little
easier when we do turn in. Any questions?'

The officers shook their heads and rose from where
they squatted on the deck or the trucks of the adjacent
guns, exchanging brief remarks with one another. All
wore grim expressions and none were under any false
illusions about their chances. Further forward the
buzz of the men eating at their action stations swelled
at this sudden, conspicuous activity aft.

Huke hung back. 'What about these damned prisoners, sir?'

'I'll see them in a minute. Get a screen put up, will

you? A canvas will do, just enough to discourage prying eyes. Ah, and post a marine sentry on its far side.'

Huke nodded. 'I've taken command of the marines myself, I hope you approve?'

'Yes, of course. I'm going to see the wounded first. Get the screen rigged and we'll find what's at the bottom of all this.'

In the cockpit Kennedy was finishing the last of his dressings. 'Twenty-three wounded, sir, five seriously.'

'How seriously?'

'Very. Two are mortal, maybe three. Deep penetration of the abdomen, vital organs in shreds, severe blood loss.'

'Bloody business.'

'Very.'

'You look tired.'

'Not used to naval surgery. Noisy business. Most of the poor devils are dead drunk. Used a lot of rum.'

'Go and get something to eat. I'm afraid we're going to start getting the ship out of this predicament.'

'Ah,' replied Kennedy. He had no idea what the captain was talking about, but was too tired to ask.

'By the bye, how is the man with typhus? I had quite forgotten him. I take it we sent him below?'

'He's here . . .'

Drinkwater followed Kennedy through the Stygian gloom. The low space, usually the mess and living quarters of the midshipmen and marines, was filled with the mutilated wounded who groaned where they lay. Kennedy's assistants were clearing away the blood-soaked cloth from the 'table' upon which the surgeon had wielded scalpel and catling, saw and suture needle. The stink of bilge, blood and fear hung heavy in the stale air. Snores and low moans punctuated the sounds of deep breathing, and the grey bundles moved occasionally as the fumes of oblivion cleared momentarily. In a corner a hammock was slung.

'How are you?' Drinkwater asked the pale blur that regarded him.

'Better than those poor bastards.'

The man's manner was abrupt, discourteous even, his accent American. Abruptly Drinkwater turned about and made for the gun deck. The canvas screen was almost rigged. When it was finished, Drinkwater, in the presence of Huke and Templeton, summoned the first of the prisoners aft.

He could not imagine why he had not realized it before, but it was impossible to conceal and it took little time to unravel, once the first tongue wagged. He was glad he had ordered the issue of spirits for, although prisoners were forbidden this privilege, such was the solidarity of the lower deck that some sympathetic souls would go to considerable lengths to supply men in the bilboes with rum, if only to help them endure the flogging all must have felt was inevitable.

In rousing sympathy, it did not much matter what a man was charged with, unless it was thieving from his shipmates. In this case few knew what had happened beyond the fact that these men had stabbed a marine and run and hidden. Cowards they might be, but a measure of sympathy had been extended by a couple of radical souls, enough to loosen a tongue or two, to the point of indiscretion, for the marines, the ship's police, could count enemies among the thirteen score of men whom they regulated.

When the interrogation of the prisoners was over, Drinkwater ordered the men taken away and returned to the bilboes. 'They are to be securely chained for tonight.'

Sergeant Danks took them off with a smart salute and an about-turn. Drinkwater turned to Huke. 'Well, Tom, here's a pretty kettle of fish.'

Even in the poor light of the battle lanterns, Huke's pallor was evident.

'I had no idea, sir.'

'And there's one missing. The ringleader, of course.'

'Malaburn.'

'An ominous name, by the sound of it,' offered Templeton nervously.

'It wasn't your fault, Tom,' said Drinkwater, ignoring the clerk. 'The truth is, there is a great deal more to this than you know. I blame myself that I didn't smell a rat the moment I heard Hopkins's Boston accent. Then, when we had the case of typhus, I should have realized that the infected man came aboard with the draft you pressed out of that merchant ship and that he was also American . . .'

'It's the damned war, sir. We've such a polyglot mob aboard here, what with Irish, Yankees, Negroes, Arabs, Russians, Finns, Swedes and that Dane, Sommer.'

'That may well be the case, but you don't know the whole story. Those Americans had only recently joined that merchantman at Leith because they had just come out of gaol. It was only just now that I recalled typhus ain't only called ship, low or putrid fever, but is also called *gaol* fever. You said yourself they offered little

177

resistance. I think the reason they were so compliant was that they wanted to be pressed.'

'*Wanted* to be pressed?' Huke repeated incredulously, 'I don't follow; why in God's name would they *want* to be pressed?'

'To get aboard a man-o'-war destined to attempt the seizure of a large arms shipment to America to support an insurrection in Canada.'

Huke whistled. 'You mean with the intention of thwarting that seizure?' He frowned and added, 'Then getting a passage home? Is that your meaning?'

Drinkwater nodded.

'But how d'you know?'

'Don't ask me how, Tom, not now; but I'm damned certain they were sprung from Dartmoor gaol for the purpose.'

'The devil they were, and how the bloody hell did they spirit themselves from Dartmoor to Leith?' Huke asked, perplexed.

'By a carter, it seems, or maybe a whole host of carters. Such men move easily about the country and for all I know belong to some Corresponding Society or seditious, republican fraternity, though I grant the thing appears impossible.'

Huke scratched his head, then shook it. 'Perhaps not.' He spoke abstractedly and then looked up sharply, as though the consideration had led him to some pricking anxiety. 'We still have to take Malaburn.'

'He will be in the hold, and every exit is barred, is it not?'

'Aye, Danks has seen to that . . .'

'Well, let him rot there for a while. At least until we've concluded this business.'

'It's true he'll not get out, sir, there's a sentry on each hatchway, but I don't like the idea, sir.'

'Perhaps not, Tom – but leave him, just the same.'

They relapsed into silence for a moment, the constrained silence of disagreement, then Drinkwater said, 'Poor Walsh. We shall have to bury them all when we get outside.'

And '*if*,' Huke added privately to himself, while Templeton, an increasingly nervous witness to these proceedings, nursed his own feelings.

'Look!'

'What is it?'

By the dim light of the stars the working parties had lowered the wreckage of the main topgallant mast, but unravelling the intricate web of tangled rigging that it had pulled down with it properly required daylight. Then, about four bells in the first watch, about ten o'clock by a landsman's time-piece, the high mountains to the north-west seemed to loom above them, closer than they remembered, a gigantic theatrical backcloth dragged forward by trolls. It was the second and more disquieting illusion of the day. A milky glow filled the sky above the mountain peaks, an ethereal and pulsing luminescence that made them all stand stock-still in amazement.

'Aurora borealis,' explained Birkbeck. 'Get back to work there! You can see what you're doing now.'

It was as though that strange phenomenon had been produced not merely for their wonder but also for their convenience. Tired though they were, the ship's company laboured with scarcely a grumble, until, long before midnight, the main was shorn of its upper spar, the broken stump drawn from the doublings and sent down to be split for kindling in the galley stove, and the lines tidied away. By the light of his lantern, the carpenter had declared it was no great thing to fish a new heel on to the old spar, and the men had been stood easy for half an hour, while spirits, biscuit and treacle were issued.

'Playing the deuce with my stores,' the purser complained.

'As you play the devil wiv our'n,' retorted a seaman within earshot, but he made no further complaint, having heard that Captain Drinkwater was no friend of peculating jobbers. Things had been somewhat different in Captain Pardoe's day . . .

At midnight the hands were sent to the capstan. The wind had fallen light after dark, though it was still foul for a passage of the narrows. Even a light breeze, funnelled between those rock buttresses, gained strength enough to prevent them making any attempt to work through under sail. The boats were hoisted out and manned. The carpenter had first had to put a tingle on the red cutter, and the launch required more extensive repairs before she could be lowered into the water again.

Ranging up under the bow, a rope was passed down into each and the boat officers, the second and third lieutenants and Beavis, the senior master's mate, fanned their charges out ahead of the frigate.

There was a faint outward current to carry them seaward, produced by streams and freshets further up the fiord, and they made slow but steady progress. By moonrise they were below the beetling crags of the narrows. After four hours Midshipman Fisher was dispatched in the white cutter with a relief crew for the first boat. Having run alongside Mr Jameson's boat and transferred his oarsmen, Fisher had the tired men of the third lieutenant's boat pull ahead, before he swung clear of the others, advancing in line abreast. Then his eye was caught by something irregular etched against the night sky. Under the black loom of the cliffs, no light came from the fading aurora. The sea beyond the gutway was a slightly less dark plane, its presence guessed at, rather than actually perceived. And Fisher was certain, as only the young can be, that something lay upon it.

'Oars,' he whispered to his men, though the grunting and straining of the men in the boats behind were plain enough. The oarsmen, eager for food and drink, ceased rowing and leaned on their oar looms. The curious craned round impatiently. 'What is it young 'un?' a voice enquired as the boat glided through the still water.

'There's a ship out there!'

'Well, why don't we just pull over an' capture it, an' make your bleedin' fortune, cully, eh?' The anonymous voice from forward was weary with sarcasm.

'Oi ain't following no little bugger whose bollocks are still up 'is arse,' another countered.

'Be quiet! Stand by! Give way together!'

With a knocking of oars, the boat forged ahead again, but Fisher did not put the tiller over.

'He's taken your advice, Harry, you stupid sod.'

'He would, the little turd.'

'Be quiet, damn you,' Fisher squeaked, uncertain whether to react to this blatant insubordination or to

181

let it pass, since the men pulled on, seemingly willing enough.

''E won't live long enough to be a Hadmiral.'

'It's that cutter!' hissed Fisher excitedly, meaning not another pulling boat but a small, man-of-war cruiser. Older heads in the boat were less eager to share the midshipman's certainty. Men stopped pulling, missed their stroke and, for a moment or two, the discipline in the boat broke down as they craned round to see where the headstrong child was taking them.

'Boat ahoy!' came to them out of the darkness, the accents unmistakably, imperiously English. 'Lie to upon the instant or I shall blow you to Kingdom Come!'

'It's that one-handed bean-pole . . .'

'It *is* the *Kestrel!*'

'I told you it was,' Fisher exclaimed gleefully.

'Well, tell that bloody lieutenant, before he shoots us!'

'Boat from *Andromeda*, permission to come aboard!'

'Come under my lee!'

They could see the irregular quadrilateral shape of the cutter's mainsail and the two fore triangles of her jib and staysail as she ghosted in towards the narrows and the Vikkenfiord.

'Put about, sir,' called Fisher, '*Andromeda's* towing out astern of us! There's a big Danish frigate and all sorts inside . . .'

They were alongside now, a rope snaked out of the cutter's chains to take their painter, and the next moment they were towing alongside.

'Come aboard and report.'

Fisher scrambled up and over the cutter's side.

'Midshipman Richard Fisher, sir, from the frigate *Andromeda*, Nathaniel Drinkwater commanding.'

'He's right enough, Mr Quil'ampton, there's a frigate comin' up ahead.'

'Put her about, Mr Frey . . .'

'What's all that noise there?' The voice of Lieutenant Huke boomed into their deliberations as he shouted from *Andromeda*'s knightheads, his voice amplified by a speaking trumpet and echoing about in the stillness.

Quilhampton cupped his good hand about his mouth: 'Cutter *Kestrel*, Lieutenant Quilhampton commanding!'

'Follow me out, Mr Q, and come aboard for orders.'

'That's Captain Drinkwater's voice,' advised Fisher.

'I know that.'

'We lay to under the trys'l, and when the weather moderated we made a good stellar observation and laid a course for the rendezvous. I guessed you couldn't afford to linger and that you had pressed on when we saw a man-o'-war's t'gallants away to the eastward, so we cracked on, thinking it was you.'

'That must have been the *Odin*,' observed Huke.

'Yes. Well, anyway, it was lucky we saw her, for it was just a question of watching her vanish. Frey, my first luff,' he explained for Huke's benefit, 'took a bearing. We ran down it and here we are. I thought we were heading for a wall of rock and was just about to put about when your young midshipmite hove out of the darkness.'

'Well, I am damnably glad to see you, James.

Forgive my lack of hospitality, but we've been cleared for action for some time now. To be truthful, I didn't expect to see you again, first on your own account, and then on ours. We've just taken a drubbing.'

Drinkwater explained the day's events.

'So we've the goods, the Dane who brought them, and the Yankees who are going to tranship them to North America all boxed up in the Vikkenfiord, eh?' Quilhampton said with an air of satisfaction, when Drinkwater had finished.

'That's certainly an optimistic view of the tactical situation,' remarked Drinkwater drily.

'Well, they might think they've the measure of you, but they don't know I'm here yet.' Quilhampton grinned enthusiastically.

'True, James, true.'

'It's certainly food for thought,' said Huke. 'Will you be able to beat out behind us?'

'Yes. She ghosts in light airs and she's fitted with centre-plates. She can point much closer to the wind than you.'

'Gentlemen,' said Drinkwater, 'we will lie to now, until daylight. Recover the boats, Mr Huke, as soon as we are clear of danger. Then let us get an hour or two's sleep. Tomorrow we will see what we can accomplish. It will be the first of the month, I believe.'

''Tis already that, sir.'

Lieutenant Huke had conceived a liking for his odd and unorthodox captain. During the crazy interlude of the great dousing Huke had noticed, as had many others, that in addition to the faint facial scar and the powder burns on one eyelid, Captain Drinkwater was disfigured by a lop-sided right shoulder and a mass of scar tissue which ran down his right arm. These were the legacy of two wounds, one acquired in a dark alleyway in the year 1797, at the time of the great mutiny, the other the result of an enemy shell-burst off Boulogne, four years later. Such marks earned their bearer a measure of respect, irrespective of rank. In a post-captain they bespoke a seasoned man.

But, on that night and for the first time, Thomas Huke considered Captain Drinkwater's conduct to be, if not reprehensible, at the very least most unwise, an error of judgement. The first lieutenant felt that the matter of Malaburn could not be left until the morning.

He excused the captain on the grounds that Drinkwater did not know the man, despite the claims he had made about their escape from gaol and extraordinary migration north. Drinkwater had not had his suspicions aroused as had Huke. As an experienced first lieutenant Huke had acquired an instinct for trouble-makers, sea-lawyers and the disobedient. There were attitudes such men struck, inflections they used when spoken to, places in which they appeared unaccountably and times when they were late in mustering. A man might do such things once or twice in all innocence, but persistent offenders were almost always revealed as falling into one or other of these troublesome categories. Malaburn had been one such, conspicuous from the first day he had come aboard at Leith.

'Provoked me,' Mr Beavis had reported back in Leith Road. The master's mate had been in charge of one of the ship's three press-gangs sent to comb the ale-houses and brothels of Leith and Granton for extra hands a few days before Huke struck 'lucky' and obtained what he wanted from the merchantman. 'Almost dared me to take him,' Beavis had expanded, 'but, like most braggarts, gave in the moment we got a-hold of him.'

There seemed little enough in the remark at the time, except to draw Lieutenant Huke's attention to the man as he was sworn in. And although Malaburn had overplayed his hand a trifle in his eagerness to get himself aboard His Majesty's frigate *Andromeda*, he had succeeded in fooling them all. Until, that is, Captain Drinkwater made his mysterious revelation, alluding to the curious desire of the Americans to be pressed. The assertion fitted not just the group lifted from the merchantman, but also Malaburn.

Thus it was that Lieutenant Thomas Huke decided not to allow Malaburn to elude his just deserts an hour longer and why he passed word to Sergeant Danks to muster half a dozen of his men at the main capstan.

Drinkwater had not wished to raise a hue and cry for the one member of the ship's company unaccounted for after the action with the *Odin* for a number of reasons. The first was that, as far as he could determine, few people as yet realized that the letting go of the anchor had been a deliberate act, rather than an accidental misfortune. The anchor had been cleared away ready for use as they closed the land, a cable bent and seized on to it. It was possible that a chance shot had carried away the lashing and it had fallen from the fore-chains. Old seamen could tell countless tales of odder circumstances; of balls hitting cannon muzzles with such exactitude that they opened them like the petals of flowers; of a shot which had destroyed the single remaining live pig being fattened for an unpopular captain, and so forth.

More important, the conspicuous arrest of the handful of men hiding on the heads had looked like the rounding up of a group of yellow-bellies, an untruth given credibility by the fact that the men were newcomers who had kept themselves to themselves and failed to court popularity with their shipmates. Their reason for doing so was now apparent to those in the know, but had not yet permeated through the ship. Doubtless the truth would get out in due course, but Drinkwater wanted his men rested, not seething with vengeful discontent that the men now clapped in the bilboes as cowards had tried to deliver them all into the hands of the enemy.

From what he could glean, his prisoners, having done what they could to incommode the British frigate, were to have escaped to the American ships in the fiord. When the Danish ship appeared, Malaburn had changed the plan, seeing a greater chance of success in the overwhelming of the *Andromeda* by the *Odin*. Drinkwater also wondered whether Malaburn had thought the British ship was retreating, that she had given up hope of cutting out the Yankees from under the Danish guns in the fort, and that the sudden appearance of the *Odin* gave him an opportunity both to destroy the British ship and to secure the escape of himself and his fellow conspirators before it was too late. It was, after all, a risky and uncertain business, being pressed into the service of King George.

If that was how Malaburn's mind had construed the day's events, he had demonstrated a commendable adaptability. Once the *Andromeda* had been brought to her anchor, confusion reigned upon her decks and her officers were distracted with the business of resisting the attack of the *Odin*. Drinkwater imagined Malaburn's party were hoping they could soon escape by getting aboard the Danish ship as she dropped alongside to board, and giving themselves up.

Whatever their expectations, and fear of a return to incarceration in Dartmoor must have been a powerful motive, their leader had been a man of determination, and if Drinkwater did not wish to stir his ship up that night, he did not wish to lose her either. What he feared most was an incendiary attack. A lone man with flint and steel could set fire to the frigate. For all her mildewed damp, there were combustibles enough to set *Andromeda* ablaze like a torch. Drinkwater had seen the fearful sight of ships burning and exploding and the thought made him shudder.

Malaburn, languishing in the dark recesses of the hold, was unlikely to cut his own throat with two of his countrymen's privateers in the offing. Why else had he preserved himself? In the morning they would winkle him out. With that thought, Drinkwater heaved himself into his cot and pulled the sheet and blankets over his shoulders. Let Malaburn stew in his own juice, believing, perhaps, that no one had noticed his absence.

Drinkwater's face was already scabbed, a thick crust which rasped uncomfortably on the pillow. The last thing he saw in his mind's eye was a spinning epaulette which diminished in size as it faded into the far, far distance.

*

'Pistols and bayonets,' Huke whispered, 'there's no room for muskets. Cold steel unless he fires, and only shoot if you are sure of hitting him. Take my word he's not just a mutinous dog, he's an enemy, a Yankee. He is aboard to make mischief and ensure this ship strikes to either those privateers we saw at anchor or that blasted Dane. So, if you can't seize him, and he resists . . .' Huke made an unpleasant, terminal squawk and drew his forefinger across his throat. 'D'you understand?'

A murmur of assent went round the little group of marines. They had a comrade to avenge. Four lanterns stood on the deck at their feet, lighting their white shirts and breeches. With their braces over their shoulders in place of cross-belts the pale ghostly figures had appeared in the gloom of the orlop to arouse the curiosity of the lesser officers quartered there. Huke had sent the inquisitive back into their tiny cabins with a sharp word to discourage their interest.

'Very well. You two go with Sar'nt Danks up the larboard side, you and you, with me to starboard.' Huke nodded and Danks bent to the padlock holding the securing bar over the aftermost grating which led down into the hold. Huke drew his own hanger, laid it on the deck and quickly rid himself of his baldric and coat. Then he recovered his sword, drew a pistol from his belt and, as Danks lifted the grating, led the party down the ladder into the hold.

On the quarterdeck, Lieutenant Mosse had the watch. He was dog-tired and would be glad to get below at midnight, but he was not insensible to the fact that, even under the easy pressure of the main and fore topsail, and a single jib, the *Andromeda* had edged closer inshore than he liked. With an effort he bestirred himself, ordered the helm put over and the yards trimmed.

As the order was passed, he was aware of groans of reluctance, but the watch mustered at their posts, the yards swung in their slings, trusses and parrels, and *Andromeda* headed out to sea.

Shortly before the watch below was due to be called, when the minutes dragged and it seemed that the march of time had slowed beyond human endurance, the tired Mosse and his somnolent watch were jerked wide-awake. What sounded like a muffled cry came to them. Its source seemed to be some way away and someone said it sounded as though it had come from the *Kestrel*, which had last showed the pale shape of her sail two miles to the south-east. Then a jacketless marine arose from the after companion with the shocking speed of a jack-in-the-box.

'Sir! Mr Huke's hurt! In the hold! There's bloody hell on down there!'

As he had raced up from the hold, the distraught soldier had raised the alarm throughout the ship. The curious officers quartered in the orlop, led by Mr Beavis, had not gone quietly to bed, but had remained clustered by the open grating. The sudden cry had stunned them, then there was a brief hiatus and the marines emerged, with Danks throwing the grating down behind him and thrusting the padlock through the hasp on the securing bar. The sudden volley of questions wakened the midshipmen and the other soldiers nearby. One of the marines nursed a badly gashed leg, another was sent into the berth deck to find Kennedy, a third to the quarterdeck. This man raised the alarm at each sentinel post, including the one outside the captain's cabin, and this sentry, aware only that the frigate was suddenly buzzing with an almost palpable anxiety, called the captain.

Drinkwater had fallen into the deep sleep of exhaustion from which he was unnaturally wrenched. Instinctively he pulled on his coat and went on deck. After five minutes of total confusion he learned that Huke had taken a party of marines into the hold to 'deal with Malaburn'.

With great difficulty he suppressed the oath welling in his throat. He was ready to damn Huke for an interfering fool, to set aside any merit the man might possess, for this contravention of orders, this unwanted display of initiative. His body ached for rest, but his heart had taken flight and hammered in his breast. He silenced the hubbub around him. 'Mr Mosse, send the off-duty watch below and stop this babble.'

'Beg pardon, sir, but 'tis almost eight bells . . .'

'Very well,' snapped Drinkwater, 'have the men relieved in the normal way.' He turned to the marine. 'What's your name?'

'Private Leslie, sir.'

'Well, Leslie, what happened? Tell us in your own words. You went into the hold to arrest Malaburn. By which hatchway?'

'The after one, sir, in the cockpit . . .'

'Go on.'

'Well, sir, we was in two parties, I was wiv Mr Huke, like, and Sar'nt Danks led the other up the larboard chippy's walk. We 'ad lanterns, like, an' bayonets and a brace of pistols. Orders was to apprehend, but to shoot if the bugger – beg pardon, sir – if 'e tried anything clever . . .'

'You were going up the starboard carpenter's walk, is that right?' Drinkwater tried to visualize the scene. The carpenter's walks were two passages inside the fabric of the ship's side enabling the carpenter and his party to get at the frigate's timbers quickly and plug shot holes. The multifarious stores stowed in the hold were inboard of these narrow walkways. The men would have started outboard of and abaft the cable tiers, then edged forward past barrels of water, beef and pork, and sacks of dried peas and lentils.

They would have been walking on gratings. Below their feet the lower hold contained barrels of water stowed on shingle ballast, and the shot rooms. It was a hellish hole, inhabited by rats and awash with bilge water, the air thick and mephitic, the lanterns barely burning.

'I was the last man in my file, sir. I could jus' see Lieutenant 'Uke, sir, wiv 'is lantern, like, when 'e gives this God Almighty screech and the light goes out. Then the bloke in front of me shouts out, turns round an' says, "Christ, Hughie, the bastard's got me, get out!" He bumps into me an' I ain't got no way out but the way I come in, and Sarn't Danks is shoutin' out from the uvver side, "What's wrong?" an' I don't know, 'cept Lieutenant 'Uke's copped it, and my mate wot's pushing me shouts out "Get back in the orlop, Sar'nt!" So out we comes.'

'And Lieutenant Huke is still down there?'

'Well, yes, sir . . .'

'Damn and blast the man!' Drinkwater muttered,

inveighing against the idiocy of the first lieutenant, but now doubting the wisdom of his own passive policy. Private Leslie thought he himself was the object of this damnation.

'I'll go back, sir, jus' give us another lantern, an' I'll go right back.'

'Yes,' snapped Drinkwater, 'you will. Give me a moment to dress. Wait outside my cabin, pass word for Danks to report to me.'

He dressed quickly, thinking while Danks stood in the darkness of the day cabin and repeated, in less detail, for he had been on the far side of the ship, what Leslie had already related.

'You didn't think of going to Mr Huke's assistance?'

A short silence followed, then Danks said, 'I wasn't sure what to do, sir. I didn't really know what had happened, except that Lieutenant Huke's dead, sir.'

'Dead? Who said he's dead?'

'Well, sir, I . . . I don't know.' The puzzlement was clear in Danks's voice. It was not fair to imply Danks was a coward. Huke's ill-conceived stratagem was too prone to confusion to blame poor humiliated Danks.

'Very well, Sergeant. Have your men remustered, all of them. In the orlop. I'll be with you directly. Send in a light.'

When Danks had gone Drinkwater finished dressing. He could do this in the dark, but he wanted light to complete his preparations. Frampton, attired in a long night-shirt, appeared with a lantern.

'Will you be wanting anything else, sir?'

'Not at the moment, Frampton, thank you,' Drinkwater said. The steady normality of Captain

Pardoe's steward stilled the racing of his own heart. He could never think of Frampton as his own man.

He went to the stern settee, lifted the seat and drew out the case of pistols. Then he sat down and, placing the case beside him, opened it, lifted out the weapons and checked their flints. Having done that he carefully loaded both weapons. He had had a double-barrelled pistol aboard *Patrician*, but these were a new pair and he thrust them through his belt. Then he stood for a moment in the centre of the cabin and retied his hair. When he had finished he drew his hanger and passed the door on to the gun deck.

A garrulous crowd had gathered in the orlop and the appearance of the captain silenced them. 'This is a damned Dovercourt, be off with you! Marines, stand fast. You there, Mr Fisher! Pass word to have the surgeon standing by. Oh, and please to lend me your dirk, young man. Here,' Drinkwater turned aside to Beavis, 'be so kind as to look after this for me.' He handed his hanger to the master's mate.

Before scuttling off on his mission, Fisher had darted to his mess and taken his dirk from its nail in the deck-beam above his sleeping place. It was a small, straight and handy weapon.

'Here, sir.' He held the toy weapon out; its short blade gleamed dully in the lantern light. Drinkwater's fist more than encompassed the hilt.

'Right, Danks,' Drinkwater dropped his voice, beckoning the marines to draw closer. 'This is what I intend to do.'

11 The Enemy Within
November 1813

Drinkwater led them below. At the bottom of the ladder he moved aside and let the marines file silently down into the hold. Then he directed Sergeant Danks and his senior corporal, Wilson, to lift the after gratings and descend into the lower hold, and as they did so the foul stench of bilge rose up to assail them. Both Wilson and Danks were armed with muskets. Behind them went two other marines, each with a lantern, followed by two men armed with bayonets. When Danks had moved out to the larboard wing, and Wilson to the starboard, Drinkwater gestured to the remaining men to fan out. Then he called:

'Malaburn! This is the captain. We know you are down here and you have until I have counted to ten to give yourself up. If you hail at that time you will be given a fair trial. If not I regard you as beyond the law, and the safety of my ship demands that I exert myself to take you at any cost. That may well be your own life.' He paused, then began to count.

'One. Two. Three . . .'

In the silence between each number he heard nothing beyond the laboured breathing of the marines still behind him.

'Five. Six. Seven . . .'

He turned. Holding a third lantern, Private Leslie was ready behind him with another marine in support, and Corporal Smyth made to take his two men up the larboard carpenter's walk to flush Malaburn from his hiding place. Drinkwater now had four groups of marines ready to move forward, two at the level of the carpenter's walk, two below, floundering their way over the shingle ballast and the casks of water in the lower hold, for Drinkwater was convinced Malaburn had taken refuge in that most evil and remote part of the ship.

'Eight. Nine. Ten. Proceed!'

Drinkwater had enjoined Smyth, advancing on the higher larboard level, not to move faster than Danks's party below him who would have far more trouble moving over the shingle ballast than those above walking on the level gratings of the carpenter's walk. Both upper and lower parties had to search each stow of stores inboard of them as they edged forward and it was five long minutes before those with Drinkwater, creeping up the starboard side, discovered the blood-stains marking the place where Huke had been wounded. The absence of Huke was both a hopeful and a desperately worrying sign. Malaburn had done exactly what Drinkwater would have done in his place: he had dragged the first lieutenant off as a hostage.

'Smyth, Danks! Mr Huke's been taken hostage!' he called, to let those on the far side of the ship know what had happened.

'Aye, sir, understood!' Danks's voice came back from beyond a large stow of sacked and dried peas.

They shuffled forward again. The shadows thrown by the lantern behind Drinkwater projected his own form in grotesque silhouette on the uneven surfaces of futtocks and footwaling. He held the little dirk in his outsize hand. It was a pathetic and inadequate weapon, but he had brought it in place of his hanger which, he had realized, would have been an encumbrance in the restricted space of this narrow catwalk.

'Nothin' yet!' shouted Smyth, and Wilson and Danks echoed the call. The stink of effluvia, bilge, dried stores, rot, fungus, rust and God knew what beside made breathing difficult. The lanterns guttered yellow, their flames sinking as they moved forward. The whining squeak of rats accompanied their scuttering retreat from this unwonted incursion into their private domain and added a quickening to the tired, low groans of the ship as she rolled on the swell.

Drinkwater's heart hammered painfully. He saw a score of phantasmagorical Malaburns, the swinging, hand-held lantern light throwing maddening shadows which moved as they did. Sweat poured off him, and he stopped to wipe it from his brow.

And then, quite suddenly, without any violent reaction of either party, he found himself staring at Malaburn. In a recess, where a large stow of barrels gave way to more sacks and these fell back, showing signs of recent removal, the American lay at bay, holding the pale form of Huke hostage. Drinkwater stopped and, without taking his eyes off the white mask of Malaburn's face, beckoned behind him with the dirk. Leslie thrust the lantern over his shoulder.

Huke lay oddly, his feet no more than a yard from Drinkwater, his legs splayed slightly apart so that

Drinkwater could see, amid the pitch-black shadows, the dark trail of blood that smeared the white knee-breeches and revealed the deep thrust of the wound in Huke's groin. Malaburn had been in the lower hold, the head of a pike through a hole in a grating waiting for the advance of the impetuous lieutenant. The wound was hideous, the pain must have been excruciating and the bleeding Huke was insensible, his face averted, lolled backwards as he lay in Malaburn's malevolent embrace.

The American had one arm across Huke's chest but the first lieutenant still breathed in shallow rasping gasps. Malaburn's other hand held a long-bladed knife at Huke's throat. In the sharp contrast of the lanternlight, Drinkwater could see the taut tendons in Huke's neck standing out like rope. Beneath them lay the vulnerable carotid artery and the jugular vein.

Drinkwater said in a low voice, 'Put your knife down.'

The blade wavered, a faint reflection of lanternlight revealing Malaburn's hesitation.

'Put your knife down, Malaburn.'

'No. I will let the first lieutenant go only if you give me your word that you will put me aboard one of those Yankee ships.'

'You know that is impossible . . .'

'You could do it, if you wanted to, Captain Drinkwater. If you gave me your word and called your men off. I trust you, d'you see.'

'Malaburn, Lieutenant Huke is bleeding to death,' Drinkwater began, trying to sound reasonable, knowing that a move of his left hand which held a pistol would cause Malaburn to react with his knife. But

Malaburn was unmoved by Drinkwater's logic.

'Your word, Captain Drinkwater,' he hissed urgently, 'your word!'

A dark suspicion crossed Drinkwater's mind. Malaburn's presumption was no quixotic plea, there was too much certainty in the man's voice. He knew Drinkwater could not give his word, dare not give it.

'Who the devil are you, Malaburn?'

'Are you all right, sir?' Danks's voice, muffled by the contents of the hold, reminded Drinkwater of the other men. Beneath his own feet, Drinkwater realized now, Wilson had stopped, aware of something happening above him.

'Stay where you are, Danks, you lobster-backed bastard,' shouted Malaburn, 'and you others, wherever you ... !'

He never finished his threat. There was a flash of light and, when Drinkwater's retinae had adjusted themselves, Malaburn's face had vanished. The long-bladed knife was lowered almost gently on to Huke's chest by the nerveless hand, and the sacks which had cradled Malaburn's head as he awaited his hunters were stained with its shattered remains.

The explosion of the musket deafened them momentarily, and the brilliance of its flash blinded them. Stunned, Drinkwater was uncertain where the shot had come from, or who had fired it. He thought himself shouting with anger, though no one seemed to hear him, and he suddenly heard Sergeant Danks's voice, no longer muffled, say with savage satisfaction:

'Got the bugger!'

Danks's disembodied face appeared above Huke's. He was casting aside sacks as he fought his way through from the far side of the ship, the long barrel of his still smoking musket visible beside him.

'I gave no orders . . .' Drinkwater began, but the words did not seem to be heard and he thought afterwards that he had only imagined them. Leslie was gently squeezing past him with a 'Beg pardon, sir . . .'

And then Drinkwater heard his own voice astonishingly loud, uttering the fact before he had apparently absorbed it. 'It's too late. He's already dead.'

He must have seen the shallow respirations cease, known when he saw that terrible, gaping wound, that Huke was dying. The vicious pike thrust was mortal, not the work of a man acting in self-defence, but the cold act of a murderer. And Drinkwater knew that it was not Danks he was angry with for so precipitately killing Malaburn, but himself, for not having dispatched him for killing a man whom Drinkwater counted a friend.

'Bring both of them out,' he ordered, desperate for fresh air and afraid he might vomit at any moment. He turned and thrust back past the other marine. 'Give 'em a hand,' he muttered through clenched teeth.

As he approached the foot of the ladder to the orlop deck he paused. He could see someone at the bottom peering forward and waving a lantern, hear a babble of curious men pressed about the coaming of the hatchway. He wiped his face and drew several slow and deliberate breaths. Then he strode out of the darkness.

'Here's the Captain . . .'

'Sir? Is that you?'

'Stand aside, if you please. They will be bringing out the first lieutenant's body in a moment, along with that of Malaburn. Pass word to have both prepared for burial.'

Then he went straight to his cabin and flung himself on his cot.

Drinkwater woke at dawn. He was cold and cramped, gritty with dried sweat and foul exertion. The stink of the hold and the discharge of black powder clung to him. He rubbed his eyes and the colours leapt before him and dissolved into the deep red of blood. Drawing his cloak about him he went stiffly on deck.

He had given no thought to the fate of the ship in the aftermath of Huke's terrible, unnecessary death. It seemed almost miraculous that this neglect had been ameliorated by the regular rhythm of the ship's inexorable routine. The realization steadied him and, as he acknowledged Jameson's salute, he saw it was raining.

'Ah'm verra sorry about Tom Huke, sir.'

'Yes. He should never . . .' He caught himself in time. He could not possibly blame Huke for his own death. 'He should never have been so zealous,' he managed.

'He was a guid first luff, sir.'

Jameson's almost pleading tone, as though explaining Tom's character for this Johnny-come-lately of a captain, was the last act of the night. It reminded Drinkwater that the junior lieutenant sought his, Drinkwater's good opinion. 'I know, Mr Jameson, I had already learned that.'

'He has dependants . . .'

201

'I know that, too.' Drinkwater shouldered the burden of command again and could almost feel the mood of the third lieutenant lighten.

'Will you gi'e Mr Beavis a temporary commission, sir?'

And with that remark the sun rose yellow behind a distant mountain, shining pallidly through the cloud and throwing a rainbow against the purple islands to the westward. The ship's routine had sustained them through the hours of darkness, and now the rigours of the naval service demanded their attention again.

'I expect so, Mr Jameson.'

Jameson seemed satisfied. The preoccupations of uncertainty were at an end. He and, Drinkwater supposed, Mr Mosse, could rest easy. He realized suddenly that he might have brought Quilhampton across from the cutter and that the fact had not escaped the two lieutenants.

'Do you think Mr Mosse is likely to be as good a first luff as Tom Huke?'

'Well, sir,' Jameson began, but then the impropriety of the thing occurred to him, as did Captain Drinkwater's arch condescension. Jameson felt put in his place and Drinkwater strode off in search of Frampton and hot water, savagely indulging in his rank.

The ship's routine, which had seen *Andromeda* safely through the night, had not proceeded smoothly. News of the irregular events in the hold had spread like wildfire and the berth deck had buzzed with claim and counter-claim, rumour and inaccuracy. What emerged as fact was that a group consisting of the pressed American merchant seamen had, by an act of what was popularly regarded as 'treachery', attempted to cripple the British ship and render her helpless under the guns of an enemy. Whatever the private and internecine tribulations which beset the company of the British frigate, it was widely understood that when in the face of the enemy they sank or swam together. Claims of American 'patriotism' were thus easily dismissed, as was any idea that Sommer had acted treacherously. They were united by the white ensign which fluttered above the quarterdeck.

During the minutes that elapsed while Drinkwater and the marines ferreted in the hold, an aimless disorder had reigned above them. In this anarchic state, with all the ship's non-commissioned marine officers in the hold, men milled about, increasingly curious, spilling from hammocks and wandering into places they would not normally visit. Even the officers were affected, waiting round the orlop hatchway, or on the quarterdeck, gossiping intently until Birkbeck began to see the dangers inherent in this general laxity.

Mr Templeton was not exempt from the effects of this electricity. He was already in a state of high excitement at the revelations of the interrogation and now, in the gloom of the orlop, he came across Greer. Somehow, unaccountably, their hands met and, encouraged by the general dissolution of order, the intensity of a mutual passion overwhelmed them. Unseen, they retreated into the fastnesses of the ship far from the after hold where they stayed throughout the remainder of the night.

An hour after dawn *Andromeda* was hove to and Huke

and Malaburn were buried. Then the yards were squared away, the sails filled, and the frigate stood inshore again. When under way, Drinkwater sent for one of the American prisoners. Danks brought the man before him.

'Who was Malaburn?' Drinkwater asked.

The American prisoner shrugged. 'I don't know. A patriot.'

'Had you seen him before you came aboard?' The American remained silent.

'Please believe me,' Drinkwater said quietly, 'I can soon make you talk. Do you know how Malaburn killed the first lieutenant? No? Then I will tell you. He waited beneath the carpenter's walk for Mr Huke to pass overhead, and then he thrust a boarding pike upwards through the grating!'

Drinkwater's words rose in tone. The man winced involuntarily and Drinkwater's voice sank to its former modulation. 'Come now; had you seen Malaburn before you came aboard?'

'I hadn't . . .'

'But others had, is that right? Shall I get one of the others?' The prisoner shrugged.

'I can hang you, you know,' Drinkwater said quietly. 'Have you seen a man hanged? The victim dances and then, when he cannot draw breath, he evacuates himself. It is not a pretty sight, but I shall do it if you do not talk.' Beads of sweat stood out upon the prisoner's pallid brow.

'Did Malaburn have anything to do with your escape from Dartmoor?'

The prisoner swallowed and nodded. He had to cough to find his voice; then he admitted, 'I'm told he did, but, honestly Cap'n, I don't know how. I didn't see him when we got away.'

'Got away? You mean from Dartmoor?' The American nodded. 'How did you get away?'

'We were a stone-breaking gang, on our way back from the quarry. The guards were bribed, I guess; we were told to stop and then our leg-irons were struck off by the guards. We left them – the guards – trussed beside the road. I didn't think of anything much at the time, except being free of going back to that gaol. I didn't see anyone at the time except the guards. I guess the whole thing was arranged. Others in the gang said they'd been told something might happen, but I hadn't. Happen I was just in the right place at the right time. It was only when we came aboard that Malaburn was pointed out to me and I was told to do what he said. When I asked why, I was told it was he who freed us from the chain-gang and that I was to obey his orders and he would see us safe back to Boston.'

'Who told you all this?'

'Hopkins, a Boston man like myself. We were taken out of a merchant schooner by one of your damned British cruisers more than a year ago. He seemed to know we were going to be released that day and what to do. The guards were quite friendly towards him and it was Hopkins who made us lash them together.'

'Hopkins is one of the others in the bilboes, sir,' put in Beavis who, with Sergeant Danks and a marine, was part of this impromptu, drum-head court martial. 'D'you want to see him?'

Drinkwater shook his head and continued his interrogation. 'You didn't see Malaburn until you came aboard this ship?'

'No.'

'And how did you get to Leith?'

'We didn't know we was going to Leith, and I daresay had we known how far it was we'd have refused. Hopkins said Bristol was closer, but orders were to lie low . . .'

'But how did you get across country?'

'We moved at night, slept rough, under the stars – that's kinda natural for us, Cap'n, if we're used to trapping . . .'

'Go on.'

'After about a week, Hopkins orders us to lie low for a day, then he comes back one afternoon with a carter, orders us into the back and tells us all is well. I don't recall where we stopped, though we stopped many times, but it was always at night in a town, and we were taken care of in a barn, or a byre, or once in a house.' The prisoner paused and seemed to be making up his mind before saying, 'We were kindly treated, Cap'n, people were mighty well disposed to us.'

'And when you arrived in Leith, you were shipped directly aboard a merchantman?'

'The brig *Ada Louise* of Hull, aye.' The American paused, then added, 'We seemed to be expected, though we had no issue of clothes.'

Drinkwater knew enough now from this and the earlier interrogation. 'Take this fellow forward again, Danks, and make sure he is secure.'

'Aye, aye, sir.'

'Mr Beavis, signal *Kestrel* for Mr Quilhampton to come aboard.'

*

'Ah, James, come in, a glass?'

Drinkwater was light-headed with a perverse and inexplicable exhilaration. Lack of sleep and the death of Thomas Huke had strung his nerves to a high and restless pitch, for he had woken with the thoughts tumbling over and over in his mind, and the short encounter with Jameson had been merely a symptom of his mental turbulence. From the interrogation of the American he had added substantially to his mental jigsaw puzzle.

He poured two glasses and felt the wine hit his empty stomach. It was, he knew, unwise to take drink in such circumstances, but such was the state of his excitement and so intense was his desire to seize those small opportunities he saw before him that he shunned the path of reason. Something of Drinkwater's state of mind communicated itself to Quilhampton.

The younger man had seen these moods of deliberate endeavour before and wondered then, as he wondered now, why he did not consider them reckless. He was certain that, in any other officer, he would have considered them so and was tempted, for an instant, to marvel at his own faith in Captain Drinkwater, but then fell victim to his professional obligation to listen and understand what was being said.

At their meeting in Leith Road, Drinkwater had told James Quilhampton the background of their mission. Now he expatiated, rationalizing the cascade of ideas that had occurred to him in the turmoil of the night.

'Something about the man Malaburn, the way he

207

spoke to me, the coolness of his actions, bespoke *purpose*, James. Don't ask me how I know, one simply forms convictions about such things. He *knew* why *Andromeda* left Leith for Norwegian waters; he sprang a group of Yankee prisoners from Dartmoor and trepanned them to Leith to help him in the business of stopping us from thwarting the American rendezvous here in the Vikkenfiord. Suborning a carter who must have been a republican accomplice, and a host of republicans *en route*, to deliver and succour them is the work of no ordinary man. Then he bribes a boarding-house crimp and spirits them aboard a ship he knows to be short of men, or pretends to be, thereby arranging for their concealment at Leith. The master or mate of the *Ada Louise* must have been in his pocket and 'tis fairly certain they were in the plot, for they issued no slops to the new hands and merely put up with their presence until the press arrived.'

'So they appeared to be brought aboard *Andromeda* in the usual manner?'

'Yes, I imagine so. Tom Huke suggested the matter had been easy.'

'Too damned easy,' Quilhampton said slowly. He paused, then went on, 'And this Malaburn knew about that Neapolitan business?'

'*Yes!* I'm damned certain he did. He knew Leith was the point of departure . . . Damn it, he must have known from the start, mark you!'

'The devil!'

'He planned to cause us to anchor and deliver us to the guns of the two American ships. Whether they are national men-o'-war or privateers matters little. Combined, they mount enough weight of metal to outgun us. Make no mistake about it, Mr Malaburn knew all about them, and us. He must have been overjoyed to see that Dane appear just as I thought we had beaten a timely retreat.'

'You knew nothing of the fort, then?'

Drinkwater shook his head. 'No. Nothing.'

'Your escaping serious damage and towing through the passage must have been what persuaded him to hide, then.'

'Yes. He had only the one chance with the men he had sprung from gaol. He could not confer much with them on board for fear of arousing suspicions and, when he appeared to have lost his opportunity, he sought to cause us maximum embarrassment. Between you and me, James, when we got clear of that confounded Dane, I was exhausted. I wanted Malaburn left until morning, but Huke . . . well, no good will come of raking the matter over again.'

'You risked him doing something desperate like setting fire to the ship,' Quilhampton said in defence of the dead Huke. 'I would probably have done what Huke did.'

Drinkwater looked at his friend, but said nothing. 'Huke has dependants,' he heard Jameson saying, as a wave of weariness again swept over him.

'But why take Huke? Why not just hide and lie low?' Quilhampton asked. 'He could, in all probability, have evaded capture and slipped overboard at any later opportunity.'

Drinkwater sighed. 'He was desperate. He did not know what other opportunities might offer. I will pay him the compliment of saying he was a determined man. Huke's appearance was fortuitous; a bad blow for Malaburn. I don't suppose he meant to kill Huke, merely to wound him in the leg, to take him hostage. He could then negotiate with me . . .' Drinkwater frowned, still puzzling over those few brief words he had exchanged with Malaburn.

'The one thing that makes no sense, James, or at least I can make no sense of it, is the fact that *he knew me*, knew my character well enough to know that if he extracted some form of parole, he thought I would honour it. That is uncanny.'

'Perhaps you imagined it, sir.' Quilhampton's face was full of solicitude. 'I don't imagine holding a hostage binds one to a parole.'

Drinkwater was touched. He managed a wan smile. 'Perhaps. Anyway it is too late now. I shall never know.' He refilled their glasses. 'Besides, we have other work to attend to.' They drank and Drinkwater added, 'I am glad you brought Frey with you.'

'That was luck. I received a letter from him the very day I left Woodbridge. Catriona brought it to me as I was in the act of strapping my chest. I wrote to him and told him to come at once. It was just as well. The lieutenant in charge of *Kestrel* at Chatham had the energy of a wallowing pig. I had his bags packed too!'

'Well,' Drinkwater cut in, a hint of impatience in his tone, 'he'll do splendidly in *Kestrel*. I want you aboard here, in command in my absence.'

'Your absence, sir?'

'You are the senior lieutenant and I must have a man here who knows my mind. I'm taking *Kestrel* back into the fiord under a flag of truce . . .'

'But, sir, I can do that! It's my job!'

'Of course you can do it, James, but I've already a good idea of what the lie of the land is in the Vikkenfiord, and there's no purpose in your taking risks, what with Catriona and the child . . .'

'But, sir . . .'

'But me no buts, James, you've already shaken my confidence in you by admitting you'd have done as Tom Huke did . . .' Drinkwater smiled and Quilhampton shrugged resignedly.

'If you insist.'

'I do. It occurs to me that the appearance of Kestrel might persuade our friends that we have been reinforced out here. I may be able to wring some advantage out of the situation. At the very least it will provide an opportunity for reconnaissance.'

'Time spent in which is seldom wasted,' Quilhampton quoted with a grin. 'I had thought for a while that you intended to withdraw.'

'I cannot with honour do that. Besides, we have an objective still to achieve, and Tom Huke to avenge.'

'Welcome aboard, sir!'

Lieutenant Frey touched the forecock of his bicorn hat and grinned broadly as Drinkwater scrambled up on to Kestrel's low bulwark.

'My dear Frey, how good to see you.' Drinkwater clambered stiffly down from the cutter's rail and shook Frey's hand.

'You damn nearly left without me, sir,' the younger man said lightly, the joke concealing a sense of affront.

'Not having my own command and occupying a rather difficult position at the Admiralty has left me

211

somewhat bereft of influence,' Drinkwater conceded, and Frey caught a gentle reproach in his voice. He opened his mouth to apologize, but Drinkwater beat him to it. 'But I've made amends by giving you command for the day. Be so kind as to pass my gig astern under tow and, by the by, d'you have a sheet or a tablecloth on board?'

'We boast a tablecloth, sir, but why . . . ?'

'Hoist it at the lee tops'l yardarm and proceed into the Vikkenfiord. A flag of truce,' Drinkwater added by way of explanation at Frey's quizzical frown.

'Aye, aye, sir.'

Frey acknowledged the order and turned away to execute it. Drinkwater stared curiously about him. The cutter had not been new when he joined her at Tilbury in the winter of 1792 and she had undergone radical structural alterations some years later. She bore the marks of age and hurried restoration: scuffed timbers, peeling paintwork, worn ropes, patched sails and dull brass-work.

'We've been attacking the binnacle with brick-dust and lamp-oil,' Frey said apologetically, 'but we were waist-deep in water on the passage and it's been a bit difficult . . .'

'It don't signify,' Drinkwater said pensively, his hand rubbing the edge of the companionway to the after accommodation from which, he noticed standing aside, the officers' tablecloth was being brought on deck by the steward. 'If you can manoeuvre under sail and fire your cannon at an enemy . . .' He looked at Frey. 'I commanded her at Camperdown, you know.' He remembered being cold and sodden as they beat about the gatways behind the Haak Sand off the

212

Texel in the days before the battle, while Admiral Duncan's fleet mutinied off Yarmouth.*

'I didn't know that, sir.'

'It was a long time ago.'

He had known Frey for ten years; the lieutenant had been a midshipman aboard the sloop *Melusine* when he had last ventured north. The boy was a man now, growing grizzled in the sea service as this long war rumbled interminably on.

'She still sails well?'

'She leaks like a sieve. She had her keel and kelson pierced for centre-plates which make her claw up to windward like a witch, but the boxes let in water and she needs regular pumping.'

'I recall them being fitted,' Drinkwater mused, then asked, 'Did you bring your paint-box?'

'Never go anywhere without it, sir,' Frey said, waving an enthusiastic hand about him. On either side the steep, dark sides of the gorge closed about them, and beyond, its surface pale and cold, the fiord lay bordered by the dark forest. 'Imagine being here, amid this splendour, without the means to record it.'

'I cannot', said Drinkwater ruefully, 'imagine what it must be like.'

And he grinned as the shadow of the gorge fell across the deck, and they entered the Vikkenfiord.

* See *A King's Cutter*.

12   The Flag of Truce
November 1813

The twelve-gun cutter *Kestrel* ran up the Vikkenfiord with a quartering wind, her huge main boom guyed out to larboard, obscuring the lie of the land and the bluff upon which lay the guns of the Danish fort. Though the British ensign flew from the peak of her gaff, the white tablecloth flapped languidly in the eddies emptying from the leeward leech of the square topsail set above the hounds. Astern, Drinkwater's gig towed in their wake.

The rain had passed and, though the threat of more lay banked up in engorged clouds beyond the mountains to the south and west, the sun blazed upon the blue waters of the fiord and the breeze set white-capped waves dancing across its surface. The low, black-hulled cutter raced downwind. She still sported two long 4-pounders forward, but her ten pop-gun 3-pounders had long ago been replaced by carronades. Frey had had these cleared away and now ordered the square topsail clewed up and furled. *Kestrel* would neither stay nor wear quickly with it still set, and Drinkwater wanted the little cruiser to be as handy as skill and artifice could make her, in case his enterprise collapsed.

Leaving the management of the cutter to Frey, he walked forward and levelled his glass at the bluff, steadying it against a forward shroud. Above the embrasures of the fort, the colours of Denmark proclaimed Norway to be a possession of the Danish crown. Drinkwater could already see the masts of the American and Danish ships, lying at their anchors in the small bay beyond the bluff and under the protection of the fort's guns.

As they drew closer, Drinkwater watched and waited for a response from these cannon. At two miles he saw nothing to indicate the sentries had seen the approaching cutter, then they were within cannon shot.

'Any signs, sir?' asked Frey, coming forward and screwing up his eyes.

'Not a damned thing,' Drinkwater muttered, his glass remaining to his eye. 'Ah, wait . . .'

For a moment he had thought the brief flash to have been the discharge of a cannon, but then the white of an extempore flag like their own appeared to hang down from a gun-embrasure, pressed by the wind against the grey stonework of the rampart.

Drinkwater lowered his glass. 'I think we may stand on with a measure of confidence, Mr Frey.'

'I'll heave to just off the point then.'

'Yes, and get the boat alongside and the crew into it as fast as possible. I don't want them coming to us.'

'Aye, aye, sir.'

Drinkwater raised his glass again and swept the adjacent coast with care. 'Time spent in reconnaissance', he muttered to himself, quoting Quilhampton, 'is seldom wasted.'

So engrossed was he in this task that the sudden righting of *Kestrel*'s heeling deck and the shift of its motion to a gentle upward and downward undulation as she came head to wind took him by surprise. The headsails shook for a moment and then the jib was sheeted down hard and the staysail sheet was carried to windward as Frey hove his charge to on the starboard tack. The bluff, with its granite coping and the dark gun-embrasures, loomed above the cutter's curved taffrail, and on her port quarter where the gig was being quickly brought alongside, the bay beyond was filled with the three ships and its sheltered waters dotted with the oared boats Drinkwater had been so assiduously studying.

Now he went aft, watched as a boathook adorned with a table-napkin was passed to the bowman and, gathering up his sword, eased a foot over the rail, stood awkwardly on the rubbing band, chose his moment and tumbled into the boat.

Barking his shins he stumbled aft with considerable loss of dignity to take his seat beside Captain Pardoe's coxswain, Wells.

'Carry on, cox'n. Make for the Danish ship!'

'Aye, aye, sir.'

They pulled away from the cutter and were soon in the comparatively calmer waters of the bay. Drinkwater coughed to catch the attention of the labouring boat's crew. 'Keep your eyes in the boat, men. No remarks to any enemy boats that may come near and', he turned to the coxswain, 'lie off a little while I am aboard.'

'Aye, sir.'

As they approached the *Odin*, Drinkwater threw

back his boat-cloak to reveal the remaining perfect epaulette on his left shoulder. He wore the undress uniform he had worn in the action of the day before. The bullion on his right shoulder was wrecked beyond repair, though Frampton had done his best when he swabbed the blood from the coat. Drinkwater stared woodenly ahead, but allowed his eyes to rove over the scene. The Danes had made good most of the ravages of the action, reinstating the foremast just as Quilhampton was doing at that moment aboard *Andromeda* beyond the entrance to the fiord.

Inshore of the Danish frigate the two American ships lay at anchor. They looked slightly less formidable upon closer inspection: privateers rather than frigates, though well armed. Between them and the Dane all the boats of the combined ships seemed to be waterborne, industriously plying to and fro. Many had stopped, their crews lying on their oars as they watched the bold approach of the enemy. They were quite obviously engaged in the business of transferring stands of arms, barrels of powder and the product of Continental arsenals destined for North America.

'Boat 'hoy!'

'Oars, cox'n.'

'Oars!' ordered Wells and the gig's crew stopped pulling, holding their oar-looms horizontally as the gig gradually lost way some fifty or sixty yards from the bulk of the *Odin*'s dark hull. Officers lined the quarterdeck while the faces of many curious onlookers, Danish sailors and marines, stared down at the approaching gig. Drinkwater stood up and doffed his hat.

217

'Good morning, gentlemen. Do I have your permission to come aboard?'

There was a brief consultation between the blue and gold figures. English, it appeared, was understood, but the matter seemed to be uncertain, so Drinkwater called out, 'I know you are transferring arms from your ship to the American vessels, gentlemen. I know also they came from France and travelled via Hamburg to Denmark. I think it will be to your advantage if I speak to your captain.'

'One of these boats coming close, sir,' growled Wells, sitting beside him.

'Take no notice,' Drinkwater muttered.

The officers above them came to a conclusion. '*Ja*. You come aboard!'

'Lay her alongside.'

'Aye, aye, sir.'

Drinkwater ascended the frigate's tumblehome, reached the level of the rail, threw his leg over and descended to the deck. With no boats on her booms the frigate's waist was wide open and the contents of her gun deck and berth deck were exposed. The bundles of sabres and muskets, boxes, bales and barrels that she carried could not be disguised. They were being hoisted out and lowered over the farther side where the boats of the combined ships were obviously loading them. His appearance had stopped the labour but, at a command, the watching men returned to work.

A tall man with a blue, red-faced coat and cocked hat stepped forward. He wore hessian boots whose gold tassels caught the sunshine, and dragged what looked like a cavalry sabre on the deck behind him.

'Kaptajn Dahlgaard of de Danske ship *Odin*. We haf

met in battle, *ja*? I see you haf a wound.' Dahlgaard gestured to the large, dark scab on Drinkwater's cheek.

'Indeed, sir, a scratch. I am Captain Drinkwater of His Britannic Majesty's frigate *Andromeda*, at your service.' Drinkwater shot a glance at the officers behind Dahlgaard. Most were wearing the blue and red of the Danish sea service. Two were not. They were wearing blue broadcloth and insolent grins. He knew them for Americans. 'And these gentlemen are from the United States, are they not?' he added, side-stepping Dahlgaard and executing an ironic half-bow at the American commanders. He was gratified to see them lose a little of their composure.

He turned his heel on them and confronted Dahlgaard, addressing him so that the Americans could not hear.

'Captain Dahlgaard, you have, I know, no reason to love my country and, from your actions yesterday, I judge you, as I judged your countrymen at Copenhagen in 1801, to be a brave and courageous officer, but I beg you to consider the consequences of what you are doing. These arms are to spread destruction in a country of peace-loving people . . .'

'I haf my orders, Kaptajn. Please not to speak of this.'

Drinkwater shrugged as though unconcerned. 'Very well, then it is necessary that I tell you my admiral will be happy to let your vessel pass, if you permit us to take the American ships as prizes.'

Drinkwater had rehearsed the speech and was watching Dahlgaard carefully. The tiny reactive muscles round the man's eyes betrayed the Dane's understanding. Here before him stood a British captain claiming to be from the frigate he had engaged yesterday. Having extricated his frigate, this man was now back in a small man-of-war cutter, hinting at the presence of an admiral in the offing. The British officer emanated an air of unmistakable confidence. Now he had the effrontery to press Dahlgaard further.

'Come, sir, what do these men mean to you? What do the French mean to you? They have occupied your country and compelled us to make war upon you. They have forced us to destroy your navy . . . would you be known as the officer who lost the last frigate possessed by King Frederick . . . ?'

The King's name seemed to rouse Dahlgaard. 'The King of Denmark is good ally of France. I haf my duty, Kaptajn, like you. You have no reason to be in Danske waters. No right to demand I surrender these American ships which are', Dahlgaard waved a hand above his head as though drawing Drinkwater's attention to the swallowtail ensigns at the fort and at the *Odin's* stern, 'under the protection of my flag.'

'Please yourself, Captain Dahlgaard,' Drinkwater shrugged, feigning an indifference he did not feel. The Danish commander impressed him as a resolute character, not one to be easily intimidated by Drinkwater's affectation of bombast. He turned to the Americans. 'I shall see you again, gentlemen.'

'I shouldn't be too sure of that if I were you, Captain,' remarked one.

'He's bluffing, Dahlgaard,' added the second. 'There ain't no British ships in the offing.'

Dahlgaard cocked his head, shrewdly weighing up Drinkwater. 'You think no?'

'No. I'm damn certain of it.'

Dahlgaard drew himself up. 'You are not welcome, Kaptajn.'

Aware that his bluff had failed, Drinkwater bowed to Dahlgaard. 'Until we meet again, Captain.' He stared about him, casting his eyes aloft and into the crowded waist. 'A very fine ship, sir. A damn pity to risk losing her.'

'We'll see about that,' drawled one of the Americans, 'there'll be three of us, you know.'

Close-hauled, *Kestrel* beat back down the fiord to meet *Andromeda*. As ordered, Quilhampton had brought the frigate through the narrows an hour after noon, cleared for action and with her upper studding sails set. A mile short of her, Drinkwater transferred to the gig and left Frey to gill about until he had exchanged places with Quilhampton. With considerable skill, Wells manoeuvred the gig under the bow of the advancing frigate so that Quilhampton had only to haul round and shiver his square sails for the gig to dash alongside.

Drinkwater met Quilhampton at the rail. 'She's cleared for action, sir,' Quilhampton said. 'Birkbeck has the con.'

'Did you clap a cable on a bower anchor?'

'Cables on both bowers, sir. And I've led two light springs outside everything.'

'Very good, James, I didn't notice them. Thank you. No dice with the Dane, but she's a formidable ship. The Yankees are privateers and spoiling for a fight, so keep out of their range. There's a deal of lumber about their decks, arms and the like, but they'll make as much trouble as they can. Try and sink their boats, but James, for God's sake keep out of trouble. I need you alive, not covered in death and glory!'

'Don't worry . . .' Quilhampton smiled, his eyes sparkling.

And then he was gone, swung one-handed down into the gig, and Drinkwater was once again absorbed into the business of his own ship.

'Don't wait for the gig, Mr Birkbeck, *Kestrel* will tow her. Let's crack on and surprise 'em. Oh, and keep her close inshore.'

'Aye, aye, sir.'

'I'm going below to shift my linen.'

He stared across the water to where the gig was rounding to under *Kestrel*'s counter. The white tablecloth was fluttering down from the cutter's bare topsail yardarm. The truce was at an end.

Captain Drinkwater was back on deck in fifteen minutes. For the second time within two hours, the bluff loomed above him as Birkbeck held the frigate's course close under the rocky prominence. This time the battery opened fire as *Andromeda* approached. Shot plunged on either bow, pierced the upper sails and parted a brace of ropes, but did no real damage. The rate of fire was slow but steady, a fact Birkbeck remarked upon.

'I fancy most of the gunners are assisting in transferring cargo out of the *Odin* into the boats,' Drinkwater observed. The next salvo, fired as they drew ever closer, passed overhead.

'Good lord, sir, they're firing *over* us. They can't depress their pieces!'

'Quite,' said Drinkwater smiling, hoping to heaven his confidence in deep water existing up to the foot of the bluff was correct.

A glance astern showed *Kestrel* coming up hand over fist and then they were past the point and the bay was opening up under their lee with the rising pine forest behind, and the muzzles of *Andromeda*'s cannon were pointing at the *Odin*.

'When you bear, Mr Mosse,' Drinkwater called as he studied the bearing of the Danish frigate.

'Fire!'

And the officers on the gun deck passed on the order.

The following wind caused *Andromeda* to carry the smoke of her broadside with her so that it was impossible to gauge the effect of the first shots. The air cleared slowly; glimpses of the enemy's masts and yards were briefly visible in the opening rents, only to be obscured as the larboard battery fired again.

Beside Drinkwater, Birkbeck was bawling orders to the topmen and waisters detailed to handle the frigate's braces and sheets as he slowed *Andromeda*, so that her guns might have the maximum effect upon their targets as she swept across the mouth of the bay and her guns emptied themselves first into the *Odin*, and then successively into the American privateers.

'Take in the stuns'ls, Mr Birkbeck!'

Drinkwater's last words were lost in the concussion of another broadside, but this time it was the enemy's and the air was again full of the buzzing of gigantic bees, of a smack and crack as a ball buried itself in the mizen mast above their heads, and the curious sucking of air as another passed close enough to affect their breathing. There was, too, the twang of ropes parting under load, followed by the whirr and thrap of their unreeving and falling across the deck. Somewhere a man screamed, but that first close broadside from the *Odin* was ragged and their own savage retaliation thundered from *Andromeda*'s side as she swept past and poured her fire into the American ships.

Above the quarterdeck the studding sails flapped like wounded gulls, were tamed by their ropes and drawn into the tops. A half-mile past the bay Birkbeck looked expectantly at Drinkwater who nodded and the helm was put down.

'Hands to tack ship! Stand by the braces, there!' Birkbeck shouted, and *Andromeda* came up into the wind. 'Mains'l haul!'

It was now that Drinkwater played the only card he held after the empty bluster about an admiral's squadron in the offing.

He had deduced that the wind which had prevailed from the south-west and died during the previous night, would very likely do the same today. He could, therefore, bear down swiftly on the anchored ships, but once he was past them, as he was now, he had two choices. He could come about on to the starboard tack and stand across the fiord as he had done the previous day, rapidly passing out of range and working slowly to windward before turning and running back again to renew the attack. By then, however, he would have lost the element of surprise.

His second choice was to come right about on the larboard tack and sail directly into the bay under the guns of an enemy, surrendering all advantages beyond that of hitting all three ships again quickly before they could recover from his first onslaught. But he would risk collision, failure to stay again, and the threat of being raked at pistol shot.

'Haul all!'

He now brought *Andromeda* round on to that potentially fatal tack and bore down into the bay. Despite the hazard of such a move he could cover *Kestrel*'s dash in among the boats by drawing the fire of the *Odin* and the Americans, and continue to inflict damage on the former as fast as his gunners could serve their pieces, for with three potential enemies, this could be no tip-and-run raid.

Puffs of smoke along the topsides of all three ships told where resistance was being organized, and columns of water rose up around them as they crabbed down to leeward, gathering way with the yards braced hard against the catharpings.

Ahead of them, already attracting fire and dividing the concentration of the enemy, *Kestrel* had danced insolently into the bay in the wake of the frigate and Quilhampton had strewn his heavy carronade shot amongst the boats. Drinkwater could see two of them awash to the gunwales, the heads of men swimming round them, then one sank, shortly followed by the other. A moment later *Kestrel*'s main boom was swung out and her hull foreshortened as she ran out of the bay towards the approaching *Andromeda* with enemy shot plunging about her.

As *Andromeda* and *Kestrel* passed on opposite courses, Drinkwater could see the little cruiser's bulwarks beaten in where she had taken punishment, but

Quilhampton waved his hat jauntily from the quarter where he stood by the great tiller with its carved falcon's head.

'Closing fast, sir,' Birkbeck cautioned, and Drinkwater looked round and nodded.

'This will do very well,' he said, staring at the height of the bluff ahead of them and the hard edge of the fort's rampart against the sky. A ball thumped into *Andromeda*'s hull and another whined overhead. 'I think we should be safe from the fort hereabouts,' he called to the master, 'bring her round now.'

'Down helm,' ordered Birkbeck, picking up his speaking trumpet. 'Hands to the braces!' he roared. Again *Andromeda* came up into the wind like a reined horse, exposing her starboard battery to the enemy.

'Fire!' bellowed Mosse.

'Stand by the larboard cat stopper!' shouted Birkbeck. 'Rise tacks and sheets! Let go!'

The starboard battery now bore on the enemy and its cannon belched fire and smoke at the *Odin* as *Andromeda*'s backed yards checked her headway and overcame it, slowly driving her astern. Her anchor bit the sand and dragged the cable out of the ship, just as Malaburn had done the previous day. But now the act was deliberate, placing the British ship not at a supine disadvantage, but with her guns commanding the enemy and strewing the anchorage with her own shot.

'Clew up! Clew up!'

On *Andromeda*'s gun deck the men of the larboard guns now moved over to assist their mates on the opposite side, and the warm cannon poured broadside after relentless broadside into the enemy ships.

But the Danish gunners had overcome their surprise and, with the two vessels now stationary, parallel and head to wind, the odds were rapidly reversed. Nor were the American ships inert and, though slightly less advantageously stationed, with lighter guns and lacking the rigid discipline of regular naval crews, their guns found the range and began punishing the *Andromeda* for her effrontery. The crash and explosion of splinters as enemy balls buried themselves in the British frigate's fabric became regular, and musket shot buzzed dangerously about.

Drinkwater was aware of men falling at their guns, of their being flung back, or thrown aside like dolls in the very act of tending their pieces. He looked up at the fort again. The guns were quiet there and he wondered if the ramparts were pierced for artillery on this side. Whether or not they were, he felt they were again too close under the bluff for carriage guns to depress. Hardly had this satisfactory thought crossed his mind than he found Midshipman Fisher at his side. The boy was shouting and Drinkwater realized that the noise of the action had deafened him. He bent to hear what Fisher had to say.

'Mr Jameson says to tell you that Mr Beavis has been killed, sir. A shot came in through the ship's side . . .' Fisher's voice was distant and Drinkwater had to stare at his mouth to understand him. He could see the tears in the boy's eyes.

'Is it bad below, Mr Fisher?'

'Terrible, sir. Collingwood's dead, sir . . .' The boy's lower lip trembled.

'Collingwood?' Drinkwater said uncertainly.

'The . . . the cockpit cat, sir.'

227

'Ah, Collingwood, yes . . . I'm sorry. Do you go and give Mr Jameson my compliments and tell him we're giving the enemy a pounding.'

'Giving the enemy a pounding. Aye, aye, sir.'

Drinkwater looked about him through the smoke. 'Mr Birkbeck?'

'Sir!'

'What d'you make of the *Odin*? We've shot away her mizen . . .'

The words were hardly uttered when there came the fatal crack of chain shot aloft. Drinkwater peered upwards and saw the whole of the main topmast tottering.

'Not again,' an anguished Birkbeck called despairingly. Aloft the falling main topgallant brought the fore topgallant with it, and then Drinkwater heard something far more serious. A deep boom came from somewhere to starboard.

'God's bones!' he swore. 'Mortar fire!'

Amid the falling shot, the smoke and confusion, it was impossible to know where that first shell had fallen. It failed to explode, so Drinkwater concluded it had fallen into the sea before its fuse had burnt down, but he knew it had come from the fort.

The second, when it came, proved lethal, exploding twenty feet above the waist, showering the entire upper deck, the tops and even those exposed in the gun deck beneath the boat-booms with shards of splintered iron.

''Tis too hot, sir!' Birkbeck exclaimed, wiping blood from his face.

'Brace the topsails sharp up, starboard tack. And set the sprits'l!'

The fore and mizen topsails, though riddled with shot-holes, were still under the command of their braces. Birkbeck ran forward among the wreckage of fallen spars and ragged sails, dragging men away from the upper-deck guns and thrusting them into line at the braces. Greer was frantically using his starter as they dragged the resisting yards round. Aloft they were encumbered by the dependent mass of the upper spars and broken mast.

Realizing that to wait many moments more would result in the destruction of his ship, Drinkwater ran forward and slipped over the rail on to the fore-chains. Here he quickly found the end of the spring Quilhampton had had prepared and, gathering up a forecastle gun's crew, sent two of them below to the hawse, to draw in the spring and secure it to the cable. Somewhere above and behind him a third shell burst with a dull thump. Drinkwater could hear men screaming, despite his impaired hearing.

Coming aft again he found the wheel shattered, the four helmsmen either dead or dying. Lieutenant Mosse lay across a quarterdeck carronade, his long and elegant legs doing a last feeble dido.

'God's bones!' Drinkwater blasphemed again, desperately casting about him. It seemed in the smoke that he was the only man alive, and then Birkbeck loomed up to report the yards braced.

'Get below and veer cable! I've a spring clapped on it and as soon as the ship's head is cast off the wind, I'll send word to you to cut it!'

Birkbeck vanished. Drinkwater could only hope the master reached the cable tier without being killed or wounded. He waited, looking up. He could see blue sky above, and the dim geometric pattern of mast, yards and rigging through the smoke. He had to force himself to think, before he worked out it would be the *Odin*.

Behind the Danish man-of-war, the outline of the bluff and the ramparts was visible as though through a swirling fog. A foreshortened faint grey arc rose slowly and gracefully above it. The mathematical precision of the thing struck Drinkwater. He could clearly see the shell that caused it, a black dot, like a meteorite in daylight. The little black sphere grew bigger with an accelerating rapidity that astonished him. He drew back cravenly, behind the insubstantial shelter of the mizen mast. Closing his eyes he rested his forehead against the thick wooden tree. Beneath his feet the ship trembled as the gun carriages recoiled inboard, were serviced and hauled, rumbling, out again. The thunder of the broadsides had broken down now. Every gun was served by its crew individually, the men possessed by the demons of blood lust, slaves to their hot and ravening artillery.

Amid the noise there was a dull thud that Drinkwater felt through the soles of his shoes, and he was aware of a faint susurration. He opened his eyes. The Danish bombardier officer cut his fuses far too erratically. The unexploded mortar shell lay at Drinkwater's feet, half-buried in the decking, its quick-match fizzing and sparking inexorably towards the funnel that carried its contagious fire into the mass of powder packed into its hollow carcass.

Perhaps a quarter of an inch had yet to burn. It puzzled Drinkwater that the unknown artilleryman had made such a mistake. Perhaps the saltpetre with which the fuse was impregnated was of inferior quality. Perhaps . . .

He regarded the thing with a detached curiosity, quite unafraid. He recalled he was supposed to be doing something; that he had initiated a course of action which had had something to do with Birkbeck.

Then smoke blew into his face as Birkbeck veered cable, and he looked up. He could see the mizen topsail above his head filling with wind as *Andromeda* altered her heading, slowly swinging as Birkbeck veered the cable and the weight of the frigate was shared by the spring. Then the wind came over the starboard bow and the ship gathered way, moving ahead.

He felt a sense of overwhelming relief as he remembered what it was he had dispatched the master to attend to. The ship would be all right; she would sail out of danger now. He could die having done his duty. 'Cut!' he yelled, aware that Birkbeck, far below, could not hear him. 'Cut!' he shouted again, and he thought he heard someone below take up the cry, but was not sure. He could do no more.

He looked at the shell again, at the rapidly shortening fuse, waiting for the explosion: then it occurred to him that he might douse it. Bending forward he pinched the hot and spluttering end between thumb and forefinger. He felt the heat sear him and transferred his hand to his mouth. He tasted bitterness, but the thing was extinguished. He bent and, with his sword blade and considerable effort, levered the shell from the splintered and cracked deck planking. Only a heavy deck beam below had prevented it from passing through and blowing up in the crowded confines of the gun deck.

He lifted the black iron sphere and, walking to the rail, put a foot on the slide of a carronade. It had ceased firing and its crew had fallen about it in positions of abandon. Some were obviously dead, their bodies mutilated by the impact of shell fragments. Others looked asleep. He heaved himself up, leant upon the hammock netting and dropped the shell carcass overboard. Then he hung there, hooked by his armpits on the cranes. He longed to shut his eyes and sleep, but he watched the plume of water raised by the splash draw astern as *Andromeda* stood out of the bay.

The butcher's bill was appalling. *Andromeda* lay at anchor on the far side of the Vikkenfiord, not far from where Malaburn had tried to deliver her to the *Odin* the day, or was it a lifetime, before. Kennedy, the surgeon, stood before Drinkwater and read from a crumpled sheet of paper.

'Messrs Mosse and Beavis; Greer, boatswain's mate; Wilson, corporal of marines . . .' Kennedy read on, thirty-seven seamen and thirteen marines dead and the list of the wounded twice as bad, many mortal.

The reproach in Kennedy's eyes was insubordinate. 'Thank you, Mr Kennedy.'

'I did my best, sir, but I cannot work miracles . . .'

'No, of course not. I don't expect that.'

'You expected it of the ship's company.' Kennedy's voice rasped harshly as he made his accusation.

Exhaustion and failure made Drinkwater lose his temper.

He turned upon his tormentor. 'I shared their exposure, damn you!'

'You've the consolation of doing your duty to your king, I suppose,' conceded Kennedy, equally angry.

'Mind your tongue, and keep your Jacobite sympathies to yourself!'

Both men stared at each other. Drinkwater was faint with hunger and exertion. He had had nothing to eat all day and Kennedy was haggard from his foul labours over the operating table. He would, he had confided to his mates, rather have tended the most corrupted fistulae at Bath than hack off the limbs or probe for shards of shell carcass, splinters of wood or grapeshot in the bodies of healthy men.

Abruptly the surgeon turned on his heel and left the cabin. Drinkwater sank into the single chair he had had brought up from the hold. Apart from dropping the cabin bulkhead, the ship remained ready for action. A bitter chill filled the cabin from the breeze that blew in, unimpeded, through the wreck of the starboard quarter gallery, battered into splinters by several cannon shot from the Yankee privateers. Drinkwater drew his cloak closer round him. His head ached and waves of blackness seemed to wash up to him, then recede again. He wanted to sleep but the cloak could no more keep out memories than the cold. He had an overwhelming desire to weep and felt a first shuddering heave.

A knock came at the door and Fisher's smoke-blackened face appeared. It momentarily crossed Drinkwater's overstimulated imagination that this was no mortal visitor but an imp of Satan.

'Beg pardon, sir, but *Kestrel*'s just come alongside.' Such had been the decimation among the officers that the midshipman was keeping the anchor watch.

'Oh, yes.' Drinkwater reproached himself for having momentarily forgotten about the cutter. With an effort he pulled himself together. 'Be so kind as to ask her commander to report aboard.' His voice cracked and he hoped the boy could not see in the gloom the tears filling his eyes.

'Aye, aye, sir . . .'

'By the way, what's the wind doing?'

'Flat calm, sir.'

'Good. Very well, cut along.'

After Kennedy, it would be good to talk to Quilhampton. James understood the brutal and unavoidable priorities of a sea-officer's duty. A few minutes later there was a second knock.

'Come in, James.'

But it was Frey who came into the bare cabin.

13   Failure
November 1813

Drinkwater knew the worst from Frey's expression. The young lieutenant was grimy from powder smoke, his cheeks smeared and pale, his eyes wild.

'How did it happen? Tell me from the beginning.'

Drinkwater hauled himself out of his chair and went to the settee placed below the stern windows. The shutters were pulled and a single battle lantern lit the unfurnished space. Lifting one of the padded settee seats he rummaged and withdrew a half-full bottle. Extracting the cork, he handed the bottle to Frey and gestured to the settee.

'The glasses are all stowed. Please, sit down . . .'

Frey took the bottle and swigged greedily, sat and offered it to Drinkwater who shook his head. Frey took a second draught and then cradled the bottle on his lap.

'We followed you directly into the bay and threw several shots among the boats with some success.' Drinkwater nodded; he remembered seeing this and then *Kestrel* running out towards them as *Andromeda* bore down into the bay to anchor and bombard the enemy ships.

'We sustained some damage from the Americans

and lost three men killed and two wounded before we extricated ourselves. Then we tacked in your wake and came back astern of you. From what we saw you achieved complete surprise. The Danes seemed uncharacteristically irresolute.'

'Their decks were cluttered with armaments they were transhipping to the Americans and they had many of their men away in the boats.'

'Yes. By the time you had come to your anchor the boats had retreated to their respective ships and I had no specific targets. As we bore down, I went aft to obtain fresh orders. The smoke from your guns drifted into the anchorage and made it difficult to see what was going on. To round your stern would have put us uncomfortably close under the guns of the Americans, so James tacked offshore a little, intending to beat back into the bay across your bow and see if anything advantageous offered.

'We managed to lay a course that not only took us across *Andromeda*'s bow, but also carried us athwart the hawse of the *Odin*. All the recovered boats were lashed alongside her starboard waist in the security of her unengaged side. It was also fair to assume the gunners on that side would be helping their mates on the other, for she was by then putting forth a furious fire.

'"We will cut those boats up, tack and get out before they know what has happened," James ordered, and in we went. I depressed our carronades and James took her in like a yacht. I had time to prime my gun captains and we swept in with terrific effect!

'I'm not certain how many of those boats we smashed but their big launch was definitely sunk, along with two cutters and possibly a third. As soon

236

as we were past, James put the helm over. We could do nothing else and . . .' Frey's voice faltered.

'You put your stern to the enemy.'

Frey nodded. 'They had woken to our presence and we received fire from their quarterdeck cannon. Langridge swept the length of the deck; James, both helmsmen and a dozen others fell. The boat in the stern davits, the binnacle and after companionway – all shot to pieces. The boom's bespattered with the damned stuff and the foot of the mains'l in tatters.'

Frey paused and shuddered at the recollection. He took another swallow from the bottle. 'We missed stays . . .'

Drinkwater could imagine the confusion. With no hand on the tiller, *Kestrel*'s rudder would have swung amidships and the turning moment applied to the cutter would have ceased. She would have sat, a perfect target, at something less than pistol shot, off the *Odin*'s starboard quarter.

'I went aft and put the helm over to make a stern board and we backed the jib, but we were too close under the land to get a true wind and she blew towards the *Odin* and paid off to starboard again, back on our former tack. We took another storm of raking fire . . .'

It was a marvel that Frey had not been hit, Drinkwater thought, watching him take a fourth swig from the nearly emptied bottle.

'Then your shot from *Andromeda* brought down the *Odin*'s fore and main topmasts and her fire slackened perceptibly. Anyway, *Kestrel* paid off fast to starboard and we cleared the *Odin*'s stern, thank God! My next problem was the Americans. The Yankees were doing their best, though their fire was nothing compared to the *Odin*'s. They soon saw us though, coming out of the smoke on the *Odin*'s starboard quarter, and quickly laid their guns upon us. I couldn't risk running under their lee, so I gybed and got her on to a broad, starboard reach . . .'

'You sailed across the bows of the Americans and across their field of fire?'

Frey tensed, nodding unhappily. 'I wanted only to get out of that accursed bay, damn it!'

'I am not judging you, my dear fellow,' Drinkwater said with a gentle resignation.

Frey relaxed visibly. 'We returned fire,' he said with a shred of pride, 'but lost our topmast and were badly hulled . . .'

'And the butcher's bill?'

'Almost half the ship's company killed or wounded, sir.'

'God's bones,' Drinkwater whispered, rubbing his hand across his face. He looked at Frey. 'And what of James?'

'It must have been instant, sir. He was quite shot to pieces . . .'

A heavy silence lay between the two men as they mourned their mutual friend. The bottle dropped from Frey's hand with a thud, recalling Drinkwater to the present. Frey drooped sideways, fast asleep. Drinkwater rose and lifted his legs out along the settee, settling him down. Then he took his cloak and laid it over Frey, tucking it in to prevent him from rolling off the narrow settee. As he took his hands away they were sticky with blood.

*

Drinkwater paced the quarterdeck. With his officers decimated and his ship requiring a thorough overhaul and reorganization, he had enough on his mind without grief and the presence of an enemy immeasurably stronger than himself not four miles away.

After he had sailed clear of the bay, he had brought *Andromeda* back across the fiord and found the shallows upon which Malaburn had so treacherously anchored the frigate only a day before. Here the ship and her company drew breath beneath the northern stars. A rudimentary anchor watch kept the deck, and most men slept, exhausted by the day's exertions.

Drinkwater walked up and down, up and down. The extreme lethargy that had seized him earlier, that had driven all thought of *Kestrel* and James Quilhampton from his brain, had left him. He felt almost weightless, as though he derived energy from the workings of his mind. He did not question or marvel at this manic activity; it did not occur to him that the news of Quilhampton's death compounded the weight of accuracy of Surgeon Kennedy's insubordinate accusation. This fateful personalization of so terrible a truth drove like a blade into his soul, and his unquiet spirit teetered on the brink of reason.

Up and down, up and down he paced, so that the men on duty, huddled in the warmest corners they could find beneath the wrecked masts, formed their own opinions as they watched the figure of their strange captain. His body was dark against the sky, the relentless scissoring of his white-breeched legs pale against the bulwarks.

'You know he pinched the fuse out of a shell,' a seaman whose battle station had been at a forecastle carronade whispered to a shivering watchmate. 'Bill Whitman told me he was as cool as a cucumber. Just looked at it for a bit, then bent over and squeezed the fuse. Then he dug the bloody thing up with his sword and dropped it over the side.'

'Christ, he's a hard bastard!'

'Makes old Pardoe look like a fart in a colander.'

'Anyway, bugger Drinkwater. I could do with a drink.'

'Couldn't we all . . .'

'He'll have had one.'

'Or two.'

They dozed into envious silence as Drinkwater's restless pacing soothed the fury of his thoughts, ordered their priority and saved him from the descent into insanity.

'Two watches,' he muttered to himself, 'Jameson and Birkbeck. First to clear the rest of the wreckage, then rig topmasts. Birkbeck will accomplish that, if we are left alone. If . . .'

He turned his mind to the problem of the enemy. He was compelled to accept the fact that yesterday's action had been a defeat. He drew no morsel of comfort from anything which Frey had reported. It was perhaps a cold consolation that the *Odin*'s fire had been furious, but Dahlgaard's countrymen had twice before impressed British seamen with their valour and this was mere corroboration. It was a bitter pill for him to swallow, to have come so close, to the point of actually observing the very muskets and sabres which would be used to ravage the peaceful settlements of Canada being lifted from the *Odin*, and to be powerless to stop their transhipment.

Had he been able to fire at the American ships, he might at the very least have reduced them to a state which no prudent commander would take across the Atlantic in winter. But the presence of the *Odin* had transformed the situation, and cost Drinkwater any tactical advantage he might otherwise have possessed.

The irony of it burned into his self-esteem. He shuddered, as much with self-loathing as with cold.

Faced with such reproach how could there be any satisfaction in knowing he had done his duty? He had spent a lifetime doing his duty and what had it availed? The war ground interminably on, the men he had befriended and then led had died beside him. His friendship seemed accursed, a poisoned chalice. He wished he had been wounded himself, killed even . . .

He drew back from the thought. What would Birkbeck do now if he was dead? The thought struck him like a pistol ball, stopping him in his mad pacing. What was *he* to do? He felt bankrupt of ideas, beyond the obvious one of slipping unobtrusively out of the Vikkenfiord. Instinctively he sniffed the air. There was something odd . . .

He had not noticed the creeping chill of dampening air. Now sodden ropes dripped on a deck perceptibly dark with moisture. The fog had come down with a startling suddenness, though its symptoms had encroached gradually.

Fog!

Even in the darkness he could see the pallid wraiths steal in over the bulwarks, wafted by the light breeze that blew the cold air from the distant peaks down over the warmer waters of the fiord.

Fog!

Hated though it was as a restriction on safe navigation, the enfolding vapour was a shroud, hiding them from the enemy. Could he spirit his ship to sea, clear of the gorge? He thought not; the fear of losing her filled his heart with dread.

Fog!

Then, as the fog enveloped them completely, the idea struck Drinkwater. Fate tugged at the cord of his despair and wakened hope.

Templeton had never before experienced so terrible an event as the action in the bay. When he learned that they had anchored to engage the *Odin* he could not understand so deliberate and foolhardy a decision, until Kennedy, up to his elbows in reeking blood, explained that it was expected of a man-of-war that she be carried into battle against all odds and that to shirk such a duty laid her commander open to charges of dereliction of duty and cowardice.

'And they wouldn't scruple to charge him either,' Kennedy said, as he completed the last suture and motioned his patient aside and the table swabbed for the next.

Templeton knew of such things in the abstract, had read a thousand reports in the copy room, but the reality had never struck him with all its terrible implications as the torn and mangled wrecks of what had, shortly before, been men were dragged on to the surgeon's extempore operating table. Convention demanded that a captain's secretary share the risks of the quarterdeck with his commander, but Drinkwater, unused to such an encumbrance, had made it known to his clerk that he expected no such quixotism.

'Besides,' Drinkwater had said, 'only you and I are privy to the exact details of this matter and, if anything happens to me, you will be best able to advise my successor. Stay below, you may be able to assist Mr Kennedy in his duties.'

Thus it was that Templeton found himself in the cockpit, among the gleaming scalpels, saws, clamps, catlings and curettes of Surgeon Kennedy's trade when the wounded began to pour below in ever-increasing numbers.

Templeton's experience of the previous day's action had, if not inured, at least accustomed him to expect the conventional brutalities of naval war. And the unaccustomed harshness of his existence since joining the frigate, the miseries of sea-sickness and the violence of the ocean had begun the ineluctable process of eroding his sensibilities. But the action in the bay produced so severe a drain upon Kennedy's resources that Templeton found himself inexorably drawn into the actual business of assisting.

Whereas on the previous day he had merely tied bandages, passed words of consolation along with a bottle among the men, and taken and recorded their names and their divisions, today he had actively helped Kennedy and his tiring loblolly 'boys' in the gruesome business of amputation, excision and debriding. He found, after a while, assisted by rum, a savagery that matched the speed of Kennedy's actions.

But nothing had prepared him for the horror of discovering Greer's white and mutilated body stretched upon the sheet spread on the midshipmen's chests, of seeing the mangled stump of Greer's right arm whose hand had so lately transported him; or the shock of the apparent callousness of Kennedy's cursory examination.

'Nothing to be done. Move him over.'

Templeton was incapable, in that awful moment, of understanding that Greer's multiple wounds were mortal, his loss of blood excessive, and that no skill on earth could staunch the haemorrhage or close those dreadful wounds.

'But he's alive!' he protested, staring in outrage at the indifferent Kennedy.

'His wound is mortal.' Kennedy's tone was brutally honest. 'I don't possess the cunning to prevent death.'

And Templeton looked again and saw the blue tint to the lips and the pallor of the formerly weathered features.

'Here.' Kennedy picked up a bottle he kept at his feet and held it out across the body. The loblolly boys dragged Greer from beneath Kennedy's outstretched arm. 'Come, bear up,' Kennedy growled, 'pull yourself together, or men will say you were fond of him!'

Templeton grabbed the bottle and averted his eyes from Kennedy. The accusation implicit in Kennedy's remark did not strike Templeton until later when, he realized, lying awake while the exhausted ship slept around him, none would make any distinction in the nature of his 'crime' as proscribed by the Articles of War. The thought added immeasurably to his burden of guilt.

'What is the time?'

Full daylight glowed through the nacreous fog as

Drinkwater woke suddenly from a deep sleep. He was sat against a quarterdeck carronade, sodden from the fog, agonized by a spasm of cramp as he tried to move.

'Eight bells, sir, morning watch just turning out, I took the liberty of mustering all hands and telling them off in two watches.'

'Well done, Mr Birkbeck, I had the same thing in mind. Now, give me your arm . . .' Birkbeck assisted him to his feet.

'Galley range is alight and burgoo, molasses and cheese are to be issued. Mess-cooks have just been piped. Purser kicked up a fuss about the cheese, but I told him to go to the devil.'

Drinkwater nodded his agreement while the blood trickled painfully back into his legs. He sought to invigorate himself by rubbing his face, but his palms rasped at the encrusted scab, which he had momentarily forgotten, and he swiftly desisted.

'You can issue spirits before you turn all hands to, and what about the officers' livestock?' he added as the idea struck him. 'With so few of them left, can I not purchase what remains so that we can get a decent meal into the men at midday? I'll add my own pullets and capons.'

'That'll put heart into the men, sir, and God knows they need it. The wardroom bullock took a cannon-shot, but he's edible. Beef and chicken stew sounds like the elixir of life.'

'Yes, it does. As for the ship herself . . .'

'We can begin to clear this lot, and the carpenter and I reckon we can step topmasts again.'

'By tonight?'

'By tonight.'

'Excellent!'

'And we've a spare tops'l just finished at Leith. Oh, I reckon she'll show enough canvas to handle.'

'Mr Birkbeck, if you achieve that I don't know what I can do for you.'

'Get me home in one piece, sir, and I'll not complain.' The master paused and looked at Drinkwater. He was unshaven and still besmirched with powder grime, the abraded scab bleeding again from one disturbed corner, the undress coat with its missing epaulette emphasizing the cock-eyed set of the captain's shoulders. With his loose hair, strands of which had escaped from the queue, Drinkwater looked like some raffish and outcast beggar.

'You'd feel better after a wash, sir,' Birkbeck offered.

'Yes, yes, I would,' Drinkwater replied, finally stirring.

'I'll pass word to Frampton.'

'I thought I might have lost him too,' Drinkwater said in a low voice, and Birkbeck, taking advantage of this moment of confidentiality, asked:

'What d'you intend to do, sir, when this fog clears?'

'How long d'you think it will hang about? There's no sign of the sou' westerly . . .'

'Glass is rising. I reckon we can guarantee today, that's why I want to crack on with the masts. Can I use *Kestrel*'s men? I've been aboard her this morning and she's very badly hulled. I doubt she can make a passage and we could use her lieutenant . . .'

Drinkwater walked awkwardly to the frigate's side above which he could just discern the cutter's truncated mast, and peered over the rail. Birkbeck drew alongside him.

They could just make out the shattered and splintered state of *Kestrel*'s upperworks.

'I don't think she's fit for much. We could burn her,' Birkbeck suggested.

'Yes, perhaps,' Drinkwater agreed thoughtfully. 'Anyway, you may have as many men as you like after I have two dozen volunteers. Call for them after they have broken their fast and do you see that you feed *Kestrel*'s crew along with our own.'

Birkbeck looked mystified at first and then horror struck. 'You don't mean to attempt something against the enemy, sir?'

'Yes, I do, and if I have not returned by tomorrow morning, Lieutenant Jameson will be in command.'

'But with respect, sir, I think we have done as much . . .'

'Give me half an hour to wash and shave, Mr Birkbeck, then ask Jameson to wait on me. Muster my volunteers at two bells. Come now, there ain't much time.'

Drinkwater left Birkbeck staring after him openmouthed.

14 A Measure of Success
November 1813

In the event, Drinkwater found his plan to use *Kestrel* quite impracticable. She had been badly hulled and even the plugs put in by her carpenter failed to stem the leaks which proved too copious for the pumps to handle without almost continual manning.

'We can't risk being betrayed by their noise,' Drinkwater remarked to Frey, who had had his wound dressed and insisted he was fit for duty.

'We could fother a sail, sir,' suggested the cutter's boatswain.

'T'would take too long, and there is much else to be done,' replied Drinkwater.

Instead they put the volunteers to emptying the cutter of her powder, and her gunner to preparing some mines, small barricoes filled with tamped powder and fitted with fuses made from slow-match.

It was not so much her waterlogged state that made Drinkwater abandon using *Kestrel* as the difficulty of approaching the enemy anchorage undetected. Although fitted with sweeps, she would be awkward and sluggish to row and difficult to keep on a precise course. The ship's boats were a different matter, but they could not carry the quantities of inflammable material that *Kestrel* could, and Drinkwater had, therefore, to modify his intentions.

When he had exchanged with Quilhampton the previous day, James had departed in Drinkwater's own gig, and had left it towing astern throughout the action. Though it had received damage in the way of splintered gunwales and a few holes in the planking, these were soon repaired with tingles, lead rectangles lined with grease-soaked canvas patches that were nailed over holes or splits.

Kestrel herself bore two boats, one slung in stern davits which had been rendered useless, but another on deck amidships which, though damaged about the transom, and with one large chunk out of her larboard gunwale, remained seaworthy. These, with an additional serviceable pulling cutter from *Andromeda*, provided Drinkwater with what he needed.

'We can't man an armada, Mr Frey,' he explained as he outlined his plan, 'but if we take advantage of this fog and do our work coolly, there is a chance, just a chance, that we may yet achieve a measure of success.'

Frey had nodded.

'Are you fit enough for this enterprise, Mr Frey? I would not have you risk your life unnecessarily . . .' Drinkwater broke off, remembering the blood on his own hand and attributing the unnatural glitter in Frey's eyes to grief and pain. He was, after all, of a sensitive, artistic bent.

Frey cleared his throat. 'I am quite all right, sir.'

'Very well, then. Do you take *Kestrel*'s boat. We know the course and will compare our compasses when we have drawn clear of *Andromeda*. I will follow in *Andromeda*'s cutter and tow the gig. The rest you already know.'

'Aye, aye, sir.'

The interview with Jameson had been more difficult. However sanguine Jameson's ambition, he had not dreamed of such rapid promotion. To find himself elevated to first and only lieutenant was bad enough, but to have command, however temporary, devolved upon him so suddenly was clearly beyond the computations of his ambition.

'But, sir, if I went in the boats . . .'

'If you went in the boats I would have no one to take *Andromeda* home, Mr Jameson. And if I am not back by midnight that is exactly what I wish you to do. Here is my written order.' He handed the reluctant Jameson a scribbled paper. 'Captain Pardoe would never forgive me for losing *all* his officers.' The bitter joke twitched a responsive smile out of the young officer. 'This is a desperate matter, Mr Jameson, one that I cannot, in all conscience, delegate to you. Should I not return on time, I wish you good luck.'

Jameson accepted the inevitable with a nod. In reality Drinkwater had abandoned reasons of state in prosecuting this last attack personally. Rather, a desire for vengeance inspired him – that, or a wish to die himself.

He had thought vaguely of Elizabeth and the children and the handful of Suffolk acres that gave him the status of a country gentleman, but they were so far away, existing in another world, that he doubted their reality at all. They were a sham, an illusion, a carrot to dangle before him. Besides, return meant also the assumption of responsibility for Huke's mother and sister, Catriona Quilhampton and her child . . .

He thrust such considerations aside. He had forfeited all claim upon the smiles of providence when, in a storm of passion, he had lain with the American widow. He had proved himself no better than the next man and could claim no especial privilege. All he could do now was to stake his own life as a tribute to the dead. They left almost unnoticed, clambering down into the boats while Birkbeck supervised *Andromeda*'s toiling company as they disentangled the shot-away spars, cleared away the raffle of fallen gear and salvaged what could be reused.

The men who had volunteered for Drinkwater's forlorn hope took their places at the oars. The looms were wrapped in rags and slushed with tallow or grease where they passed the crutches and thole pins. In every spare space the small barricoes of powder, jars of oil and impregnated rags lay in baskets. In the stern sheets, alongside the boat compasses and in two tinplate boxes in which officers usually kept their best hats, slow matches glowed. The tin boxes bore the names *Huke* and *Mosse*.

'Give way.'

'Give way.'

The boats drew away from the ship, paused while Drinkwater and Frey conferred over their respective compass headings, and then settled down to the rhythmic labours of the oarsmen.

Drinkwater had no intention of trying to run straight into the anchorage. The vagaries of the compasses, particularly in these high latitudes, and the risks of being detected dissuaded him. He knew this was a last chance, knew too that once Captain Dahlgaard had discharged the remainder of his cargo and the fog had cleared, *Odin* would set off in pursuit of the British frigate.

Instead, he had laid off a course which would take them beyond the bay, striking the coast north of the anchorage. This would allow them to drop back along the shore towards the enemy, encountering the American ships first. Dahlgaard, he argued, would be as exhausted as he was himself and preoccupied by completing the transfer of the shipment of arms and equipment, refitting his ship and preparing for sea. At the very least, Drinkwater's attack of the previous afternoon must have incommoded this plan to a degree. Frey had mentioned the *Odin*'s loss of her fore and mainmasts, and he himself thought the mizen had been shot away earlier.

As the boats glided over the still waters of the fiord, these considerations obsessed Drinkwater. Beside him Wells sat attentively, watching the man in the bow who held the end of a length of spun yarn. The other end was held in the hand of a bowman in Frey's boat, so that, paying out and heaving in, as the boats made small variations from their rhumb-lines, they kept in contact. At first it proved awkward and cumbersome, but after ten minutes or so, the men settled to their strokes and, just in sight of each other most of the time, they pulled along in line abreast.

Drinkwater had given orders for the strictest silence to be maintained in the boats and after an hour's hard work, in a brief clearing in the fog, he waved at Frey. Both boats ceased rowing and, with the oars drawn across the gunwales, they ran alongside, willing hands preventing them from coming into contact. Astern of Drinkwater's boat the empty gig ran up under their transom and Wells put out a hand to prevent it colliding.

'Rum, I think, Mr Frey,' Drinkwater murmured in a low voice, and was gratified to see the men grin. Volunteers they might be, but they brought with them no guarantee of success.

'No more than another mile, by my reckoning.'

Frey nodded, and Drinkwater noted the high colour of his cheeks. It was probably the effect of the damp chill, he concluded, munching on a biscuit and sipping at a small pewter beaker of rum.

Resting in silence they all heard the noise, a regular knock-knock, as of oars.

'Guard-boat,' whispered Drinkwater, hoping to Almighty God it was not an expedition bound on a reciprocal mission to their own ships. They listened a little longer. Drinkwater thought he heard background noises of men speaking, and of them labouring at some task, but dismissed them as wishful thinking. They sat still as the sound died away, the men shivering as the fog chilled their sweat-sodden bodies.

'Let's be getting on, then,' he ordered quietly, and the boats were shoved apart, the oars pushed out and the first strokes taken. A few minutes later, with the spun-yarn umbilical between them, they had taken up their former stations. Only the chuckle of water under the bows of the three boats and the dip and gentle splash of the oars marked their progress.

Their arrival was less well organized, for the loom

of smooth boulders ahead of Frey's boat caused her coxswain to put his tiller over and she ran aboard her sister with a clatter and an outbreak of muffled invective. Then the towed cutter ran up astern and struck Drinkwater's boat with a second thud, so that the ensuing confusion took a moment or two to subside.

Frey's boat edged ahead and found a second boulder and then a steep shingle beach which rose swiftly to a gloomy forest of pine and fir. They ran the boats aground and Drinkwater ordered them all ashore. While the men relieved themselves, Drinkwater checked the slow matches. The foggy damp and the need for silence had dissuaded him from any ideas of striking flint and steel. Happily, the matches still burned.

Satisfied that he could do no more, Drinkwater strode off to ease himself. Above the smooth stones of the beach, the ground grew soft with fallen needles and the air smelt deliciously of resin. Outcrops of rock broke through here and there, and were fronded with ferns, but an awesome and sinister stillness pervaded the forest, and he was glad to retreat to the water's edge, where the men talked in low voices.

'Silence now.' The babble died down and, when all were reassembled, Drinkwater asked quietly, 'Any questions?' There was a general shaking of heads.

'Back into the boats. Line ahead, Mr Frey.'

Frey's boat led, out beyond the rocks then turning to starboard, edging along the shoreline. From time to time they had to shorten oars, even trail them, as they glided between the massive boulders that, smoothed by ice and water, had been cast aside as glacial moraine thousands of years before.

As they worked their way south-west, Drinkwater

gradually became aware that he could see the shore and the dark shapes of the trees more and more clearly. Their tops moved languidly in the beginnings of a breeze, no longer grey monotones, but assuming the dark and variegated greens of which he knew them to be composed. The fog was lifting.

Then, almost it seemed in the sky itself, the topgallant yards of the first ship appeared above them. It was the American privateer anchored closest inshore.

Ahead of them Frey, whose boat still ghosted through the clammy vapour, had seen this apparition and altered course towards it. With a surge of jubilation, Drinkwater realized that though the fog was dispersing, the shift of wind which caused it had merely altered the relative balance of nature. He had seen sea-smoke in the Arctic years before, and now his boat pulled happily through it as it clung to the surface, rising no more than ten or fifteen feet, exposing the top-hamper of the enemy while concealing their own approach.

He made a gesture to Wells and the coxswain leaned on the tiller. Drinkwater's boat pulled out to pass Frey and edge round the enemy, clear of her and obscured by the low fog. They could see the grey loom of the American ship and then lost sight of Frey as his boat dropped alongside and merged with her.

From on board he could distinctly hear a voice sing out, 'Lower all, handsomely! Avast! Come up!' The accent was unmistakably American and Drinkwater was immeasurably encouraged by this, for they were clearly still loading cargo.

Drinkwater felt his own sleeve being plucked and swung round. Wells was pointing ahead, to where the next ship was looming. Her hull seemed more distinct, the sea-smoke less dense. An empty boat lay under her stern davits, and a rope ladder dangled invitingly down from an open stern window. As they closed it, they could see the boat was picked out in white and blue, with some fancy gold gingerbread work along her quarters. Beneath the windows the privateer's name was carved, gold letters on a blue background: *General Wayne*.

Without a word, the coxswain ran alongside, the bowman caught the painter round a thwart on the enemy boat and several oarsmen manoeuvred the trailing cutter alongside their own unengaged side.

A moment later two men were swarming up the ladder, the first signalled the cabin was empty and then there was a general scramble as men clambered aboard, helped to lower lines and hoisted the combustible stores they had brought with them. They lifted the inflammables in through the cabin windows. Drinkwater motioned for the barricoes of powder which would form the explosive mines to be rolled towards him and flung back the rich carpet that was spread across the deck of the cabin to reveal the hatchway to the lazarette below. He was crouched beside it when the cabin door suddenly opened. The American commander Drinkwater had last seen aboard the *Odin* stood transfixed in the doorway. The look of insolence he had shown on the former occasion was gone, and now he wore an expression of incomprehension which turned rapidly to alarm.

Drinkwater had had his back to the door as he inspected the hatch. Fitted with a bar and hasp, this would have been padlocked under normal circumstances. But the ship had been in action and the padlock had not been replaced. The carpet, however, had been roughly pulled back over the hatchway with its loose bar and Drinkwater had been in the act of lifting the bar clear when the American had appeared.

Even as the Yankee commander opened his mouth, Drinkwater struck. Twisting with all his strength he straightened his legs, swinging upwards from his crouching position, the bar in his hand. The blunt edge struck the American violently, winding him so that he buckled forward. One of the seamen grabbed him, drew him into the cabin and shut the door.

For a moment not a man moved, but no alarm was raised outside and Drinkwater had his hanger at the man's throat as he gasped for breath.

'Get on with it!' Drinkwater hissed, and the tableau dissolved, the men tearing off the lazarette hatchway and stuffing it and the cabin full with the mines, powder and oil-soaked rags.

Drinkwater bent to the American. 'I'm going to save your life and I'm going to gag you, then you go down into my boat. One false move and you are dead. Do you understand?'

The American commander was still gasping for his breath, but he nodded and Drinkwater grabbed a passing seaman. 'Give me your kerchief. Now, you are to take this man back to the boat . . .'

From somewhere beyond the window a dull thud sounded: Frey's party had either been discovered or had begun their work of destruction.

'Out, you men!'

They seemed to take an interminable time to scramble back through the open stern window. Drinkwater could hear cries of alarm on deck and the pad-pad of running feet. Any moment now and there would be someone reporting to the privateer's commander.

'Ready, sir.' Wells had the hat-box open and the slow-match in his hand. Drinkwater nodded and the match was touched to the first of the three mines. When its fuse was alight, Drinkwater dropped it into the lazarette. 'Get out!' he ordered. 'Get back to the boat!'

The shouting on deck had increased. He took the slow-match and touched it to the protruding fuse of the second mine and rolled it into a mass of rags. The third he had just ignited when the door opened for the second time:

'Cap'n Hughes . . . what the hell . . . ?'

Drinkwater's pistol ball smashed into the man's chest, flinging him backwards, his breastbone broken. Drinkwater threw the weapon after it and made for the window. Below him the men were tumbling into the boat and beyond them there was an orange glow which leached through the last of the fog and grew as he watched. Frey's party had been successful and the American privateer astern of the *General Wayne* was well ablaze.

'Hey! Look!'

The voice came from above, where the *General Wayne*'s people had run aft to see what had happened to their consort and who now, staring down, saw the British seamen climbing out of their own ship and into the strange boats trailing astern.

'The bastards have been aboard of us!' The voices were outraged, surprised and affronted.

'They've been in the bloody cabin!'

'Here, get me a rifle!' Above Drinkwater's head the urgent sound of hurrying footsteps passed to and fro.

'Pass some muskets, quick!'

Drinkwater could see the men settle at their thwarts and Wells looked up at him, his face anxious and expectant. Drinkwater waved his boat away, unwilling to shout and betray his own presence. The coxswain looked nonplussed and Drinkwater made violent, swimming motions. Wells understood; the initial oar strokes of the boat's crew coincided with the report of a musket from the quarterdeck above.

'Another shot and your cap'n's a dead duck!' Wells roared defiantly, his arm round the wild-eyed figure gagged beside him.

'Christ! They've got the cap'n!' an American voice warned.

This last confusion gave Drinkwater the momentary respite he needed. He glanced back into the cabin. The fuses on the mines sizzled, that on the first he had lit must almost have burned through. The last thing he noticed, as he turned back to the window, was the tin hat-box and the name *Thos. Huke* executed in white upon its black-japanned surface.

Climbing on to the window ledge, he dived into the sea.

The water was shockingly, numbingly cold. He surfaced, gasping, and drew a great, reflexive breath. A ball smacked into the water close by, and he struck out wildly. Another raised a short, vicious spurt of water alongside his head and he felt a sharp blow to his arm, but no pain as he plunged on.

Then his tormentors stopped, blown upwards as

the first powder-packed barrico exploded and counter-mined the others with a terrific roar, setting the whole after part of the *General Wayne* ablaze. Dully, he realized what had happened and rolled over on to his back.

The stern of the American privateer appeared in black silhouette against the blaze. He could see the apertures of the stern windows within which the fire rapidly became an inferno. The mines had blown the decks upwards and flames shot skywards, licking hungrily at the mizen rigging, taking hold, then racing aloft. Around the stern dark objects of debris, animate and inanimate, fell into the cold and crystal waters of the fiord.

He turned away. To his left the other privateer was on fire, sparks and cinders rising rapidly from her as the flames, little yellow flickers at first, grew redder in their intensity as they rose up her rigging. It was like some over-blown and monstrous firework display. The neat and ordered lines of the rigging were displayed to perfection by the racing flames, holding their accustomed pattern for one brilliant, incandescent instant, and then falling away in ashen dissolution.

He no longer felt cold. Somewhere to his right he could hear English voices. One of them called his name. He shouted back.

It was with considerable difficulty that they dragged him shivering into the boat.

He was still shuddering so badly three hours later that he could not level his glass at the burning ships, but fumbled and dropped the telescope. The cold water had struck deep into his body. The damaged muscles of his old shoulder wound ached with breath-taking pain, the scab on his cheek had softened and partly sloughed off. As he warmed through, the enlarging capillaries began to bleed again. Oddly, he felt nothing of the slight flesh wound, where the Yankee musket-ball had galled his arm.

It was almost dark and the fog had gone, but he needed no lens to watch as the two privateers blazed against the sombre background of the forest behind them. He derived no satisfaction from the sight; only a loathing for what he had accomplished.

'You *must* go below, sir,' Kennedy insisted, almost manhandling Drinkwater from his position by the mizen rigging. 'Frey has a rare fever from his wound, and if you don't take care of yourself upon the instant, I cannot answer for the consequences.'

Drinkwater submitted, and allowed himself to be led off.

'We have neither the men nor the boats to tow out through the narrows,' he heard Birkbeck saying as he stumbled below, leaning on Kennedy's shoulder.

And the words mocked his success as Kennedy and Templeton wrapped him in warmed blankets and plied him with hot molasses.

15 The Fortune of War
November 1813

Drinkwater had no idea how long he slept, only that when he was woken he regretted it, that Jameson's face was strange to him, and he wished to be left alone. He closed his eyes, seeking again the oblivion of sleep.

'Sir, you must wake up! Sir!'

Jameson shook the cot. It made Drinkwater's head ache and with the acknowledgement of pain came memory. He shook off the luxury of oblivion.

'What is the matter?'

'The Danish frigate, sir, the *Odin*, she is under weigh!'

Drinkwater frowned. 'Where is the wind?'

'In the north, sir.'

'The north!' Drinkwater flung his legs over the edge of the cot and realized he was completely naked. Jameson averted his eyes.

'What o'clock is it?'

'Four bells, morning watch.'

Ten in the morning! He had slept the clock round and more! Why had they not woken him? What had they been doing? 'Pass word for my servant and then you had better beat to quarters. We shall have a battle this morning.'

But Jameson had gone and he was talking to himself.

The two frigates presented an odd sight as they stood down the fiord, both heading for the narrows and the open sea beyond. But this was a deceit, for neither could leave the other behind; the honour of their respective flags denied them this escape, so their almost parallel courses converged slightly, to a point of intersection some half a mile before the gorge, where the matter between them must be decided.

Their unusual aspect was caused by the mutual damage they had suffered and inflicted. It was some consolation to the watching Drinkwater that he had cut up his opponent so badly, for she bore no mizen topsail, her aftermost mast supporting a much-reduced and extemporized spanker, and although her main and foremasts bore topsails, that on the fore-most was a diminutive, a former topgallant. Clearly the *Odin* possessed insufficient spars to replace all her losses. Drinkwater shut his glass with a decisive snap and summoned Jameson and Birkbeck. They conferred in a huddle beside the starboard hance.

'We have one opportunity, gentlemen. Our lack of manpower . . . well, I have no need to emphasize our disadvantages. I shall exchange fire and run directly aboard him. He has the weather gauge, but with that rig he will find it impossible to draw ahead of us. Mr Birkbeck, you will remain on the quarterdeck and handle the ship. Mr Jameson the starboard battery. I will lead the boarders. The topmen are to grapple, then seize us yard-arm to yard-arm. The matter will be decided on her deck. Very good. To your posts and good fortune.'

Drinkwater turned away. 'Sergeant Danks?'

The marine sergeant hurried over and Drinkwater explained his intentions. 'Volley fire as we approach, then, when we close, let the men fire independently. When I give the order to board, half your fellows are to follow me, you are to remain on board in command of the rest and cover our retreat if we are driven back. Understand?'

'Aye, sir. Odds will follow you, evens stay with me.'

'And tell the men in the tops to mind their aim. Fire ahead of us, not into our backs!'

'Aye, aye, sir.'

Danks went off and Drinkwater studied his enemy again. His fears on waking had been unjustified, for he had come on deck flurried and anxious to find Birkbeck had the matter in hand, his re-rigging as complete as skill and artifice could make it and the anchor a-trip.

'I told you, sir,' Birkbeck had said when Drinkwater complimented him, 'I am quite keen to get home all in one piece.'

They had been under weigh within moments of Drinkwater's appearance on deck and now the two frigates were running neck and neck, *Andromeda* drawing slightly ahead.

'That'll change when we fall under her lee,' Drinkwater muttered to himself.

'What will? Our speed?'

He looked round to find Frey beside him. The young lieutenant had been at some pains to repair the ravages of battle to his uniform.

'I heard there was to be an action, sir.'

'Yes, but you are not fit . . . What about your wound? Your fever?'

'I'm as fit as you, sir,' Frey said quietly. He looked astern. 'What happened to *Kestrel*?'

Drinkwater regarded his young colleague and their eyes met. There was the glitter of resolution in Frey's and Drinkwater sighed, then smiled.

'A master's mate named Ashley volunteered to bring her in with a prize crew. He's on our larboard beam.'

Frey craned round and saw the man-of-war cutter. 'Ah, yes. I wonder what their chances are?'

'Less than fifty-fifty.'

Drinkwater did not say that he would never have let Ashley go had not the odds against their own survival been considerably shorter. Ashley carried a hurriedly written report of proceedings and a secret, enciphered dispatch. Both had been prepared by Templeton at Drinkwater's dictation while he had dressed.

Drinkwater looked at Frey. 'Very well. Do you keep an eye on things here. I'm going to take a turn below.'

He descended to the gloom of the gun deck. The gunners were, to a man, gathered about their cannon, staring at the enemy through the open ports. Behind the guns the powder-monkeys crouched, trying to see between the men. Standing at the bottom of the ladder, Drinkwater was struck by the lack of numbers. The larboard guns were almost unmanned. Shackled amidships were the chained American prisoners. Drinkwater had quite forgotten them. His memory seemed, these days, to be fickle in the extreme.

Further forward, beside the mainmast, Lieutenant

Jameson was studying the enemy and haranguing his men.

'He's going to open fire any moment, my lads. When he does I want him to feel the weight of our metal in one blow.'

A murmur of appreciation greeted this speech. Someone forward, in the eyes of the ship, cracked a joke, and Drinkwater heard the expressions of mirth roll aft.

'Make 'em eat shit, Jamie!' another called, and a good-natured laugh broke out again.

'No, no,' Jameson called, never taking his eyes off the enemy. ''Tis too soft.'

The filthy jests went on, bolstering their courage. This was a Jameson Drinkwater had never met, but would be glad of in the coming hour. He abandoned any thought of addressing these men and made to return to the quarterdeck. The sudden movement attracted attention. Midshipman Fisher saw him and touched the brim of his ridiculous hat. Others caught sight of their captain and the whisper of his presence passed along the line of guns like a gust of wind through the tops of fir trees. Jameson became aware of it and straightened up.

'Don't let me distract you, Mr Jameson, I merely came to satisfy myself that you were ready,' he called.

'We're ready, sir, aren't we, my lads?'

'Aye, we're ready!' They broke out into a cheer. It was foolish; it was utterly beyond reason and it was pitifully affecting. Drinkwater stood stupid with emotion and, although stoop-shouldered beneath the beams, he raised his damaged hat in solemn salutation. Then he turned and ascended into sunshine as the cheers of the gunners below followed him.

The noise was taken up on the upper deck. The men at the forecastle guns, those mustered at the mast and pinrails and stationed on the quarterdeck at the carronades and the wheel, began to cheer.

He let them be, let their enthusiasm subside naturally and, walking to the ship's side, wiped the moisture from his eyes as unobtrusively as possible. He was a damned ninny to be seduced by such stupidity, but he could not prevent himself from feeling moved.

Sniffing, he looked again at the enemy; she was much closer now.

The line of the *Odin*'s opened gun-ports suddenly sparkled, then faded from view, obscured by the smoke from her broadside. Shot whined overhead, fell short or thudded into their side before the sound rolled down upon them.

He heard Jameson's order and *Andromeda* shook to the simultaneous discharge of her own battery. Plumes of spray rose up along *Odin*'s waterline and a cannonade which was to last for twenty long minutes began.

Shot smacked home, the faint trembling of the hull betraying a ball burying itself in the frigate's stout oak sides; ropes parted aloft; more holes appeared in the already tattered sails with an odd, sucking plop; explosions of splinters lanced the deck and the hot breath of cannon shot made them gasp. The business of dying began again; men screamed and were taken below.

'I believe you're boarding, sir.'

'What?' Distracted, Drinkwater looked round to see Templeton beside him.

267

'I understand it is your intention to board the *Odin*.'

'Yes.'

'It is my intention to accompany you.'

'The devil it is . . .'

Drinkwater looked at the clerk. Was he pot-valiant? Drinkwater could smell no liquor on his breath, and Templeton winced as the starboard battery fired again. Templeton had not occupied much of Drinkwater's time or attention during the last fortnight. He had been summoned when required, which had not proved often, and for the most part had been left to his own devices and desires. He looked somehow strange, different from the man who had stood in his room in the Admiralty, but then Quilhampton was dead and Frey was a changed man; so, he supposed, was he. If Templeton wished to prove himself it was his own affair, and who was Drinkwater to judge him for taking a nip to fortify his nerves?

'Very well, Mr Templeton, if that is what you wish. I should have sent you with Ashley in the *Kestrel*, but I shall be glad of all the support I can get.'

'Thank you.' Templeton moved away and stood by the mizen mast, selecting a boarding pike from the rack. Six feet away a ball from the *Odin* crashed into the bulwark between two larboard carronades and a spray of musketry spattered aboard, killing a marine and wounding a gunner. Drinkwater saw Templeton jerk with involuntary reaction.

The distance between the two ships was closing rapidly now. It must have been obvious to Dahlgaard what Drinkwater intended, but the Danish captain made no attempt to draw off and pound his weaker opponent.

'Edge closer, Mr Birkbeck, then go at her with a run, we're falling under her lee!'

Shot thumped into *Andromeda*'s planking and the enemy's upperdeck cannon belched langridge at them. The iron hail swept whistling aboard, taking Drinkwater's second hat from his head. He drew his hanger. He was conscious now of only one burning desire, to end this madness in the catharsis of a greater insanity.

'Now, Birkbeck! Now!'

Andromeda was losing ground quickly as the *Odin* masked her from the wind, but Birkbeck had the measure of the situation and put the helm up the instant the guns had fired a broadside. The British ship swung to starboard with a slow and magnificent grace. Her bowsprit rode over the Dane's waist and the dolphin striker lodged itself in the *Odin*'s main chains. The impetus of the *Odin* caught the lighter ship and drew her alongside, so the first impact of the collision was followed by a slewing of the deck; then the two ships ground together, locked in mortal combat, a tangle of yards and hooked braces aloft, their guns muzzle to muzzle below.

From the corner of his eye Drinkwater caught a glimpse of a grapnel snaking out as he clambered up on the rail and stepped over the hammock netting. Other men were gathering, anticipating his order:

'Boarders away!'

He could never afterwards remember those few vulnerable seconds as he scrambled aboard the *Odin*, beyond realizing that the Danish frigate had two feet more freeboard than her adversary and he had to climb upwards. It was always something of a mystery as to why the defenders of a ship did not find it easy to repel attackers coming aboard in so haphazard a manner. A mystery, that is, until one considered the encumbrance of the hammock netting which was designed to form a breastwork behind which sharpshooters could be stationed, but which almost perfectly masked an attack made up the ship's side.

Sometimes a ship would hoist boarding nettings, but neither had done so, perhaps each to facilitate their own attacks. Astride the *Odin*'s hammock netting Drinkwater discharged his pistol into the face of a Danish marine, then leaned down and thrust his hanger at a gunner waving a pike. The pike ripped his sleeve and, gripping the hammocks with his legs as though on horseback, he jabbed the discharged pistol barrel into the man's eye. As his victim fell back, Drinkwater stood, swung both legs over the netting and, grabbing a mizen shroud with his left hand, slashed a swathe with his sword and jumped down on to the *Odin*'s deck in the space thus provided.

Other men tumbled all about him, a 'veritable cascade of seamen and marines', he afterwards wrote in his full report of proceedings, Templeton among them, keening in a curious, high-pitched squeal as he cut dangerously left and right with his sword.

' 'Ere, watch it, Mr Templeton,' somebody sung out, clear above the howls of rage and the screams of the dying.

Drinkwater engaged a second Danish marine, cut at the man's forearm and winged him, advanced a half step and grasped the musket's muzzle, ducking under the bayonet and jabbing his hanger at the soldier's stomach. The man cried out, though his voice was lost in the general bedlam and Drinkwater was conscious only of the gape of his mouth. The musket dropped between them, Drinkwater withdrew and slashed down at the marine's shoulder as he fell, parried a pike and felt the flat of a cutlass across his back.

He half-turned as the weapon was thrust again, flicked his own hanger and pricked the seaman's hand as he lunged with the clumsy cutlass. The severed tendons cost the man his grip. Drinkwater grunted with the speed of his response, raised his sword-point and, as though with a foil, extended and withdrew. Blood ran down the hapless sailor's face and his breath whistled through his perforated cheek as he fell back.

A musket or pistol was discharged close to him. Drinkwater felt the fierce heat from its muzzle and a stinging sensation in his ear. He cut right, parried a sword thrust and bound the blade; bellowed as he thrust it aside and slid forward, driving his sword home to the hilt in the soft abdomen of a man he had barely seen in the press of bodies.

He was conscious of an officer, of two officers, threatening him from the front in defiant postures. He was running short of wind, but Templeton was on his right and he shrieked, 'Here, Templeton, to me!'

Drinkwater engaged, crossed swords and felt the Danish officer press his blade. Drinkwater disengaged with a smart cutover, but was thwarted as the Danish officer changed his guard. Drinkwater dropped his point and reverted to his original line, extending without lunging. The Dane grinned as he parried high and extended himself. Drinkwater was drawing his breath with difficulty now, he ducked clumsily and fell back, expecting a swift *reprise*, but the Dane would not be drawn and stood grinning at the panting Drinkwater.

Drinkwater's puzzlement was brief. On his flank Templeton was whirring his blade with such fanatic energy that his opponent was confused, or would not be drawn, and maintained a defensive position.

Then, in the hubbub and confusion, Drinkwater realized, drawing breath in the brief and timely lull, that the two officers were defending a man seated behind them in a chair.

It was Dahlgaard and he was pale as death, a pair of pistols in his lap.

'Captain Dahlgaard!' Drinkwater shouted, 'I see you are wounded! You can do no more! Surrender, sir! Strike your flag and stop this madness!'

'No!'

The officer from whom Drinkwater had just escaped howled his commander's defiance.

Drinkwater fell back a step. Templeton had drawn off and suddenly pulled a pistol from his belt. He fired at the officer he had been fighting and, as the Danish lieutenant fell, he stepped quickly forward and thrust savagely at Dahlgaard.

The officer who had defied Drinkwater's call to surrender, seeing what was happening, made to strike Templeton but lost his balance.

Drinkwater was on him, lunging forward with such speed that he, too, lost his footing and slammed into the Dane, his hanger blade snapping as he drove it home.

As Drinkwater fell to his knees something struck him on the shoulder. The blow was not hard. He sat back on his haunches and looked up into Dahlgaard's face. The Danish captain's eyes were cloudy with pain, his face wet with perspiration. Blood ran from the new wound Templeton had inflicted in his upper arm. Between these two men, instigators of the carnage all about them, Dahlgaard's young lieutenant was pinioned to the deck by Drinkwater's broken sword-blade.

Breathing in gulps, Drinkwater realized the injured Dahlgaard had struck him with one of his pistols. It had already been fired.

'I strike my flag,' Dahlgaard called, his voice rasping with agony.

'You surrender?' Drinkwater gasped, uncertain.

Dahlgaard nodded. '*Ja, ja,* I strike.' The Dane closed his eyes.

'They strike!' shrieked Templeton. 'They strike! They strike!' And heady with victory Templeton ran aft to cut the halliard of the Danish ensign.

Wearily Drinkwater heaved himself to his feet. He felt the madness ebb, heard the cheering as though it came from a great way away. He was sodden with sweat and breathing with difficulty. Lightly he placed his hand on Dahlgaard's shoulder.

' 'Tis the fortune of war, Captain Dahlgaard, the fortune of war.'

Dahlgaard opened his eyes and stared up at Drinkwater, blinking. 'He was my sister's son, Kaptajn Drinkwater, my sister's only son . . .'

And Drinkwater looked down at the body which lay between them, oblivious of Templeton who bent over the *Odin*'s taffrail, the blood-red and white Danish colours draped about him, vomiting into the sea below and weeping in a rage at his own survival.

16   To the Victor, the Spoils
November 1813

Lieutenant Frey climbed wearily out of the boat, up the frigate's tumblehome and over the rail on to *Andromeda*'s quarterdeck.

'The Captain's in the cabin, Frey, and asked if you would report when you arrived.'

Frey nodded to Lieutenant Jameson and went below. He found Drinkwater sitting having a dressing changed on his arm by the surgeon.

'Help yourself to a glass, Mr Frey, you look quite done in.'

'He still has a fever,' put in Kennedy.

'I'm fine, Kennedy, just a little tired.'

'Who isn't . . . ?'

'I didn't know you had been hit, sir,' Frey said quickly, restoppering the decanter.

'It's nothing. A scratch. A Yankee galled me as I swam away from the *General Wayne*. My exertions yesterday reopened it . . .'

'It needed debriding', said Kennedy severely, 'before it became gangrenous. Your face is a mess, too; you'll likely have a scar.'

'Stop clucking, Mr Kennedy. Thanks to your superlative skill, I will mend,' said Drinkwater, silencing the surgeon. 'Now, Frey, tell me about your expedition, what of the two Americans?'

'The *General Wayne* burned to the waterline and settled where she lay. The other, the *Hyacinthe* – a French-built corvette – drifted ashore after her cable burnt through and then blew up. Her remains continued to burn until there was little left of her, or her contents. As for the matter of the truce, I had no trouble in landing my party. The commandant of the fort, a Captain Nilsen, or some such, is making ready to receive the wounded from the *Odin*. He was especially solicitous for Captain Dahlgaard. I understand they are related in some way.'

Drinkwater recalled Dahlgaard's dead nephew and dismissed the morbid thought. 'And you mentioned the *Kestrel*?'

'Yes. They seemed relieved not to have been entirely deprived of a means of communication with Bergen, or Copenhagen for that matter. I formed the impression that the Americans are an acute embarrassment to them.'

'I am truly sorry for the Danes,' Drinkwater said. 'Captain Dahlgaard was a most gallant officer . . .'

Kennedy sniffed disparagingly at this assertion. Drinkwater ignored the man's infuriating importunity.

'And what arrangements have you concluded?'

'That all the Danes are to be landed and that we hand over the *Kestrel* immediately prior to our departure. A truce is to obtain until we are seaward of the narrows, thereafter they may communicate with Bergen.'

'Very well. In the circumstances we must count that as satisfactory. Captain Dahlgaard may be sent ashore as soon as is possible.'

'I took the liberty of permitting the one launch left to the Americans to pull out immediately and take off the worst of the wounded.'

Drinkwater nodded. 'That was well done. Birkbeck has completed his survey of *Kestrel* and has condemned her as totally unfit for further service. Properly we should destroy her, but I do not think their Lordships will judge us too harshly for leaving this place with a measure of magnanimity towards our beaten foe.'

Kennedy sniffed again as he completed his work.

'Physician, I suggest you heal yourself', said Drinkwater, 'instead of making that ridiculous noise.' Kennedy scowled as he added, 'Thank you for your solicitude.'

Frey watched the surgeon leave and turned to Drinkwater. 'Sir, there is a matter of considerable importance I have to discuss with you . . .'

'If it is to do with a prize-crew . . .'

'No, no! Though I should like to know what arrangements you are intending.'

'You will take the *Odin* home. We will stay in company and make for Rattray Head, thereafter I will signal Leith, or London, depending upon the circumstances. But come, what is this matter of such importance?'

'Gold specie, sir.'

Frey breathed the words with a quiet satisfaction, as though not daring to frighten them away. Comprehension dawned slowly on Drinkwater.

'Aboard the *Odin*?'

Frey nodded conspiratorially. 'I was in a lather of apprehension whilst I was away, but it is quite safe.

Captain Dahlgaard had made especial provision for it and I do not think many of his people knew. It was in a small lazarette below his cabin . . .'

'And had, I think, come out of a similar lazarette in the *General Wayne*,' said Drinkwater, remembering the empty space into which he had rolled the little barrels with their lethal filling of fine-milled black powder. 'But how did you come by it?'

'When we boarded and you attacked aft,' Frey explained, 'my party went for the wheel and then the gun deck. I had hoped to take the gunners in the rear, but too few of our fellows followed me. Most of the Danes on the upper deck fell back on their quarterdeck and we got below without encountering much resistance. The gun deck was reeking with smoke and we got the hatches down amidships and aft before, I think, anyone was aware of our presence. When I secured the after hatch to prevent anyone coming up from below, we were seen and set on by the aftermost gun crews. There were about a dozen men with me at that time including Fisher and we had a hard few moments of it, being hopelessly outnumbered and totally unsupported.' Drinkwater could imagine the scene: the noise and confusion; the Danish gunners blazing away, half-deafened, the gun deck full of smoke and then someone spotting the strange intruders.

'Go on,' he said.

'It was curious, but the Danes had left the after bulkhead down. Fisher got the cabin door open and we retreated into Dahlgaard's quarters, leaving four of our number outside. None of the after guns in there were manned . . .'

'Well I'm damned! I never noticed, but forgive me; do go on.'

'Dahlgaard had emptied the cabin space of furniture, though, and it struck me that there was a reason why he had not completely cleared the after part of the ship for action. At the time I gave it no further thought, beyond welcoming the respite, expecting the Danes to burst through the flimsy door at any moment. In fact the fire beyond the bulkhead slackened and then ceased. A few minutes later, things having fallen silent, we ventured out to find the ship had struck her colours. I think those men who were not still at the guns had been called away to defend the upper deck just at the point when you gained the upper hand.'

'Go on.'

'After you left me prize-master I posted guards and went back into the cabin to seize the ship's papers. Dahlgaard had left a bunch of keys, a pair of pistols, a telescope and a number of other articles one would have supposed he ought to have had disposed about his person. I found them on the stern settee. I tried the keys and found they fitted the usual lockers and also a lazarette hatch. I think Dahlgaard underestimated us, sir, thought he could dispense with the aftermost guns in order to preserve intact what lay below his cabin.'

'The specie?'

'Yes. A dozen chests of it. Gold ingots . . . I have no idea how many.'

'And you placed a guard on it?'

'Mr Fisher. I locked the poor fellow in. I have just been aboard, before reporting to you. He is all right; he stuck to his post after I impressed the importance of it upon him, though he is very hungry.'

'Does he know what he is guarding?'

Frey shook his head. 'No, not exactly; only that it is important.'

'Twelve-year-old boys take much for granted, including the presumed wisdom of their elders, I'm glad to say. And the Danes made no attempt to regain it, not even during your negotiations?'

Frey shook his head. 'No. I thought better than to draw their attention to it.'

'Quite.' Drinkwater frowned, then said, 'Perhaps Dahlgaard and his lieutenants were the only ones to know of it, and I suppose the Americans themselves may well have physically shifted the stuff. The fact that it was concealed in wooden boxes would have prevented all but a few officers from knowing its true nature. It would also explain the protracted length of time taken to tranship that cargo. I imagine Dahlgaard insisted the Americans surrender the gold before he released the arms. There was certainly much toing and froing between the ships, and the *Odin* would have been stuffed with the arms shipment. Her crew must have been heartily sick of having their freedom impeded by so much cargo.'

Frey looked puzzled. 'I'm sorry, Frey,' Drinkwater added, 'you ain't party to all the ramifications of this business. I will tell you all about it when we anchor in British waters.' Drinkwater smiled wanly. 'You'll have to possess your soul in patience until then, but suffice it to say the Danes were only acting as carriers, which may explain their indifference to the gold's fate. It was destined for Paris, not Copenhagen.'

'Ah, I see. Payment from the Yankees to the French for the arms being shipped into the American privateers.'

'Exactly so.'

'And kept damn quiet by those Danish officers in the know.'

'Yes.'

'I imagine there can be few of them left,' Frey said, 'judging by the carnage on deck.'

'No.' Both men were briefly silent, then Drinkwater returned to the matter in hand. 'You had better take Danks and four marines with you as a special guard. Keep Fisher, take Ashley and pick your prize crew, sixty men. We will weigh as soon as possible. Rattray Head is to be the rendezvous.'

'You don't wish to tranship the specie aboard here, sir?'

Drinkwater shook his head again. 'No. The fewer people who know about it the better. It is safe enough in your hands. Besides, I don't want to wait a moment longer.' His last sentence was an excuse. The truth was, there was something obscene about the thought of tucking the gold under his own wing.

'I rather think you have made your fortune, sir.'

Drinkwater shook his head again. 'I doubt it. I'll lay a guinea on it becoming a droit of Admiralty, Mr Frey, but you may at least have the commission for carrying it.'

And a brief gleam of avarice came into Frey's eyes, the first manifestation of mundane emotion since he had announced the death of James Quilhampton.

Mr Templeton looked up at the figure silhouetted against the battered remains of the stern windows. The seated clerk was shivering with cold and persistently glanced at the blanket forming an inadequate barrier to the open air which whistled with a mournful moan through the shot-holes in *Andromeda*'s starboard quarter.

Captain Drinkwater's silence grew longer, past the point of mere reflection and into an admission of abstraction. Templeton coughed intrusively. Drinkwater started and looked round.

'Ah . . . yes . . . Read what you have written, Templeton,' Drinkwater commanded.

'To the Secretary, and so on and so forth,' Templeton began, then settled to read: 'Sir, I have the honour to report . . .'

Head bent and stoop-shouldered beneath the deckhead beams, his hands clasped behind his back, Drinkwater paced ruminatively up and down the shattered cabin as Templeton's voice droned on through the account of the past weeks. He was compelled to live through those last hours in Quilhampton's company and forced to recreate from the spare words of his report the frightful minutes crawling through the hold in search of Malaburn. Finally Templeton concluded the details of the final action which culminated in the capture of the *Odin* as a prize of war.

'. . . And having, subsequent to a survey by Mr Jonathan Birkbeck, Master, condemned the *Kestrel*, cutter, as unfit for further service, her stores and guns having been removed out of her, she was, by my order, turned over to the enemy as an act of humanity in order that communication might be opened with Bergen and the removal of the wounded to that place be effected.

'Having taken in my charge the former Danish

frigate *Odin* and placed on board a prize crew, Lieutenant Frey in command, the said *Odin* did weigh and proceed in company with HBM Frigate *Andromeda*, leaving the Vikkenfiord shortly before dark . . .'

'Very well. Add the date.' Drinkwater paused while Templeton scratched.

'Is that all for the time being, sir?'

Drinkwater had yet to account for the dead, to write their collective and official epitaph.

'Yes, for the time being. It is getting dark.'

'The evenings draw in swiftly in these high latitudes, sir.'

'Yes,' Drinkwater replied abstractedly. 'It is time we were gone, while this favourable breeze holds.'

'Mr Birkbeck says the glass stands very high and the northerly wind will persist for many days.'

'Does he now?' Drinkwater looked at Templeton as if seeing him for the first time in weeks. Templeton was not usually prone to such abject ingratiation. 'You are taking an uncommon interest in nautical matters, Mr Templeton.'

'Sir?'

The sarcasm struck Templeton like a whip and he turned his face away, but not before Drinkwater had seen the unaccountable effect his words had had. Nor could Templeton disguise the withdrawing from his sleeve of a pocket handkerchief.

Drinkwater was about to speak, then held his peace. He had been too hard on a man not inured to the fatigue of battle. A man of Templeton's sensibilities might receive hidden wounds, wounds of the mind, from the events of the last few days. For a moment Drinkwater looked at his clerk, remembering the rather supercilious man who had brought the news of Bardolini's landing that night at the Admiralty. Drinkwater felt the stirrings of guilt for, had he not insisted that Templeton sail aboard *Andromeda*, the wretched fellow might never have been subjected to the rigours of active service.

They had gone through much since, much that should have brought them closer, but Drinkwater felt a constraint between them; they no longer enjoyed that intimacy of communication which had marked their relationship in London. Something between them had diminished and failed to withstand the manifold pressures of life at sea. Perhaps it was merely the distance imposed by the isolation of his rank, and yet Drinkwater felt it was something more subtle. And with the thought, Drinkwater realized he felt an intuitive dislike of Templeton.

The dull boom of a gun, followed by another, echoed across the water. It was the agreed signal that Frey was ready to weigh, though it made Templeton start with a jerk.

'That is all for now, Mr Templeton.' Drinkwater watched the clerk shuffle unhappily forward, blowing his nose, bearing his own weight of guilt and grief.

Drinkwater threw his cloak about his shoulders, clamped his damaged hat upon his head and went on deck. He could not dismiss the unease he felt about Templeton, aware of his own part in the clerk's transformation. Something had altered the man himself, and Drinkwater felt an instinctive wariness towards him. It was a conviction that was to grow stronger in the following days.

*

The two ships stood down the fiord in line ahead, the symmetry of their sail-plans wrecked by battle. *Andromeda*'s jibboom was shortened from her impact with the *Odin*, and both frigates bore an odd assortment of topsails on a variegated jumble of jury-rigged spars.

Already the high bluff with its fort and the burntout wrecks of the two American privateers had faded in the distance. They seemed now to have no existence except in the memory, though Drinkwater wondered how the Danish garrison were coping with the influx of wounded and the encumbrance of numerous Yankee privateersmen. He wondered, too, whether Dahlgaard had survived his wounds, or whether death had claimed him as well as so many others.

On either hand the mountains and forests merged into a dusky monotone, and the waters of the fiord, though stirred by the breeze, were the colour of lead. Even the pale strakes of their gun decks, yellow on *Andromeda* and buff on *Odin*, were leached of any hue; nor were the white ensigns more than fluttering grey shapes at the peaks of the twin spankers, for Drinkwater had forbidden *Odin* to fly her colours superior to those of Denmark while they remained in Norwegian waters.

'I dislike gloating, Mr Frey. You may play that fanfare when in a British roadstead, but not before.'

They could judge him superstitious if they liked, but he had tempted fate enough and they had yet many leagues to make good before crowing a triumph.

The shadow of the narrows engulfed them. In the

twilight, they moved through an ethereal world; the cliffs seemed insubstantial, dim, almost as though seen in a fog, except that beyond them lay the distant horizon hard against a sky pale with the washed-out afterglow of sunset.

Then, as they cleared the strait and left the Vikkenfiord behind them, as the grey and forbidding coast began to fall back on either side and the vast ocean opened about them, they saw the last rays of the setting sun strike the mountain summits astern. It was, Drinkwater recalled, how they had first spied them. For a moment it seemed as though the very sky had caught fire, for the jagged, snow-encrusted peaks flashed against the coming night, then vanished, as the western rim of the world threw its shadow into the firmament.

Drinkwater turned from contemplating this marvel and swallowed hard. Birkbeck came towards him.

'Course set sou'west by south, sir. Should take us clear of Utsira before dawn.'

'I hope so, Mr Birkbeck, I hope so.'

' 'Tis a damnable coast, sir, but we've been lucky with the fog. Just the one day.'

'Yes. We've been lucky.'

They stood for a moment, then Birkbeck said, 'I hope you don't mind my saying, sir, but Pardoe would never have done what you did.'

Drinkwater stared blankly at the master. Then he frowned. 'What's that?'

'He'd have drawn off after the first encounter . . .' Seeing the bleak look on Drinkwater's face, Birkbeck faltered.

'Perhaps he would have been the wiser man, Mr

Birkbeck,' Drinkwater replied coldly. Had it all been worth it? So many dead: Quilhampton, Mosse, that marine corporal – Wilson, the boatswain's mate Greer and so many, many more: Dahlgaard, his sister's son, and the Americans. He was reminded of the fact that he still had American prisoners, though he had returned the Yankee privateer commander to the fort under Frey's flag of truce.

Birkbeck looked nonplussed, then said, 'Beg pardon, sir, I meant no offence . . .'

'There was none taken.'

'Well, I'll . . .'

'Go below, Mr Birkbeck. You have done your utmost and I shall remember your services. Is there anything in my gift that I might oblige you with?'

Even in the gloom, Drinkwater could see Birkbeck brighten. 'I should like a dockyard post, sir, if it ain't asking too much.'

'I will see what I can do. Now, do you go below and I will keep the deck until midnight.'

'There's no need . . .'

'Yes there is. I have much to think about.'

Time seemed of no account as the ship, even under her patchwork sailplan, leaned to the breeze and seemed to take wing for the horizon. The northerly wind was light but steady, and bitterly cold, fogging their exhalations and laying a thin white rime on the hemp ropes as the night progressed.

Drinkwater paced the windward quarterdeck, no longer unsteady on his legs, but with the ease of long practice and the nervous energy of the sleepless. The sky was studded with stars, the great northern constellations of Ursa Major and Cassiopeia, Cygnus, Lyra, Perseus, Auriga and, portentously, Andromeda, rolled about Polaris, beneath which lay the terrestrial pole. Across the heavens blazed the great swathe of the Milky Way. Such was the cold that their twinkling seemed to the watching Drinkwater to be of greater vigour than was customary.

About four bells in the first watch he became aware of the faint luminosity to the northward that marked an auroral glow. It was so faint that he thought at first he had imagined it, but then he became aware that it was pulsing, a grey and pallid light that came and then faded. Slowly it grew more intense and concentrated, turning in colour from a deathly pallor to a lucent green, appearing not as a nebulous glow but as a defined series of rays that seemed to diffuse from a distant, invisible and mysterious polar source.

For some fifteen or twenty minutes this display persisted and then the rays subsided and consolidated into a low, green arc. This in turn began to undulate and extend vertically towards the zenith so that it hung like some gigantic and diaphanous veil, stirred by a monstrous cosmic wind which blew noiselessly through the very heavens themselves. To men whose lives were spent in thrall to the winds of the oceans, this silence possessed an immense and horrible power before which they felt puny and insubstantial.

The sight overwhelmed the watch on deck; they stared open-mouthed, gaping at the northern sky, their faces illuminated by the unearthly light, while the frigate *Andromeda* and her prize stood south-east beneath the aurora.

17   The Return

December 1813–January 1814

'So, you bring home a prize at last, Captain Drinkwater.'

Barrow peeled off his spectacles and waved Drinkwater to a chair. A fire of sea-coal blazed cheerily in the grate of the Second Secretary's capacious office, but failed to take the chill out of the air. Outside the Admiralty, thick snow lay in Whitehall, churned into a filthy slush by the wheels of passing carriages. Icicles hung from every drainpipe and rime froze on the upper lips of the downcast pedestrians trudging miserably along.

Drinkwater sat stiffly, feeling the piercing cold in his aching shoulder, and placed his battered hat on the table in front of him.

'Is that a shot hole?' Barrow asked inquisitively, leaning forward and poking at the cocked hat.

'A musket ball,' Drinkwater said flatly, finding the Second Secretary's curiosity distasteful. 'I fear my prize is equally knocked about,' he added lest his true sentiments be too obvious.

'I hear the Master Shipwright at Chatham is much impressed with the *Odin*; a new ship in fact. There seems little doubt she will be purchased into the Service. I don't need to tell you we need heavy frigates as cruisers on the North American station.'

Drinkwater nodded. 'Quite.'

'You do not seem very pleased, Captain.'

'She has already been purchased at a price, Mr Barrow.'

'Ah, yes. I recollect your losses. Some friends among them, no doubt?'

'Yes. And their widows yet to face.'

'I see.'

Drinkwater forbore to enlarge. He was filled with a sense of anti-climax and a yet more unpleasant duty to attend to than confronting Catriona Quilhampton, or Tom Huke's dependent womenfolk.

'Coming from Norway,' Barrow continued, 'you will not feel the cold as we do! The Thames is frozen, don't you know. It has become such a curiosity that there is a frost fair upon it in the Pool.'

'I saw something of it as I came across London Bridge.'

'Indeed. Well, Captain, the First Lord desired that I send for you and present the compliments of the Board to you. Whatever the cost it is better than losing Canada; imagine that in burnt farmsteads and settlements, the depredations of Indians and the augmentation of American power.' Barrow smiled and replaced his spectacles. One hand played subconsciously with a pile of papers awaiting his attention. The profit and loss account of the Admiralty was, it seemed, firmly in credit and John Barrow, fascinated by a hole in a sea-officer's hat, was satisfied.

'You will not have heard all the news, I fancy,

though it is run somewhat stale by now.' Barrow's high good humour was so buoyant that it threatened to become infectious.

'News, Mr Barrow? No, I have heard nothing.'

'Dear me, Captain, we must put that right at once. Boney was trounced at Leipzig in mid-October,' Barrow explained. 'Schwarzenburg's Austrians refused battle with the Emperor, but attacked his marshals in detail and forced the French to concentrate on Leipzig. With Blücher attacking from the north, Schwarzenburg pushed up from the south, leaving Bernadotte to advance from the east. *He* dallied, as usual, waiting to see which way the wind would blow, but Bonaparte sent a flag of truce to discuss terms. The delay allowed the Russians to reinforce the Allies and the attack was resumed next day with the odds two to one in the Allies' favour. At the height of the battle the Saxons and Württembergers deserted Boney and, with the game up, he began to withdraw across the River Elster. He might have got away, but the single bridge was prematurely blown up, and in the ensuing chaos the French losses were gargantuan – over two hundred and fifty guns alone! Since then thousands of men have straggled, conscripts have deserted in droves and the French garrisons in Germany are isolated. The 26,000 men at Dresden have surrendered and typhus is said to be raging in the camps of the Grand Army!'

Drinkwater suppressed a shudder at the mention of that fearful disease, but was unable to restrain his interest. 'And what is the news from Spain?'

'Wellington is across the Pyrenees,' Barrow declared, his eyes shining, 'he deceived Soult by crossing an "impassable" but shallow channel of the River Bidassoa. He entered France and forced the Nivelle in November, a month after Leipzig! I tell you, Captain, it is now only a matter of time.'

'And what of Marshal Murat?'

Barrow barked a short, derisive laugh. 'King Joachim has retired to Naples to raise troops, but is, in fact, in contact with the Austrians.' Barrow paused and smiled. 'So you see, Captain, we have not entirely lost the services of a Secret Department in your absence.'

There was a sleek complacency in Barrow's patronizing which irritated Drinkwater after the rigours of his short but violent voyage. Nor had the Second Secretary yet finished the catalogue of Allied triumphs.

'And you will be interested to know that King Joachim', Barrow pronounced the title with sonorous irony, 'has not only concluded a treaty with Vienna, but also one with His Majesty's government, as recently as last week.'

'I see. Colonel Bardolini would have been pleased.'

'Bardolini?' Barrow frowned. 'Oh, yes, I recollect; the Neapolitan envoy. Well, at all events, Captain Drinkwater, the Board are most gratified with the success of your cruise, and not displeased that you have enjoyed a measure of personal success.'

'That is very civil of the Board, Mr Barrow.' Drinkwater bestirred himself; much had happened in his absence. 'Please be so kind as to convey my thanks to Lord Melville and their Lordships.'

Barrow inclined his head. 'Of course.'

Drinkwater rose and reached for his hat. The

inferred message in Barrow's complimentary speech was less subtle than Barrow imagined. Drinkwater was not to expect a knighthood for taking the *Odin*; moreover, the Admiralty Board considered he should be satisfied with his prize-money. The gold was indeed a droit of Admiralty, having originated in Britain in the first place, as payment for wheat sent to Wellington's army in Spain two years earlier.

Drinkwater cleared his throat. 'I should like to ask for a dockyard post for Birkbeck, my sailing master, Mr Barrow, and a step for Mr Frey,' he said.

Barrow frowned. 'He is getting his percentage for carrying the specie as you requested in your report.'

'He is an excellent officer, Mr Barrow, a competent surveyor and first-rate water-colourist. Please don't forget', he added, with an edge to his voice, 'that several officers have died upon this service.'

Barrow opened his mouth, saw the harshness in the eyes of the sea-officer before him and cleared his throat. 'Frey, d'you say?' He made a note of the name. 'Then perhaps I might find something for him.'

'I should be obliged.' Drinkwater was satisfied, unaware of the effect his expression had had on Barrow. His time at the Admiralty had not been entirely wasted. He would not otherwise have known of Barrow's predilection for exploration. 'Good-day to you.'

'Good-day.' Drinkwater had reached the door when Barrow called after him, 'Oh, by the way, what happened to that clerk Templeton? I did not see his name among the dead or wounded.'

'He is well,' Drinkwater replied, adding evasively, 'he has taken furlough.'

'He has lodgings off the Strand, if I recall aright. Lived there with his mother in some decayed style, I believe.'

'Indeed.'

Drinkwater did not wish to pursue the matter and was in the act of passing through the door when Barrow went on, 'You may tell him there is still a place for him in the copy room. We still need a good cipher clerk – though not so often now.'

'I will tell him,' replied Drinkwater, 'though I am not certain he wishes to return to the copy room.'

'Very well. That is his affair. Good-day to you, Captain.'

'Good-day.'

Drinkwater walked down Whitehall towards the Abbey. He was deeply depressed, for Templeton was no guest of his, but had been held at the house in Lord North Street against his will under the close guard of Mr Frey.

The fate of Mr Templeton had been the last strand in the splice. And, ironically, he had been the means by which the rope's end had come unravelled in the first place, with his news of Bardolini's arrival at Harwich. And, Drinkwater thought savagely, pursuing his nautical metaphor, the last strand had been the most difficult to tuck.

He had attended to all the incidental details of the affair. He had buried Quilhampton as he had buried Huke, along with all the dead that had not been unceremoniously hurled overboard during the action fought with the *Odin*, sending their weighted bodies to the deep bed of the Vikkenfiord as he read the burial service, culminating with the psalm, 'I will lift up mine eyes unto the hills: from whence cometh my help . . .'

The cold and distant mountain summits had mocked him in his grief.

And he had dutifully written to Mosse's father, and to Huke's sister and asked permission to wait upon her and her mother; he had discharged into the hands of the military the American prisoners who had been Malaburn's confederates. They, in due process, would be returned to Dartmoor gaol.

And still there was Templeton.

The vague unease which Drinkwater had felt towards his confidential clerk had, he now knew, been founded on half-realized facts and circumstantial evidence that the preoccupations of those desperate days in the Vikkenfiord had driven from his immediate consideration.

When, however, the light northerly winds persisted and promised them a cold but steady southward passage, Drinkwater had had more leisure to mull over the events of recent weeks. The high pressure of the polar regions extended the length of the North Sea, bringing to England a bitter, snow-girt Christmas and to London the novelty of a frozen Thames.

Ice settled, too, about Drinkwater's heart.

He had wondered who had murdered Bardolini, attributing the crime to one of the many spies Napoleon maintained in London, as he had suggested to Castlereagh's under-secretary, but the cunning and co-ordination of Malaburn's actions, the appearance, compliance and ready impressment of those Americans, the sabotaged gun breeching, the certainties inherent in Malaburn's conduct in that last, fatal encounter, all argued something more sinister, more organized. He became obsessed with the notion of a conspiracy.

Drinkwater could not evade the question of what he would have done had Danks not so peremptorily shot Malaburn. With Huke dead, Malaburn had overplayed his hand, but with Huke still alive, Drinkwater did not truly know what he might have done.

These events, isolated in themselves, were but elements in the desolation of the last weeks. Their linkage was circumstantial, no more part of a conspiracy, in fact, than Herr Liepmann's report of a quantity of arms arriving at Hamburg. And yet, for so fatalistic a man as Nathaniel Drinkwater, the train of isolated occurrences wanted only a catalyst to link them as certainly as Bardolini's intelligence had led *Andromeda* to the American privateers anchored in the Vikkenfiord.

Two days south from Utsira, Mr Birkbeck had placed the catalyst in his hand.

'I'm afraid I opened it, sir. I had no idea what it was, but I think you should see it.'

Drinkwater knew what it was the instant he saw the package in Birkbeck's grasp. It had been in his office at the Admiralty, then in the house in Lord North Street. Now . . .

'Where did you find it, Mr Birkbeck?' he had asked quietly.

'In the hold, sir.'

'Malaburn.'

'It has an Admiralty seal . . .'

'Yes, yes, I'm much obliged to you.' Birkbeck had

relinquished the canvas parcel and retreated, his curiosity unsated.

Drinkwater knew Malaburn had seized the papers from his London house, but how had this American known of the house, of Bardolini's presence there, or of the Neapolitan's significance? And while the contents of the package had no direct bearing upon the business of King Joachim or the shipment of arms to the Americans for the invasion of Canada, they contained information which, in the hands of Napoleon's chief of police, Savary, the Duke of Rovigo, could betray those persons in France well disposed to the cause of Great Britain, among whom was Madame Hortense Santhonax.

Holding the package after Birkbeck's departure, Drinkwater was almost shaking with relief at having nipped the betrayal of Hortense and her network in the bud, and then he found the answer to the half-formed question which had plagued him.

Apart from Drinkwater himself, only one person existed who could have drawn so fine a thread through this mystery: Templeton.

It came to him then, aside from the formal, everyday loyalty, those tiny fragmented clues, invisible to all but the suspicious and even then almost imperceptible.

He remembered Templeton's subtle attempt to play down the value of Liepmann's intelligence report from Hamburg; remembered Templeton had not broadcast the news of Sparkman's letter concerning Bardolini to the copy room, and had had difficulty concealing his satisfaction when Drinkwater himself, in an act of uncharacteristic high-handedness, had burnt Sparkman's letter. Finally he remembered

Templeton's consternation when he learned he was to sail with Drinkwater. He must have been sick with anxiety as to the outcome of events throughout the whole passage, Drinkwater concluded.

It was true that Templeton had witnessed the Americans letting go the anchor to deliver *Andromeda* to the guns of the *Odin*, but that had been a somewhat circumstantial occurrence, Drinkwater concluded. Moreover, in the aftermath of that event, Templeton had been singularly unhelpful in identifying the culprits. Only their own hiding on the knightheads where Huke had discovered them had revealed who they were.

It was clear they knew very little of what was going on, and had acted according to Malaburn's instructions, as well they might, for he had spirited them out of prison and seemed set fair to get them aboard homeward-bound American ships! Malaburn himself had taken pains to keep out of trouble during that first action. Drinkwater had no doubt now that Malaburn had been below throughout the event with the dual objective of avoiding the Danish fire and compressing the cable when sufficient had run out. Why his absence at his battle station had not been reported, Drinkwater would never know, but some dilatoriness on the part of, say, the twelve-year-old Mr Fisher, would seem to provide an answer.

It was not difficult in a man-of-war for a seaman of experience, as Malaburn clearly was, to avoid Templeton, who was himself penned up with the officers. Templeton had given no hint of any foreknowledge of an acquaintanceship with one of the crew, but God knew what anxieties, hopes and fears had made Templeton act the way he did. Templeton's presence may have given the American agent a great deal of anxiety, but Malaburn could not expect events to fall out too pat. He had had the greatest run of luck in collecting his chain-gang from Dartmoor and shipping it so neatly to Scotland to be pressed promptly by the assiduous Huke!

Moreover, Drinkwater remembered angrily, Malaburn had so nearly been successful.

He had not arrested Templeton immediately, but waited until *Andromeda* anchored at the Nore, observing his clerk for any clues of apprehension. On their arrival he had instructed Templeton to accompany him to London, implying his service aboard the frigate was at an end. With the crippled *Odin* sent up the Medway to the dockyard, Drinkwater made out a written order to Frey to turn the prize over to the master-shipwright and join him. Leaving Birkbeck in charge of *Andromeda*, Drinkwater had prepared to post to London, intending to take Frey and Templeton. There was nothing remarkable in the arrangement.

Frey had joined Drinkwater as he emerged from the fine red-brick residence of the Dockyard Commissioner where he had been finalizing details for the reception of the two ships. A post-chaise awaited the three men.

'Ah, Frey, you are on time.'

'Good afternoon, sir. It's damnably cold.'

They shook hands and Drinkwater turned to Templeton. 'I appear to have left my gloves, would you mind . . . ?'

'Of course.' Templeton had returned towards the house.

'Frey,' Drinkwater had said in a low and urgent voice, 'I want you to accompany me to London. I've made the necessary arrangements for the *Odin*.'

'Is it the *Kestrel*, sir?' Frey had asked anxiously. As the senior surviving officer of the cutter, Frey was naturally concerned with their justification for handing over the little ship. He feared a court-martial.

'No, no. Listen . . .' but Templeton was already returning, holding Drinkwater's full-dress white gloves.

'Just do exactly what I say!' he had hissed vehemently, then swung round to Templeton. 'Ah, Templeton, obliged, thank you.'

'You had dropped them in the hall.'

Drinkwater had grunted. Now they were ashore again Templeton had resumed his old familiarity. It bespoke his confidence. Drinkwater clambered aboard and was followed by the others. A moment later the chaise swung through the Lion Gate and on towards Rochester and London.

Drinkwater had waited until it was almost dark before he struck. He affected to doze, killing off all chance of conversation as the chaise lurched along, passing through a succession of villages. Frey, though consumed with curiosity, obediently held his tongue.

Templeton had stared out over the snow-covered countryside. Surreptitiously watching him, Drinkwater sought to read the man, but Templeton remained inscrutable, unsuspecting.

As a grey twilight spread over the land and the chaise rocked on towards Blackheath, Drinkwater stirred from his mock stupor. He could no longer endure the sharp angularities of the pistol in the small of his back and drew it with slow deliberation.

Templeton, himself half asleep by then, was unaware of anything amiss until Drinkwater, having given Frey's foot a sharp kick, pulled the hammer back to full cock with a loud click.

'Mr Templeton,' Drinkwater said, 'consider yourself under arrest.'

'What the devil . . . ?' Templeton made to move, but Frey seized his arm and held it while the clerk ceased struggling and subsided. Drinkwater watched Templeton's eyes close in resignation and saw his Adam's apple bob nervously above his stock.

'You deceived me, Mr Templeton,' Drinkwater said, 'you were in contact with Malaburn, were you not? You informed him of the purpose and whereabouts of Bardolini, and you are an accessory to the man's murder. You told Malaburn of the purpose of our voyage, you were aware that the package of papers was removed from my office and secreted at my house . . .

'Well, have you nothing to say?'

Templeton shook his head. His mouth had gone dry and he could not speak.

'Is this how you served Lord Dungarth? Leaking secrets to the enemy? Is that how Dungarth was blown up and lost his leg? Did you betray him to the French?'

'No! No, never!'

'So when did you start this?'

'I . . .' Templeton licked his lips, 'I never betrayed Lord Dungarth. I never trafficked with the French.'

'Only with the Americans, eh? Is that right?'

Templeton said nothing.

'Your silence is eloquent, Templeton, and enough to condemn you.'

'Sir . . . Captain Drinkwater, I know you for a man of sensibility, my intention was not murder, I meant only . . .'

'Meant only what?'

Templeton's features worked distressfully in the gloom. He breathed heavily and wiped the back of a hand across his mouth.

'Sir . . . sir, I beg you . . . my mother . . .'

He had looked desperately at Frey and then lapsed into a sobbing quiescence from which Drinkwater had been unable to rouse him. In the end he had abandoned the attempt.

'I am taking you to my house,' he had said. 'You will be held there for the time being.'

'Is that a good idea, sir?' Frey had asked, speaking for the first time, his face bleak with suppressed emotion.

Drinkwater had nodded. 'For the time being, yes. You will look after him until after I have decided what is to be done.'

Night had fallen when they crossed the Thames. The light of a young moon and the gleam of the lamps mounted on the parapet of London Bridge to illuminate the carriageway shone on the white expanse of the frozen river.

'Stap me,' Frey had said, breaking the dolorous silence, 'I wish I'd my paint-box!'

On arrival at the house in Lord North Street they had hustled Templeton quickly inside and upstairs to the bedroom which Bardolini had once used.

'Leave us a moment,' Drinkwater had said to Frey, after he had dismissed the impassive Williams, and Frey, with a glance at the trembling Templeton, had done as he was bid.

Downstairs, the manservant had ushered Frey into the withdrawing-room. Frey settled before a roaring fire quickly conjured by Williams, who poured him a glass of oporto. The young lieutenant sat and stared at the magnificent portrait above the fireplace, marvelling at the skill of the artist. The lady was fair and beautiful and her lovely face seemed to glow in the imperfect candlelight. He had no idea who she was, nor what her relationship had been with Captain Drinkwater. He had had no idea, either, that Drinkwater possessed such a house; the knowledge seemed another mystery to add to the sum of extraordinary occurrences of recent weeks. He wondered whether Drinkwater would vouchsafe him some further explanation when he came downstairs. He knew that Captain Drinkwater had, from time to time, some connections with secret operations and felt that the death of James Quilhampton had elevated Frey himself to the post of confidant. For the moment he was lost in admiration of the work of Mr George Romney.

So abandoned to contemplation had he been, that Drinkwater startled him. 'She was the Countess of Dungarth,' Drinkwater had explained, helping himself from the decanter. 'The wife of the former head of the Admiralty's Secret Department. This was formerly his house. Your health, Mr Frey. Now tell me what is troubling you.'

Frey had been recalled to the present. 'That man, sir.'

'Templeton? What about him?'

'Shouldn't we turn him over to the constables? If what you say is true, he is guilty of treason, of trafficking with the enemy . . .'

'You are concerned he might escape, that the bedroom is no Newgate cell, is that what's troubling you?'

'Yes it is, in part.'

Drinkwater had sighed. 'I owe you something of an explanation, my dear Frey. You are the only man I can trust in this matter and it must be settled quietly. Forgive me, it is an imposition I would rather not have laid upon you.'

Drinkwater had then related to Frey an account of the arrival of secret intelligence from Naples and of the subsequent disappearance of Bardolini. He told of the sabotage in the Vikkenfiord, of his belated suspicions, of the too pat pressing of the Americans and the mischief they had wrought under Malaburn.

'It was an assumed name, I think, and a flash one, a punning which might have spelled the end for all of us.'

'What do you think he intended to do, if he had not let go your anchor?'

'To set us on fire when we were conveniently close to the American ships and he and his accomplices could escape in a boat. Had he lain low in the hold, he might just have achieved it. He was a resourceful fellow, this Mal-a-burn, he staked a great deal on chance and he nearly won . . .'

Drinkwater did not wish to dwell on how close his own laxity had come to promoting this course of events, nor on what he owed to Thomas Huke whose unnecessary death would reproach him for the rest of his life. The two men were lost in silence for a moment, contemplating what might have happened.

'And Templeton?' Frey had prompted at last. It did not seem to be over until Templeton was dealt with.

Drinkwater stirred and poured another glass for both of them.

'There has been enough blood spilled in this whole wretched business. We have both lost a friend in James, and only you and I know of Templeton's guilt. Let us sleep on it.'

'But he might escape from that room.'

'He might murder us in our beds, it's true, and if he does escape,' Drinkwater shrugged, 'well, what does it matter? It's over now.'

'But *why*, sir? I don't understand.'

' 'Twas a temptation more than he could bear. Consider the matter.' Drinkwater sighed; his conversation alone with Templeton had borne out all his suspicions and answered most of his questions. 'Templeton is an intelligent fellow,' Drinkwater went on, 'skilled, dedicated. For years he toils miserably upwards in the sequestered corridors of the Admiralty, a world of internecine jealousies between pettifogging minds. He finds himself close to secrets of state, unlocks some of them with his ability to decrypt reports at speed. He learns from Lord Dungarth, and later myself, of his true worth, yet he is paid a pittance. He is surrounded by glory and yet not one iota is reflected upon him. You are an artist, Frey, a man of, what did he call me? Of sensibility; surely you can see how such a life could corrode a proud spirit and leave him vulnerable to seduction?'

Frey had stirred uncomfortably, but held his tongue.

'Templeton, I suspect,' Drinkwater went on, 'was as much led astray by Malaburn's gold as Malaburn's promise of a new life. D'you think Templeton was a high Tory or the member of a Corresponding Society, a secret republican? For him America means opportunity, another chance away from our world of privilege and patronage, of jobbing and perquisites, of the eternal English *kow-tow*. I didn't have to ask him if this is true, though I have spoken to him of it. I know it myself; I feel it in my bones, and so, if you're honest, do you.

'No, leave Templeton to his conscience, and the workings of providence. He can do no harm now.' Drinkwater had paused, then said, 'This is a damnable war. It has lasted all my adult life. Quilhampton joined me as a midshipman and was shot to pieces. Now we have a new generation, boys like little Fisher weeping over cats, but bred to war, inured to war like me. I am weary of it, sick to my very soul, Frey, and I am burdening you unreasonably with my confession.' Drinkwater smiled, and his face was oddly boyish.

'Not at all,' Frey said uncertainly, 'not at all. I recall something Pope wrote . . .'

'What is that?'

'"Sir, I have lived a courtier all my days, And studied men, their manners and their ways; And have observed this useful maxim still, To let my betters always have their will."'

'So, you feel something of it too, eh?' Drinkwater smiled again. 'Anyway, my dear fellow,' he said, rising and stretching stiffly, 'I have asked for you to be given a step in rank. You will be a Commander before too long.'

'Is that to purchase my silence in the matter?' Frey had asked quickly, looking up.

Drinkwater laughed. 'Only incidentally. But yes, it binds you to the system and compromises you. Like marriage and family, it makes you a hostage to fortune.'

Drinkwater crossed the room and drew back the curtains. 'Good Lord, I thought it had grown warmer and blamed the wine, but it is raining outside.'

Frey became aware of the hiss of the deluge, then Drinkwater closed the curtains and faced him. 'I think it is time for bed.'

Frey tossed off his glass and stood up. 'Good-night, sir.'

'Good-night. I hope you sleep well.'

'I'll try.'

'Lock your door,' Drinkwater said with a laugh.

When Frey had gone, Drinkwater poured another glass and sat again, to stare into the dying fire as the candles burned low. It was already long past midnight and he would confront Mr Barrow later that day. Finally, after about an hour, he rose, went into the hall and opened the front door. In the street a cold rain fell in torrents; peering out into the hissing darkness, Drinkwater smiled to himself. Turning back into the house he left the door ajar and went quietly upstairs.

Outside Templeton's room he drew a key from his pocket and unlocked the door. He stepped inside; rain beat upon the uncurtained window and he could faintly see Templeton, still dressed, lying upon the bed.

'Captain Drinkwater . . .?' Templeton's voice faltered uncertainly. 'Captain Drinkwater, is that you?'

It suddenly struck Drinkwater that Templeton expected to be executed for his crime of treason, murdered perhaps by Drinkwater himself as Bardolini had been assassinated. Instead, he stood motionless and silent beside the open door.

'I tried to get myself killed in the boarding of the *Odin*,' Templeton said desperately.

'I know,' Drinkwater replied quietly.

'What . . . what do you intend to do?'

'Nothing,' Drinkwater murmured, stepping aside from the doorway, 'now be gone.'

The Frost Fair
26 January 1814

Upon the frozen Thames in the Pool of London,
between London Bridge and the Tower, there had
been a great frost fair for some six weeks. Tents containing circus curiosities and human freaks had been
set up, stalls selling everything from patent nostrums
and articles of cheap haberdashery to roasted chest-
nuts were laid out in regular 'streets'. Open spaces
were cleared for skating and the populace displayed
every scale of talent from the inept to the expert. An
émigré fencing master gave lessons with épée or foil to
ambitious counting-house clerks, while rustics exercised at single-stick. Bloods rode their hacks on the
ice, caracoling their slithering mounts in extravagant
daring for the admiring benefit of credulous belles.
Fashion rubbed shoulders with the indigent upon the
slippery surface, and many a dainty lady lost her dignity with her footing, to the merciless merriment of
her acknowledged inferiors.

Whores and pick-pockets abounded, preying on
the foolish. Silly young blades were helped to their
feet and simultaneously deprived of their purses.

Good ales were served from barrels set upon stands

on the ice, whole sheep were spit-roasted and consumed with the relish that only cold weather can endow. London was entranced, captivated by the spectacle.

On the night of 25 January, the night Templeton was released, the warmth of an approaching depression brought heavy rain. This raised freshets in the Thames valley to the west of the capital. The following day the thaw set the frozen river in sudden motion. Tents and stalls were swept away, along with their customers and the curious promenaders whom even six weeks' revelry could not deter.

In the days that followed, far downstream, amid the samphire bordering the salt-marshes of the Kent and Essex shores, the bloated bodies of the drowned washed ashore.

Among them was the unrecognizable corpse of Templeton. He had been quite drunk when the ice melted.

Author's Note

In 1813 Norway was a possession of King Frederick of Denmark, and occasional raids on its coast were made by British cruisers operating in northern waters.

As a result of the second expedition against Copenhagen in 1807, the Danish navy had been very largely destroyed by the British, though a fleet of gun-vessels and one or two men-of-war remained in commission, along with a large and effective fleet of Danish privateers. Subsequent actions between the British and the Danes became notorious for their ferocity.

The Danes also lost the island of Helgoland which, at the entrance of the Elbe, became a forward observation post for the British, and an entrepôt for British goods destined for the Continent to break the embargo imposed by Napoleon (a fact I have used as the basis for *Under False Colours*). The island remained in British hands for a century.

After the French Emperor's disastrous Russian campaign, the loyalty of his marshalate was severely shaken. Several of these men, who owed their fortunes to Napoleon, made overtures to the Allies. One, Marshal Bernadotte, became heir presumptive to the Swedish crown and, as a result of his joining the

Allied camp, was later ceded Norway, afterwards becoming king of the entire Scandinavian peninsula.

Less successfully, Joachim Murat, King of Naples and Marshal of France, 'the most complete vulgarian and poseur', according to Carola Oman, but an inspired if vainglorious leader of cavalry, opened a secret communication with the British government in the autumn of 1813 with a view to retaining his throne in the event of the fall of his brother-in-law, Napoleon. His rival, the Bourbon King Ferdinand of the 'Two Sicilies', retained the insular portion of his dual kingdom under British protection. Murat's overtures resulted in a treaty with London signed on 11 January 1814. It availed him little; he was shot by his 'subjects' in the following year, and the odious Ferdinand returned to his palace in Naples.

The ambivalent posture of the Americans in their brief war with Great Britain was at odds with their single-minded ambitions towards Canada. Thirty thousand Loyalists had settled in New Brunswick after the War of Independence, a living reproach to the claims of the patriot party, and it was the avowed aim of the war-hawks in Congress to assimilate these and simultaneously liberate the French Canadians from the yoke of British tyranny, to the considerable advantage of the United States.

Between the new and the old worlds lay the Atlantic Ocean, dominated by the Royal Navy which, despite receiving a bloody nose from the young United States' Navy, was by 1813 reasserting its paramountcy. Nevertheless, American privateers continued to operate with impunity and the British were equally equivocal in their attitude to American

311

trade, particularly when it affected the supply of Wellington's army in the Iberian peninsula.

Napoleon, moreover, took an interest in American affairs (his youngest brother Jerome married an American and their grandson was later Secretary of the US Navy, though the lady herself was later repudiated in favour of a Württemburg princess). Napoleon had sold Louisiana and the Mississippi valley as far west as the Rockies to the United States in 1803 with the prescient remark that the Americans would 'fight the English again'. His secret diplomacy thereafter applied pressure to bring about this highly desirable state of affairs.

With Britain contributing 124,000 muskets, 18.5 million cartridges, 34,500 swords, 218 cannon, 176,600 pairs of boots, 150,000 uniforms and an additional 187,000 yards of uniform cloth to the Allied armies for the Leipzig campaign, a similar arrangement between the French and the Americans in exchange for wheat does not seem improbable.

That knowledge of such a deal should form the 'guarantee' of Joachim Murat's good faith and a pledge of his suitability for a throne forms the basis of this story.

Both the British and the American governments were quite indifferent to the fate of merchant seamen, and those Americans lodged in Dartmoor remained incarcerated until long after the signing of the Peace of Ghent ended the war. On 6 April 1815 a riot broke out which left seven American prisoners dead and fifty-four wounded. It is believed that among the dead were a handful that had earlier escaped and been recaptured.